2002

CLUB
EST. 1923

Hart O'Brien
The rugged bomb tech with nerves of steel returns home to Mission Creek to help uncover the Lone Star Country Club bomber, only to discover that his old flame works at the club. Can Hart ever convince Joan to give him a second chance?

Joan Cooper
A night of passion transformed this spoiled society princess into a loving and responsible mother. But when she is confronted with her long-ago love, can Joan continue to ignore the passion she feels for Hart? Will she reveal the secret she's kept from him for ten years?

Helena Cooper
Joan's spunky preteen daughter takes an instant liking to the bomb tech from Chicago. He's an old friend of her mom's, so he's gotta be "way cool." So why does her mom turn white as a sheet every time Helena talks to Hart?

Chief Benjamin Stone
Hart's arrival in Mission Creek screws up all the police chief's plans for the future—Step One: Woo Joan and her daughter. Step 2: Do whatever it takes to clean up the Lone Star Country Club mess once and for all. NEW Step 3: Get rid of know-it-all bomb tech....

Dear Reader,

Once again, Intimate Moments invites you to experience the thrills and excitement of six wonderful romances, starting with Justine Davis's *Just Another Day in Paradise*. This is the first in her new miniseries, REDSTONE, INCORPORATED, and you'll be hooked from the first page to the last by this suspenseful tale of two meant-to-be lovers who have a few issues to work out on the way to a happy ending—like being taken hostage on what ought to be an island paradise.

ROMANCING THE CROWN continues with *Secret-Agent Sheik,* by Linda Winstead Jones. Hassan Kamal is one of those heroes no woman can resist—except for spirited Elena Rahman, and even she can't hold out for long. Our introduction to the LONE STAR COUNTRY CLUB winds up with Maggie Price's *Moment of Truth.* Lovers are reunited and mysteries are solved—but not all of them, so be sure to look for our upcoming anthology, *Lone Star Country Club: The Debutantes*, next month. RaeAnne Thayne completes her OUTLAW HARTES trilogy with *Cassidy Harte and the Comeback Kid,* featuring the return of the prodigal groom. Linda Castillo is back with *Just a Little Bit Dangerous,* about a romantic Rocky Mountain rescue. Finally, welcome new author Jenna Mills, whose *Smoke and Mirrors* will have you eagerly looking forward to her next book.

And, as always, be sure to come back next month for more of the best romantic reading around, right here in Intimate Moments.

Enjoy!

Leslie J. Wainger
Executive Senior Editor

Please address questions and book requests to:
Silhouette Reader Service
U.S.: 3010 Walden Ave., P.O. Box 1325, Buffalo, NY 14269
Canadian: P.O. Box 609, Fort Erie, Ont. L2A 5X3

Moment
of Truth
MAGGIE PRICE

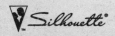

INTIMATE MOMENTS™

Published by Silhouette Books

America's Publisher of Contemporary Romance

Special thanks and acknowledgment are given to Maggie Price for her contribution to the LONE STAR COUNTRY CLUB series.

 SILHOUETTE BOOKS

ISBN 0-373-27213-8

MOMENT OF TRUTH

Visit Silhouette at www.eHarlequin.com

Printed in U.S.A.

Books by Maggie Price

Silhouette Intimate Moments

Prime Suspect #816
The Man She Almost Married #838
Most Wanted #948
On Dangerous Ground #989
Dangerous Liaisons #1043
Special Report #1045
　"Midnight Seduction"
Moment of Truth #1143

MAGGIE PRICE

turned to crime at the age of twenty-two. That's when she went to work at the Oklahoma City Police Department. As a civilian crime analyst, she evaluated suspects' methods of operation during the commission of robberies and sex crimes, and developed profiles on those suspects. During her tenure at OCPD, Maggie stood in lineups, snagged special assignments to homicide task forces, established procedures for evidence submittal, even posed as the wife of an undercover officer in the investigation of a fortune teller.

While at OCPD, Maggie stored up enough tales of intrigue, murder and mayhem to keep her at the keyboard for years. The first of those tales won the Romance Writers of America's Golden Heart Award for Romantic Suspense.

Maggie invites her readers to contact her at 5208 W. Reno, Suite 350, Oklahoma City, OK 73127-6317. Or on the Web at http://members.aol.com/magprice

To Marie Ferrarella and Beverly Bird, my fellow
Lone Star Country Club cohorts in all things nefarious.

To Pam Newell, mother of five,
for patiently providing awesome "daughter/mom" advice.

To Officer Kip Higby, certified bomb technician,
Boise Police Department, for invaluable information
on all things explosive.

Chapter 1

What the hell am I doing here?

The thought hit Hart O'Brien the instant he steered his rental car up the Lone Star Country Club's drive, where long afternoon shadows slanted across shrubs laden with eye-popping yellow blossoms.

He knew his uneasiness wasn't due to the fact his destination was the site of a bomb blast. An expert on explosive devices, he was accustomed to the Chicago PD sending him wherever his expertise was most needed. Yet, no way could Hart write off *this* trip to Mission Creek, Texas, as just another assignment. Not when the last time he'd laid eyes on the place, both he and his mother had been running from the law.

That's why he'd been surprised when Spence Harrison called the CPD's bomb squad. Ten years ago Spence had subsidized his law school tuition by working alongside Hart as a groundskeeper at the posh country club. When Hart fled town with barely the clothes on his back, he regretted not saying goodbye to one of the few friends his vagabond lifestyle had enabled him to make.

Spence was now Lone Star County's District Attorney. A D.A. with big problems, from what Hart could tell from the few details Spence gave over the phone. Problems that required untangling by someone with an insider's knowledge of police work and explosives.

Now, two days after agreeing to act as the D.A.'s liaison to the police task force investigating the Lone Star bombing, Hart was back in the city to which he'd sworn he would never return.

Ignoring the signs for valet parking, he pulled into the lot near one of the tennis courts. Against his will the image rose in his mind of a willowy dark-haired young woman with long, bronzed legs lobbing balls across that court.

Jerking his mind free of the memory, he tightened his grip on the steering wheel and fought the urge to drive away. In his logical, cop's brain, he could find no reasons *not* to stay at the Lone Star in the room Spence had reserved for him. Although there were reasons, they were all emotional and were way below the surface. That's where he planned to leave them.

He climbed out into the warm March breeze, then slid the car keys into the pocket of his well-worn khakis. A high-pitched squeal from a far corner of the parking lot caught his attention. Two young girls—one with a blond ponytail, the other with waist-length dark hair—raced on bicycles. The dark-haired girl jammed on the brakes, sending her bike's rear wheel skidding. She blazed a triumphant grin. Cute kid, Hart thought with a faint smile.

Raising the trunk lid, he hefted out his suitcase and field evidence kit. He headed up the pristine drive lined on both sides by shrubs heavy with purple and white peonies, some he and Spence had planted during their stint as groundskeepers.

The knots in Hart's gut tightened the closer he got to the clubhouse. He would rather walk toward a madman's ticking bomb than spend time at a place that held memories that were capable of snapping out at him like fangs. Still, he'd given Spence his word. He would do the job.

When he was halfway up the drive, the clubhouse came into full view.

The old and elegant wooden building, the original structure, sat beside the four-story brick addition that had been added years later. To Hart the combination of old and new seemed to exude power and wealth. As did the man and woman alighting from the sleek, black Jaguar parked beneath the covered portico. While the man handed his keys to the parking valet, the woman, clad in a trim white jumpsuit, glided through the front door. After the man followed her inside, a bellman began unloading a mountain of leather luggage from the Jaguar's trunk.

During Hart's phone conversation with Spence, the D.A. mentioned that the Lone Star was now more than just a private country club. It had evolved into a world-class resort. Very exclusive. Very private.

Heart-stoppingly expensive.

Hart shook his head. The place might ooze money out of its pores, but that hadn't stopped some slime from setting a bomb that killed two people and caused significant structural damage.

"Take your bags, sir?" a bellman offered.

"Thanks, I can handle them," Hart said, then stepped into the elegant lobby, its ceiling soaring two stories above his head. He paused, sweeping his gaze across what seemed to be the same intermittent groupings of leather chairs and sofas that formed private seating areas. As always, long, flowering stalks spilled color and scent out of slim stone vases positioned on sturdy pedestals. Attractive art in massive frames continued to line the walls at precise intervals. Yet changes had been made.

A fountain now sat in the lobby's center, its water bubbling over the petals and stems of brass magnolias. Like the floor and nearby columns, the fountain had been built from the pink granite native to the area. The club's transformation into a resort had no doubt necessitated the concierge's desk and long, rose-toned registration counter located to Hart's right. Behind the counter, clerks wearing starched white dress shirts and identical blue blazers conducted business. At one end of the counter stood the man and woman who'd arrived in the black Jag.

Hart strode to the counter, settled his suitcase and evidence kit on the floor. A young blond-headed male clerk with strong, clear-cut features stepped to help him.

"We're expecting you, Sergeant O'Brien," the clerk said after keying Hart's name into the computer. "Your executive suite is ready."

Hart looked up from the registration card the clerk had placed on the counter. "I don't need a suite, executive or otherwise. A plain room will do."

"Mrs. Brannigan chose the suite specifically for you."

"Mrs. Brannigan?"

"Our general manager. She wants to welcome you personally."

"Nice of her," Hart murmured, turning his attention back to the card. He wondered what the Brannigan woman would say if she knew one of the club's former presidents had accused him of stealing money from the golf shop's till.

"I'll call Mrs. Brannigan," the clerk said, reaching for a phone. "She'll be here by the time I finish your registration."

"Fine." Hart completed the card, dashed his signature on the bottom, then slid it across the counter.

"Mrs. Quinlin," said a warm, soft voice to his left. "Welcome to the Lone Star. It's a pleasure to meet you."

Hart froze. *That voice.* He knew that voice. Had spent a couple of months lying awake at night, thinking he might go crazy if he never heard it again.

Throat tight, he forced himself to turn toward the end of the counter where the couple who owned the Jaguar stood. A hot ball of awareness settled in his gut as he took in the woman clad in a snug, icy-pink jacket and matching trim skirt that showed off her legs. Those endless, perfect legs.

Setting his jaw, Hart studied her. At eighteen Joan Cooper had been vividly pretty with an open, carefree spirit. Now, a man could take a glance at the woman and see a long, cool brunette with a throat-clenching body and touch-me-not look about her. But *he'd* touched. Throughout one long hot summer night, he'd touched her plenty.

"I've scheduled your itinerary for Body Perfect according to the instructions you faxed." Joan's glossed mouth curved as she handed a pink folder to the woman wearing the white jumpsuit. "Your stress recovery program with Hans starts at eight in the morning."

While the couple moved toward the bank of elevators across the lobby, Joan stepped to the counter. "Karen, be sure Mrs. Quinlin gets a wake-up call at seven-thirty."

"I'll take care of it, Ms. Cooper."

Cooper. Hart had heard she'd jumped immediately from him to a hotshot Dallas attorney. Although he'd never learned the lawyer's name, odds were almost nil Joan had married a guy with the same last name as hers.

Flicking a look at her left hand, Hart noted her ring finger was bare. Divorced? he wondered, feeling a nasty little streak of satisfaction at the thought.

As he stepped behind her, Chanel No. 5, like a whiff of warm flowers, slid like a haunting memory into his lungs. Bitter satisfaction instantly transformed into the dull ache of regret.

"Hello, Texas," he said quietly.

Joan went utterly still at the sound of the male voice, as deep and clear as brandy, coming from behind her. A voice from the past. At one time, she would have given everything—*anything*—to hear that voice again.

Now it put the fear of God inside her.

With blood roaring in her head, she forced herself to turn. And felt everything slip out of focus when her gaze locked with eyes as green as summer leaves. This isn't happening, she told herself.

But it was. The realization of how very real Hart O'Brien was shot a shudder down the length of her spine and onward to bury itself behind her knees.

He stood so close she could have reached out and touched him. Touched the man whom she had once wanted more than she'd wanted air to breathe. The man she had loved above life. The man who had told her he loved her, then turned his back and walked away forever. Resentment bubbled up instantly. Just as quickly she shoved it back. She couldn't afford the indulgence of resentment. Not when Hart's presence threatened so much more than just her pride.

She stared back at him, struggling for words that wouldn't come. His face was thinner than it had been ten years ago, the hollows of his cheeks deeper. His body was trim, muscled and looked hard as granite. A dark-green polo shirt, open at the neck, revealed curling auburn hair as rich in color as the hair he wore short and brushed back from a straight hairline. His casual shirt, well-washed khaki slacks and scuffed loafers would give most men a relaxed appearance. Hart looked anything but relaxed as he stood watching her, his eyes as sharp as a sword.

"Hello, Hart," she said, finally finding her voice. This isn't happening, she told herself again. Can't happen.

"It's been a long time, Texas."

"Yes, it has." Despite the blood pounding in her cheeks from his use of his private nickname for her, Joan kept her voice cool, devoid of emotion. Her gaze flicked to the counter where no customers lingered and two pieces of luggage sat unattended. Surely he wasn't checking in. Surely not. Please, God, no.

"Are you a guest here?"

"Yeah." One side of his mouth lifted in an insolent

curve she remembered well. "You wondering how a guy who lived in a trailer park on the outskirts of town can swing a room here?"

"I...no. Of course not." She stood perfectly still, her gaze locked with his. Around them the sounds of muted conversation, the click of heels against pink granite, the bubbling of the fountain all faded into nothingness. Nothing mattered, except the knowledge that Hart's presence could destroy the secure world she'd so carefully built.

A cold fist of apprehension tightened her chest. Had he found out? Did he somehow know the secret she had guarded for so many years?

"What brings you back to Mission Creek?" she asked, thankful she managed to keep her voice businesslike, neutral.

"Work. I'm a cop. Spence Harrison called and asked me to join the bombing investigation."

She blinked. "*You're* the bomb tech?"

He slid a hand into one pocket of his khakis. "My official title is hazardous devices technician. But bomb tech will do."

Joan forced her swirling thoughts to the information the general manager had given in the previous day's staff meeting. "From Chicago? You're with Chicago PD?"

"Yes to both questions."

"I see." Dread lodged in her stomach. The bombing had occurred ten weeks ago. Chief Ben Stone had told her in confidence that his officers on the task force had no firm suspects. No leads. Nothing. There was no way of knowing how many more weeks, or even months the investigation might drag out. "How long do you expect to stay here?"

"As long as it takes to figure out who set that bomb. And put them behind bars."

On that terrible morning she had heard the bomb's thunderous explosion. *Felt* it. Then watched in sheer horror while rescuers battled flames while pulling survivors—and victims—from the devastation. When she'd heard Spence had called in a bomb expert, relief had risen in her like a wave. Finally someone might find the killer still at large.

Hart angled his chin. "Do you have a problem with me being here?"

Her relief that the terror might soon end with the bomber's arrest battled against the danger Hart's presence held for her.

Regarding her steadily, he crossed his arms over his chest. "Since you seem to have suddenly lost your voice, it looks like you do have a problem."

"On the contrary," she countered, keeping her gaze locked with his. "I don't think anyone in Mission Creek will get a good night's sleep until whoever set that bomb is in custody."

"That's to be expected."

"I'm just surprised to see you after so many years. To find out that you're the Chicago bomb tech we've been expecting." She needed to breathe, but she couldn't quite remember how. "I had no idea you were a police officer."

"And I didn't know you were back in Mission Creek." His gaze flicked to the small brass name tag above her left breast. "What do you do here?"

"I manage Body Perfect."

His gaze did a slow skim down her, then up. "Body Perfect?"

Her nerves shimmered as if he'd touched her. "The ladies' spa." Lifting a hand to her throat, she settled her fingers against the point where her pulse hammered as if she'd spent hours lobbing balls across a tennis court. If she stood there much longer, her legs would buckle.

"Speaking of my job, you'll have to excuse me. I have paperwork to deal with—"

"Joan, I see you're already making our important guest feel at home." Her blond hair teased to poofy heights, Bonnie Brannigan swooped in wearing a fire-engine-red suit that fitted her voluptuous curves like a dream. Widowed, and a grandmother several times over, the Lone Star Country Club's exuberant general manager held equal favor with club members, guests and employees.

"Yes," Joan said, giving silent thanks for Bonnie's arrival. Realizing her hands were trembling, she curled her fingers into her sweating palms. Her knees were water. She had a great deal to think over, but her mind simply wouldn't connect. She needed to go somewhere quiet. Someplace where she could wait for the sick feeling of dread churning in her stomach to settle. Someplace where she could figure out what in heaven's name to do about this man who had stepped so suddenly from the past.

Joan slicked the tip of her tongue over her dry lips. "Bonnie Brannigan, this is Hart O'Brien from the Chicago Police Department."

Beaming, Bonnie shook his hand. "My goodness, Sergeant O'Brien, you're a gorgeous one, aren't you?"

Hart flashed a grin that closed Joan's throat. How many times during that long-ago summer had she been dazzled by that grin?

"That label suits *you,* Mrs. Brannigan, not me," Hart commented.

"And charming, too," Bonnie added with a delightful laugh. "Police officers are as common around here as cattle tracks in a pasture, but I can't say all the officers I know are charming. Can you, Joan?"

"No. Bonnie, I was just explaining to Sergeant O'Brien that I have paperwork to deal with. You'll excuse me?"

"Sure thing. You run on, dear. I'll take good care of one of Chicago's finest."

Joan shifted her gaze to Hart. "Good afternoon, Sergeant."

"See you around, Texas."

Chapter 2

Hart kept his eyes on Joan's retreating form while she moved across the lobby toward the bank of elevators. Despite her pink high heels, her walk was still the smooth, fluid glide of an athlete. Yet, he could tell by the stiffness of her shoulders she was as tense as wire.

Even after she stepped onto an elevator and the doors slid closed, he kept his gaze focused there while memories that still oozed blood stormed through him. He hadn't known, hadn't realized so much bitterness still simmered inside him, just below the surface.

He knew that Joan, too, had her own emotions to deal with.

The surprise he'd seen in her eyes that had quickly transformed into stunned incredulity was understandable. A logical reaction to someone suddenly appearing without warning from one's past.

Hart narrowed his eyes. More was going on with her, though. As a cop he knew all about body language. Joan's had been stiff, defensive. Serious stress, he thought. And he'd seen something more than mere surprise and stunned incredulity in those whiskey-dark eyes. Panic. Glints of panic.

Why, he wondered? They'd had no contact for a decade. What the hell did she have to feel panic about?

"'Texas'?"

The curious lilt in Bonnie Brannigan's voice had Hart switching his mental focus to the Lone Star's general manager. "What?"

"You called her Texas." Bonnie's blue eyes glittered with a meaningful look. "Obviously, you and Joan know each other."

"We ran into each other the summer I worked here."

"That's right." Bonnie waved a slim hand that sent the small gold charms clattering on the thick-linked bracelet circling her left wrist. "Flynt Carson—this year's club president—mentioned you'd been a groundskeeper here years ago."

Hart didn't know Flynt Carson personally, but anyone who spent any time in Mission Creek knew of the Carsons. The Wainwrights, too, for that matter. The families controlled two of the largest ranching empires in Texas. From what Hart remembered, sometime in the twenties Carson and Wainwright ancestors had deeded a thousand acres each of adjoining land to create the Lone Star Country Club. After that, a vicious feud split what most had considered an unbreakable bond between the families. As recently as ten years ago that feud still festered.

Bonnie nodded. "Flynt said you worked here the same summer as Spence. Imagine that. He's now the district attorney and you're a police officer. A bomb expert."

"Mrs. Brannigan—"

"Bonnie."

"Bonnie, I learned a long time ago that it's best to clear the air with people. I left my job here because the man who was that year's club president accused me of stealing money from the golf shop's till. If you were around here then, you maybe heard about it.''

"I was a member then—my late husband played golf every day.'' Bonnie tilted her head as if to gain a new perspective. "If he had heard about money stolen from the golf shop, he'd have mentioned it. So would a lot of other people. I never heard a thing about it.''

Hart stood silent while his anger built. *He* knew he hadn't stolen money, but back then he'd been too young and green to realize Zane Cooper had lied about that to chase him out of town. Until this moment he hadn't realized there had probably never been money missing from the golf shop's till.

Bonnie pursed her mouth, painted the same traffic-stopping red as her suit. "So, if there actually was money stolen, did you take it, Sergeant O'Brien?''

"Hart. No. I've never taken anything that didn't belong to me.'' He slicked his gaze toward the elevator in which Joan had disappeared. Except her, he conceded. She had never been his. Never *intended* to be his, past that one night.

"Well, Hart, I've got a real fondness for men who don't beat around the bush. You're obviously one of 'em.'' Bonnie shifted her stance to give ample room to a bellman wheeling a brass cart piled with luggage. "I appreciate you getting that out in the open. Since you've worked here before, you probably know that old secrets have a long life around this place. If you don't clear the air, you're liable to find yourself knee-deep in some awkward situation before you realize it.''

"Yes, ma'am.'' Hart's thoughts flashed back to the scene that had played out between himself and Joan's father. Awkward wasn't the half of it. "That's why I told you.''

"Now that you have, let's put it to rest. What's important is the reason you're back in Mission Creek.''

"I agree,'' Hart said, banking down any emotion. He

had come here, intending to keep his mind on business. Now that he knew it wasn't just memories of Joan he would have to deal with—but the woman herself—he was even more determined to control his thoughts. Since there was no more serious business than a bomb, he doubted he would have a problem. "I'd like to look at the crime scene now."

"I thought you would," Bonnie said, her eyes going somber. "That's one reason I wanted to know when you arrived. I told the desk clerk to have your bags sent up to your suite. I also contacted Captain Ingram and asked him to join us at the site."

"Captain Ingram?" Hart asked while Bonnie led the way across the lobby.

"Yance Ingram. He's a retired Mission Creek PD captain." As she spoke, Bonnie escorted Hart beneath a graceful arched entry into a wide hallway, its floor a long sweep of the same cool pink granite as in the lobby. "Yance now runs the club's security operation. All the police officers report to him."

"You have commissioned cops instead of civilians working security?"

"Yes. Our whole force is off-duty Mission Creek police officers."

Hart's thoughts went to the vague mention Spence had made about two MCPD cops who'd kidnapped a little boy who had survived the bombing. One of those cops had died during apprehension, the other committed suicide. In another case, two cops were charged with attempted murder. Hart planned to get the details about those incidents when he and Spence met that night.

Hart gave Bonnie a sideways glance as they made their way down the long hallway. "Does having all those cops around make you feel safe?"

"Before that bomb exploded it did." She paused before a makeshift wall of plywood that stretched along the remaining length of the corridor. Nearby was a plywood door, secured by bright silver hinges, a hasp and padlock. "I'd feel a whole lot safer if one of 'em figured out who set the bomb," she added, sliding a key from the pocket of her jacket. "It's been over two months, and everybody around here is feeling more and more unsettled. Knowing that the bomber is still free has cost a lot of people to lose sleep. Including me."

"I've tracked down my share of bombers. I'll do all I can to find this one."

She patted his arm. "You don't know what a relief it is to have someone with your expertise here. When Spence called and asked me to book your room, he said you might need to spend a lot of time at this scene." As she spoke, she handed the key to Hart. "Keep this for as long as you need it."

"Thanks." He glanced at the padlock. "Who else has access to this site?"

"Captain Ingram and I are the only Lone Star staff members. Yance mentioned that all the officers on the bombing task force also have a key."

Hart slid the key into the padlock, twisted it, then pulled open the plywood door. The smell of doused ash, sour and acrid, instantly swept into the hallway.

"Oh, that smell." Cringing backward, Bonnie rubbed a hand across her throat, tears brimming in her eyes. "Every time I get a whiff of that smoke everything about that horrible day hits me again."

When he saw how her face had paled, Hart instantly swung the door closed and gripped her elbow. "Do you need to sit down?"

"No. No, I just need a minute to steady myself."

"Bonnie, something like this can't help but get to you. I can check the site, then ask you any questions I have later."

Nodding, she pulled a lacy handkerchief from the pocket of her suit jacket. "By now I shouldn't get so emotional. It's just... The people who died—Daniel and Meg

Anderson—were salt of the earth. Of the survivors, their son, Jake, was the most seriously injured. He's only five. The sweetest little boy you'd ever want to know.''

Since color had settled back into her cheeks, Hart dropped his hand from her elbow. ''How is Jake doing?''

''Fine. Better.'' Dabbing at her eyes, Bonnie took a deep breath, then forced a watery smile. ''Adam and Tracy Collins, a lovely couple, have given him a home. They've put the wheels in motion to adopt him.'' Bonnie shifted her gaze down the hallway. ''Here's Yance Ingram now.''

Hart turned. The man striding toward them was medium height, toughly built and compact. He had a round face and a neatly cropped mustache the same dark brown as the hair that had receded halfway down his head. Midfifties, Hart judged when the retired cop got closer. Dressed in a starched white shirt, red tie, blue blazer and gray slacks, Ingram looked comfortable and competent.

''Yance, thanks for meeting us,'' Bonnie said. ''This is Sergeant Hart O'Brien from the Chicago PD bomb squad.''

''Pleasure, Sergeant,'' Ingram said. When he extended his hand, light glinted off the small gold pin in the shape of a lion affixed to his right lapel. ''Glad you're here. Any help we can get on solving this bombing is welcome.''

Hart returned the man's brisk, sure handshake. ''I hope I can help.''

''I spent twenty years on the job, and I never saw anything as terrible as this,'' Ingram said. ''I'm not proud to know that some bastard managed to sneak a bomb in here on my watch. You can damn well bet I let my security people know that, too.''

Ingram turned to Bonnie, his eyes softening. ''Why don't I take over and give Sergeant O'Brien a rundown on things while he has a look at the scene? When we're done, I'll give you a call.''

''I appreciate that, Yance.'' Turning back to Hart, Bonnie squeezed his arm. ''I'll just run up and make sure everything's perfect in your suite.'' Her mouth curved. ''We're going to take good care of you here at the Lone Star. So good you'll be tempted to call your boss and tell him you're staying forever.''

Hart gave a meaningful look at the huge diamond that glittered like the tail of a comet on Bonnie's left ring finger. ''If some man hadn't already laid claim to you, I'd make that call right now.''

She chuckled. ''Oh, you're a devil, Hart O'Brien. A real devil.''

Hart waited until Bonnie disappeared down the hallway, then shifted his gaze to Ingram. ''She could charm a dead man.''

''You've got that right. We're going to miss Bonnie like hell when she leaves.''

Hart arched a brow. ''Leaves for where?''

''She's decided to quit her job when she marries C. J. Stuckey—he's a rancher with a huge spread east of town. The Lone Star board offered C.J. a dues-free lifetime membership if he can talk Bonnie into staying on after they're married.''

''Think he can?''

''Not so far,'' Ingram said. ''She claims she intends to stay home and tend to C.J. Lucky man, is all I can say.''

''I agree.''

Ingram nodded toward the plywood door. ''You ready to have a look at the crime scene?''

''Ready.'' Hart swung open the door and gestured for Ingram to step in before him.

''This room is…*was* the Men's Grill,'' the retired cop explained across his shoulder as Hart followed him in. ''Part of the original structure. If what's left of the walls could talk, they'd tell you about the hundreds of big-money land, cattle and oil deals they'd seen sealed over grilled Texas beef, whiskey and cigars. Sad to say, a lot of the Lone Star's history went up in smoke the morning that bomb went off.''

The security chief flicked on a bank of portable lights sitting just inside the door. "The club brought these in to help the lab boys see what they were doing," Ingram explained. "They'll stay here until this investigation is wrapped. So feel free to use them. Move them around wherever you need them."

"Thanks."

With the stink of smoke hanging in the air, Hart took in his surroundings while particles of soot and dust danced in the bright beams. He saw immediately that the explosion had occurred somewhere near the rear of the restaurant, blowing outward toward where he stood. The chairs and tables nearest him had been toppled by the force of the blast, but left intact. Across the room, the furniture was reduced to splinters. Throughout the restaurant, pieces of charred ceiling, insulation and boards had rained down, crisscrossing on top of the furniture and floor.

Ingram shifted his stance. "Has the D.A. already briefed you on the specifics of what happened? Given you copies of the reports?"

"No. I told him I wanted a look at the scene first. Gather my own impressions."

Usually at a fresh bomb scene, hot spots, jagged glass, nails and other debris made moving around treacherous. Those times Hart wouldn't take a step before pulling on the pair of steel-soled boots he kept in his field kit. Here, though, the scene was ten weeks old. The lab techs who had worked it had cleared a narrow footpath as they dug through the rubble.

Hart followed that path, snaking around toppled tables and chairs and other charred debris toward where the damage visibly worsened. Getting closer, he thought.

A few inches from a gaping hole in a wall, he found the crater. The shallow depression measured about four feet across. Crouching, he narrowed his eyes. Although the illumination from the portable lights on the far side of the restaurant was dim, he could see that the blast had ripped through the wood flooring but had barely chipped the concrete slab below. A shallow crater was characteristic of a low-velocity blast.

The ache that began working its way up from the bottom of Hart's skull told him volumes about the bomber's explosive of choice. Frowning, he rubbed at the back of his neck.

"You okay?"

"Yeah." He rose, stepped back from the crater. "A dynamite headache, is all."

"*Dynamite* headache?"

"There's traces of nitroglycerine in the crater."

Ingram's eyebrows slid up his broad forehead. "How the hell do you know that?"

"Nitro gives some people, including me, a headache. Has to do with its instant ability to thin blood."

"Okay, Spence Harrison hasn't briefed you on what happened. You haven't read any lab reports on the bomb. From what I hear, there's a lot of explosives out there these days. Why do you automatically assume the bomber used dynamite?"

"I'm not assuming anything. First, when it comes to explosives, nitro is used almost exclusively in dynamite. Finding nitro in any other type of explosive would mean the bomber used something pretty far-fetched and exotic." Hart gave his neck another rub. "Second, I get hit with a headache at a scene, I'm 99 percent sure I'm dealing with a dynamite bomb. Third, this bomb left a shallow crater, the type of blast commensurate with dynamite. The crater's size confirms what the ache in my head is telling me."

"I'll be damned," Ingram murmured. "You're right, Sergeant. The bomber used a nitroglycerine-based dynamite."

Turning, Hart glanced though the jagged teeth of a gaping hole in what was left of the restaurant's rear wall. Beyond the hole was a dark, yawning expanse where the worst of the fire had raged. He knew the dynamite itself wouldn't have sparked the flames unless an accelerant had been present.

He looked at Ingram, who had moved in and now stood a few yards away. "What started the fire?"

"Beyond that wall is the fried remains of the billiards room. Had big, megaexpensive pool tables, thick mahogany paneling on the walls, leather sofa and chairs, a lot of brass antiques. A real man's room."

"None of those things started the fire."

"I'm getting to that." Ingram pointed a finger. "A janitor's closet was there, sandwiched between the Men's Grill and the billiards room. At the time of the blast, it was filled with cleaning supplies, cans of paint and thinner."

"Paint and thinner? I expect the fire marshal had something to say after his people found out about that."

"Yeah. Everybody agrees—the stuff shouldn't have been in there."

"Why was it?"

"A paint crew was scheduled to start work on the kitchen the day after the bombing. When one of the crew members hauled in their supplies, he stuck everything in the closet where it'd be handy to the kitchen when they started the job the next day."

Hart slid his hands into the pockets of his khakis. "So, when the bomb exploded behind the closet, the blast ignited everything flammable inside, blowing flames out into the billiards room."

"You got it, Sergeant." Ingram ran a hand over his balding head as if smoothing down hair that was no longer there. "Some of the club's board members wanted the painter gone. His name's Willie Pogue and he's not exactly the most sterling employee around here. Bonnie talked the board out of firing him. He's got a wife and new baby, and a case of guilt a pasture wide. Nobody had to tell Pogue his carelessness made things worse."

"A lot worse," Hart agreed.

"Even so, I sided with Bonnie. We don't need to spend our time hammering some guy for an innocent screw-up. We need to find the sick scum who planted the bomb."

Unless Pogue *was* that scum, Hart thought. And he stacked the accelerant in the closet to intensify the damage.

Adding Pogue to the list of items he planned to bring up with Spence, Hart looked back at Ingram. "Other than the two fatalities and their injured son, how many people were hurt?"

"Fifteen. That includes club members and wait staff. Thank the Lord none were hurt worse than little Jake Anderson." Ingram checked his watch. "You going to spend a lot of time in here tonight? If so, I can give you a hand with whatever you need."

"Thanks, I'm almost done for now." Ingram had been nothing but congenial and cooperative. Eager. Still, Hart had worked hundreds of investigations; he knew that many things were not as they appeared on the surface. Things or people. When he worked this scene, he intended to do it alone.

He shifted his gaze back to the crater. Like all bomb investigators, he paid attention to details. He moved slowly and methodically, building puzzles often made of many small pieces over postblast investigations that lasted weeks, sometimes months. This investigation was no different. He would find out everything there was to know about the dynamite bomb that had exploded out a pressure wave with the capacity to kill in one-ten-thousandth of a second. Then, if luck and evidence were on his side, the remnants of that bomb would lead him to its maker.

That wasn't the only puzzle he intended to piece together, Hart realized as the image of Joan slid uninvited from a dark corner of his aching brain. He thought again about the flash of panic he'd seen in her eyes as she faced him across an expanse of ten years. Why panic? he wondered again. Why the hell *panic?*

At one time his love for her felt as though it was killing him. He'd gotten over her long ago, and he had no intention of taking a ride on that same roller coaster again. Still, he was curious. So much so that he intended to find the reason for that panic before he left Mission Creek.

Hours later Joan tucked the last of her laundry into a dresser drawer. Tightening the belt of her silky white robe, she eased a hip onto the edge of her pillow-piled bed.

"It's nine o'clock," she said to her daughter, clad in leopard-spotted pajamas and sprawled on her stomach crosswise on the peach-colored comforter. Propped up on her elbows, the young girl leafed through the pages of a family photo album.

"I think I'll use this one of you." Helena pointed a red polished fingernail at a photograph in the center of a page. "It looks the most like me. Grandma Kathryn took this picture of you, right?"

"Yes."

The photo showed a nine-year-old Joan, dressed in pink tights and tutu. Positioned in the center of the stage at the Mission Creek Grade School, she stood on the tips of her toes in pink satin *pointe* shoes, her arms twined exquisitely above her head. Her childhood dream of becoming a prima ballerina had faded the instant she took her first tennis lesson.

Joan's mouth curved. "Your grandma had a new camera that night. I think she snapped two entire rolls of film during the three minutes I spent on stage. I wasn't even the star."

"I miss Grandma Kathryn."

"I do, too, sweetheart," Joan said softly. Her grandmother's death a year ago had devastated Helena. Joan knew that her own father's rapidly failing health also hung heavy on her child's mind. Helena didn't need any more emotional trauma in her life right now. Which would be exactly what she would get if Hart O'Brien learned the truth.

Dread clamped a vise on Joan's chest, making it almost impossible to breathe. With an unsteady hand, she stroked her palm down Helena's long dark hair that streamed to her waist. "I think the two pictures you've picked are good choices for your Brownie project," she managed.

Helena plucked up a photo of herself dressed in similar ballet attire that she had already removed from a different photo album. "I'm standing in an *arabesque* position instead of *en pointe,* like you," she said, studying the photo. "But that's okay. Mrs. Rorke said to bring a picture of ourselves and a picture of one of our parents doing the same activity."

"We're both dancing ballet, so you've got it made," Joan said, then closed her eyes. There was no way Helena could have chosen a photo of her father doing anything, because there were no photos. None. When Helena had first asked why, Joan told her that her father had been gone so soon after they'd fallen in love there hadn't been time for pictures. That was basically the truth, except Joan had been the only one in love.

"Mom, can we take these albums with us the next time we visit Grandpa Zane?"

Blinking, Joan forced herself to concentrate on Helena's question. "I'm not sure he would look at them, sweetheart."

"Well, if he *did* look, maybe that would help him know who we are again. He's in a lot of these pictures, too." Flipping pages, she touched her red fingertip to several photographs of her and her grandfather smiling together. "Maybe seeing them would help him remember us. If he could do that, maybe he'd get well. I just want him to get better."

Joan slid an arm around her daughter's thin shoulders, grasping her in a tight hug. The Alzheimer's that had slowly taken over Zane Cooper's mind had robbed Helena of the only father figure she had ever known. "Did anyone ever tell you that you're one special kid?"

"Grandpa Zane did all the time before he forgot who I was," Helena said wistfully.

"He was right. And the next time we visit him at Sunny Acres we'll take one of the albums with us."

"Girl Scout's honor?"

"Girl Scout's honor." Joan dropped a kiss on Helena's head, drawing in her child's sweet, clean scent. "Now, it's time to go to bed in your own room."

"I'm not sleepy. Can't I look at the pictures a little longer?"

"No." Rising, Joan rearranged the throw pillows to one side of her bed. "Tomorrow's a school day," she continued as she nudged down the comforter and sheets. "And I have to get up early and meet a new client. In fact, I've got several new clients scheduled to begin programs at the spa, so I have to be there early every morning this week."

Not for the first time Joan sent up silent thanks that, when the Lone Star Country Club evolved into a nationally known resort, the board of directors added living quarters for upper-management employees. Joan's moving into one of those suites meant Helena could come home each day directly after school, instead of going to day care. Joan smiled at the thought of the checklist her nine-year-old daughter had made for herself. Each afternoon after her homework was done, Helena touched base with certain employees on her list to see if they needed her help. From assisting with swim classes to stuffing envelopes to folding napkins in the restaurants, Helena had her routine so perfected that Joan could pretty much check her watch and know Helena's exact whereabouts any given afternoon.

"How early do you have to leave for the spa?" Helena asked.

"Even before your ride to school gets here." Joan gathered the albums off the bed and slid them into the bookcase beside the tufted slipper chair that matched her comforter. "You'll have to come up to my office each morning and tell me goodbye, okay?"

"Okay."

"Oh, I almost forgot. Chief Stone called and invited us to a cookout at his house tomorrow night."

"Can I play Frisbee with Warrant?" Helena asked, referring to the chief's golden retriever.

"I doubt I'd be able to stop you." Two months ago Ben Stone had surprised Joan by asking her to dinner. He was forty-five to her twenty-eight; growing up, she had thought of him only as a police officer. Now she was cognizant of him as a handsome, attractive man. One whom she sensed would soon like their relationship to move into intimacy. That was a step Joan wasn't sure she wanted to take.

She slid a finger down Helena's nose. "Chief Stone said to tell you he's making your favorite homemade ice cream."

Helena grinned. "Chief Ben makes almost as good chocolate ice cream as Grandma Kathryn used to."

"Off to bed, now," Joan said, giving Helena a firm but loving tap on the bottom.

Reluctantly Helena crawled off the bed and made her way out the door.

Joan followed, saying, "I'll turn off the lights in the living room, then come in and kiss you good-night. Be sure and brush your teeth before you climb into bed."

"Okay, Mom."

Fifteen minutes after kissing Helena good-night, Joan stood on the dark balcony that jutted off her living room, staring at the starry night sky. The cool little breeze that swirled the hem of her silky white robe around her ankles made her shiver.

The suite she and Helena lived in was on the club's third level. Before dinner Joan had used the computer in her office to look up which suite Bonnie Brannigan had reserved for Hart. That suite was on the same level, three doors away.

Stepping to the waist-high railing, Joan leaned, counting each separate balcony where ivy and geraniums spilled over the wrought-iron railing. Her gaze settled on Hart's suite. The drapes were closed in both the living room and bedroom. She could see no light seeping around the edges.

She eased out a breath. Ten years ago she'd been eighteen, broken-hearted and pregnant, and would have given anything to have him near. Anything to have just known where he was.

And what would she have done if she had known? she asked caustically. Gone after him and begged him to want her? Begged him to love her the way she did him? Begged him to want and love the child she was carrying?

Hart had walked out on her. All her going after him would have done was enhance the despair and mortification she had felt when she realized his claiming to want and love her was a lie.

She shoved at a wisp of hair the breeze batted against her cheek. Ten years ago she had made a vow not to let her unborn child down. To give her the best life possible. To protect her.

Joan had no idea what kind of man Hart O'Brien had become. She could not second-guess what he might do if he discovered Helena was his daughter. Ignore his child? Befriend her? Walk away as easily as he had done ten years ago, leaving Helena with a shattered heart?

No, Joan thought as the need to protect welled inside her. Hart O'Brien had made his bed a long time ago. He had stepped on her own heart, but he wasn't getting a shot at Helena's.

For the first time Joan gave thanks for her parents' unending need to maintain appearances. That need had motivated them to send her to stay with her aunt in Dallas when they found out she was pregnant. When she brought Helena home to Mission Creek, Joan had learned her parents had told everybody she'd had a whirlwind romance with a Dallas attorney who had died weeks after they'd eloped. Everyone in Mission Creek had accepted the story. Joan had done nothing to change that. Why should she? Why not protect her child from the stigma of being illegitimate?

Everyone believed Helena's father had died before she was born. There was no reason Hart shouldn't believe that, too.

No reason to tell him Helena was his.

Chapter 3

Hart said goodbye to Yance Ingram outside the bomb crime scene, then rode an elevator, complete with a small, tinkling chandelier, to the third floor. There he unlocked the door to the executive suite Bonnie Brannigan had reserved for him. The sumptuous rooms were full of mahogany furnishings, Oriental rugs and silk drapes the color of burnt sugar. The suite sported two televisions, a stereo system and a full bar setup.

For Hart the opulent surroundings represented the height of irony. His previous living quarters in Mission Creek had been a cramped, going-to-rust trailer, which he and his mother shared on the outskirts of town. Then Vonda O'Brien had been a truck-stop waitress, existing in a hazy world of bourbon and country music. For years she had blocked Hart's efforts to get her off the bottle, claiming she was happy the way things were. Content to drift from town to town just as she'd done years before when she'd been a vocalist for a country-western band. Growing up,

Hart hadn't had a choice but to accept his mother's itinerant lifestyle.

Things had changed the day their car broke down in Mission Creek.

Tired of being on the move, sick of having nothing, he told Vonda they were settling down, and began a campaign of bullying her to go into rehab. He'd hired on at the Lone Star, determined to have some sort of normal life.

The day he first laid eyes on Joan Cooper dashing across a tennis court, he had forced himself to ignore the lust that punched through him. Forced himself to dismiss her sassy smile and the way she tossed back her dark hair. Told himself that a rich-girl, poor-boy romance had disaster written all over it. He had managed to keep most of his thoughts and his hands off Joan until that night she came to him. The curves that had driven him nuts for months had been covered only by skimpy shorts and a white halter top. Mad with desire, he had taken what she offered. And fallen in love in the process. He'd been fool enough to think that somehow, some way, he could keep her in his life.

Hours later he and Vonda had fled Mission Creek. If Zane Cooper's phony accusation that Hart had stolen money had been the man's sole threat, Hart would have dug in and defended himself. But Cooper had an ace in the hole—a hot check Vonda had written and a buddy on the sheriff's department willing to haul her in. With his mother in trouble, Hart had to get her away from there. Later, after he got Vonda settled near her stepbrother in Chicago and attending AA meetings, he had tried to contact Joan. That's when he found out she'd gotten married.

"Christ," Hart muttered. Even after so long he felt a remnant of the anger and hurt pride that had burned away the last of his innocence. Knowing those events still had the power to reach out and grab him by the throat had his temper rumbling all over again. He had spent ten years making something of himself. He didn't need reminders of a past that was best forgotten.

And he had to figure that was how Joan felt, too. After all, she'd heard her father's claim that the man she'd given herself to was a no-good thief. The shame she'd probably felt back then would have been enough for one lifetime.

Shame, Hart thought, his eyes narrowing. Could he have been wrong about her reaction to him this afternoon? Was what he'd read as panic actually been shame? His cop's instincts, honed over time, had always proved infallible. Still, emotion usually didn't taint those instincts.

Biting back frustration, he unpacked, then stowed his field evidence kit in a walk-in closet the same size as the sparkling-tiled bathroom that boasted a round sunken tub. That done, he returned to his rental car and drove though the clear moonlit night to the address Spence Harrison had given him.

Ten minutes later Hart pulled up to the curb in front of a Victorian house with a wraparound porch.

"Nice digs," he said as Spence headed into the kitchen for beer. Hart made himself comfortable on the leather couch that faced a dark fireplace with a burnished wood mantel and marble edging. On each side of the couch sat a matching leather wing chair. A thick-legged coffee table piled with neat stacks of file folders sat in front of the couch. The warmly lit room's overall impression was of old polished oak and leather, a place of comfort to settle in and relax.

"Glad you like the place," Spence commented when he strode back into view. Holding two long-necked beer bottles between the fingers of one hand, he loosened the knot on his crimson tie with the other. "The woman who owns this house is a widow. When I heard she wanted to rent out the entire top floor, I grabbed it."

"Smart move," Hart said, accepting the bottle Spence handed him.

"It's a plus that this place is only a couple of blocks

from the courthouse.'' Spence set his bottle on the coffee table, stripped off his navy suit coat and draped it over the far arm of the sofa. Out of the corner of his eye, Hart caught a glint of reflected light. He noted the small gold pin in the shape of a lion affixed to the coat's lapel. Yance Ingram had worn an identical pin.

"Sorry I couldn't meet you at the Lone Star when you got in," Spence said.

"No problem." While Spence settled into a chair, Hart sipped his beer, letting the ice-cold brew slide down his throat. "You said you had some sort of dinner event to-night."

"At which I gave a speech. The minute I wound things up my pager went off. I had to stop by my office on the way here to take care of a problem with a search warrant one of my assistants authorized. I got here five minutes before you drove up."

"That kind of schedule doesn't make for much of a social life."

"What the hell is a social life?"

Hart chuckled. "Good question. I wouldn't know one if it jumped up and bit me on the butt."

Spence took a draw on his beer. "Hard to believe it's been ten years since we slaved as groundskeepers at the Lone Star."

"Yeah." Spence Harrison hadn't changed much over those years, Hart decided. His friend still had the lean, powerful build that complemented his six-foot frame. He wore his thick brown hair in the same style, although now it was cropped close on the sides. It was his eyes that seemed different. More than just fatigue shone in their dark depths. Ingrained anxiety had settled there. Which, Hart supposed, was the reason Spence had asked him to come to Mission Creek.

Setting his beer on the table beside the couch, Hart leaned forward. "I took a look at the bomb site after I checked in."

"And?"

"Someone built a nitroglycerine-based dynamite bomb which they planted behind a closet filled with various accelerants. Since that's all I'm sure of at this point, why don't you fill me in on what you know?"

"It isn't much. Two days after the bombing the police chief—Ben Stone—organized a task force. Ten weeks later they still have nothing. No firm motive. Or solid suspect. Right now the cops are a million miles away from closing the case."

Hart wasn't a homicide detective, but he knew the first rule of any homicide investigation: look for a link between the victim and the killer. "Bonnie Brannigan said the people who died in the blast were salt of the earth. Have the cops come up with a reason anyone might want to kill them?"

"No. The police searched Dan and Meg Anderson's house and found nothing suspicious. The task force combed through their bank records, checked their safe deposit box, talked with co-workers, friends, the IRS and the state tax people. No red flags popped up. Nothing to make anyone think something nefarious was going on. No indication that either of the Andersons was being black-mailed or had a gambling problem. The way it looks, they'd be the last people anyone would have a reason to kill."

"Did they have a reservation that day at the Men's Grill?"

"No. One of the club members chatted with Dan outside the restaurant. He said he and Meg had decided to eat there on the spur of the moment. Even they didn't know they'd be there."

"Who *was* supposed to be there?"

"I was, for one."

Hart arched a brow. "Did you make a reservation?"

"No, but it wouldn't have been hard to figure out I would be there." As he spoke, Spence gave the back of his neck a long, slow rub. "During my stint in the marines I served under a lieutenant colonel named Phillip Westin. So did four other buddies of mine from Mission Creek. A couple of days before the bombing, Westin called me, Flynt Carson, Tyler Murdoch and Luke Callaghan to let us know he was flying in and staying overnight at the Lone Star. Westin had already scheduled a tee-time for all of us to play golf. He'd also made a reservation for us to eat in the Men's Grill after the game."

"Westin made those arrangements before he was even sure all of you would be available?"

"He didn't have to ask first. During the Gulf War, Flynt, Tyler, Luke, myself and another man named Ricky Mercado were captured in enemy territory. If Westin hadn't helped us escape, we'd have died. He knows all he has to do is ask and we'll be there for him. Anytime. Anywhere."

Hart narrowed his eyes. "Something tells me Westin wasn't making a social call here."

"Right. He stopped over on his way to Central America. Mezcaya specifically."

"The unrest there has made a lot of headlines. Why was Westin headed there?"

"To join a joint mission between our government and the British to take down the terrorist group, El Jefe. Have you heard of them?"

"Yes." Hart settled his elbows on his knees. "Terrorists are partial to using bombs, so my unit gets memos from the FBI, DEA and ATF on all known terrorist groups. From what I've picked up, El Jefe is Mezcaya's answer to Columbia's Cali cartel."

"Right. Lately El Jefe has been flexing its muscle. The Brits want to take down the group because its thugs have started roaming across the border and terrorizing citizens of Belize. The U.S. wants El Jefe because of the increase in drugs coming from Mezcaya into Mexico, most of which get smuggled into the U.S."

"So, El Jefe would have had ample reason to stop Westin from joining the mission," Hart reasoned. "A bomb would have not only killed him, but sent a message to others that it's not smart to screw with El Jefe."

"Correct."

Hart pictured again the devastation he'd seen at the crime scene. "The bomber planted the device near the rear wall of the Men's Grill. Was that near Westin's reserved table?"

"Yes. Right next to the table where a waitress seated Daniel and Meg Anderson."

"What about timing? Where was your group when the bomb went off?"

"On the trellised walkway behind the club house. Our golf game took longer than expected so we would have gotten to the Men's Grill about ten minutes after the time Westin scheduled the reservation." Spence shook his head. "That's the sticking point for me, Hart. There's no way to exactly time a golf game. My gut tells me word of Westin's mission leaked. The four of us whom he called knew a couple of days ahead of time he'd be at the Lone Star. So did everyone working at the front desk, the golf shop and in the Men's Grill. That's plenty of advance notice for one of El Jefe's thugs to set up the bombing. But since the bomb went off so close to the time set for Westin's reservation, I can't say for sure he was the target. If he was, the bomber sure didn't leave himself a very big window of opportunity."

"You're supposing the bomb went off when the bomber meant for it to."

Spence frowned. "Of course."

"It's not rare for a bomb to explode before or after it's intended to, so you have to take that into consideration," Hart responded. "A lot depends on the skill of the person who builds the device. Luck, both good and bad, also comes into play. I've lost count of the calls I've answered where an unsuspecting bystander touched a bomb and caused it to detonate prematurely. Sometimes you don't even have to touch an explosive device to set it off. Walk across a carpet or wear too much nylon and static electricity can detonate a certain type of bomb. Show me a female bomb tech and I'll guarantee you she never wears pantyhose on the job.''

''Christ.'' Spence sent him a long look. ''How do you do it?''

''What?''

''Purposely walk *toward* a ticking bomb. You do that, knowing the thing could kill you if you touch it the wrong way, make the wrong decision or cut the wrong wire.''

''With my training, I'm not in any more danger than a patrol cop who responds to a domestic disturbance,'' Hart replied. ''Speaking of career choices, your being the D.A. guarantees you a few enemies. Have you put anyone with explosives experience in prison? Especially someone who got out recently?''

''My staff checked. Other than you, the only person I know with explosives experience is Tyler Murdoch. Since he was also in Westin's party, I doubt Ty planted a bomb designed to blow himself up along with me.''

''Good point.'' Hart sipped his beer, going over what Spence had told him so far. ''What about Ricky Mercado?'' he asked after a moment. ''You said he served in the marines with you, but Westin didn't include him in the golf game. I remember hearing talk about the Mercado branch of the Texas Mob. Is Ricky a part of that family?''

''Yes. Westin didn't call Ricky because there's bad blood now between him, Luke, Flynt, Tyler and me. Has to do with Ricky's dead sister.''

Hart glimpsed the shadow of regret that passed over Spence's eyes. ''Do I need to know about that for this investigation?''

''No. I know Ricky as well as I know myself. He didn't plant that bomb because of what happened among all of us in the past. It's possible, though, that someone else in the Mercado family was behind the bombing."

"For what reason?"

"Did Bonnie mention Meg and Daniel Anderson's son to you?"

"Yes. Kid named Jake, right?"

Spence nodded. "Minutes before the bomb exploded, Jake walked out of the Men's Grill to find the rest room. He took a wrong turn and wound up opening a door that leads outside. He saw two men dragging bags out of one of the clubhouse's back doors and loading them into a car."

"What kind of bags?"

"Some sort of green cloth or canvas bags." Spence's mouth hitched upward on one side. "Jake thought the bags looked like the one he'd seen Santa with. The kid thought the men were Santa's helpers."

"Did these so-called elves spot Jake?"

"Yes. They slammed the door in his face. Then the bomb went off."

"I take it the police tried to find the bag men?"

"They interviewed employees and club members. If anybody knows who they are, they're not saying."

"Which leads us back to the Mercados. Do you think the bag men belong to the mob?"

"It's possible. What if those bags were stuffed with money? Or drugs? That would point to illegal activity going on at the Lone Star. Maybe someone on the inside stopped cooperating in that activity, and the mob planted the bomb to either kill them or scare the hell out of them."

"Hearing that makes me wonder about trusting anyone who works there."

"That thought has crossed my mind several times." Spence rose, walked to the fireplace and stared into its dark mouth. "The guys with bags could have also been cops."

Hart sat back in his chair. "When you called, you said an MCPD cop had committed suicide, another is also dead, and two others are charged with the attempted murder of a fellow officer. What in God's name is going on with the police?''

"Hell if I know. All I can say for sure is there's a problem inside the MCPD. I just don't know how big a problem." Spence scowled. "After Jake got out of the hospital, a cop named Ed Bancroft snatched him and his adoptive mom. Bancroft's partner, Kyle Malloy, was also in on the kidnap. Luckily, help got to Jake and his mom in time. Malloy got killed in a struggle and Bancroft was arrested. He clammed up, wouldn't say a thing, then hanged himself in a holding cell."

"Did Jake ID him or Malloy as one of the men he saw with the green bags?''

"Jake isn't sure." Spence paused. "There may be even more going on with the cops. The local rec center hired a basketball coach, an ex-con by the name of Danny Gates. He used to work for the Mercado mob."

"Used to?''

"Used to," Spence confirmed. "He's gone straight. Gates and a cop named Molly French developed a rapport with a teen named Bobby Jansen—goes by the name Bobby J. After he figured out he could trust Danny and Molly he started opening up."

"The kid gets close to an ex-con *and* a cop?''

"Strange combination," Spence agreed. "A couple of weeks ago, Bobby got beaten and wound up in the E.R. Before he went into surgery he managed to tell Molly he'd been working for some bad guys. Because of Danny and Molly's influence, Bobby decided to go straight. The bad guys got wind of that, beat him and left him for dead. Bobby told Molly the guys were cops who belong to a group called the Lion's Den."

"Damn." Hart pulled at his lip, staring into space as his mind worked. "What happened after Bobby got out of surgery?" he asked after a moment. "Did he I.D. the two men who beat him?"

"Bobby went into a coma during surgery and hasn't regained consciousness. When Molly French started digging into Bobby's assault, someone took a shot at her. Later two of her fellow officers and a nurse involved with one of those cops, named Beau Maguire, tried to kill French. Maguire's gone underground. His nurse girlfriend and his partner are in jail, keeping quiet."

Snagging his beer, Hart rose and walked to the opposite side the fireplace from where Spence stood. "You a member of the Lion's Den, too?"

Spence's eyes narrowed. "Why the hell do you ask?"

Hart gestured with his bottle toward the arm of the couch. "There's a gold pin shaped like a lion on your suit coat's lapel. Yance Ingram has one, too."

"That pin, my friend, is an award conceived years ago by Mission Creek's then mayor and city council."

Hart gazed at the small gold lion pin, then looked back at Spence. "What did you do to earn yours?"

"Before I became D.A., I did pro bono work for the battered-women's shelter."

"What about Ingram? What good deed did he do?"

"You'll have to ask him. Like I said, the award has been in existence for years. You'll spot a lot of lion pins around Mission Creek."

Hart nodded. "This Officer Molly French, is she on the up and up?"

"It's Detective French now. You can trust her. I can't say that about other cops because I don't know what's going on inside the P.D. *If* anything."

"If?"

"I've lost count of the calls I've gotten from the public demanding the police make an arrest on the bombing. I know that's one reason I'm feeling pressure. But that's not the only problem here. Maybe the four cops were a rogue group operating inside the department. Or maybe they're the tip of an iceberg that's just surfacing."

Rolling his shoulders, Spence walked to the nearest

chair and sat. "That's why I called you, Hart. You know about bombs. You know how a police department operates. I need you on the inside, telling me what's going on."

"Why isn't Molly French doing that?"

"She is. Still, she can only dig so much. If there are more corrupt cops, it's possible she's being watched. Don't forget someone took a shot at her. In my mind she's in danger and needs to lie low."

Hart leaned a shoulder against the mantel. "What about the department's top cop? Do you think he's righteous?"

"I don't have a reason to think he isn't. Ben Stone was born here, he's been chief for years. Nothing like this has ever happened on the force. No evidence ties him to the Lion's Den."

"How did he take it when you told him you want to put your own representative on his task force?"

"Ben said they need all the help they can get."

"That could be the PR spin. If I was a Mission Creek cop, I'd get my back up if I couldn't solve a case and somebody came in from the outside to look over my shoulder. Some big-town guy."

"Ben Stone's in a tight spot, just like I am. He's getting pressure from the mayor, city manager and the Lone Star's board of directors to get the bombing solved and the crime scene released so the club can get on with remodeling. Ben's people have had a ten-week shot at this and they've got nothing. Ben wants the case solved. Period. Who gets credit for that isn't a prime consideration."

"Stone understands I work for you? That I report only to you?"

"Yes. He's agreed to give you access to all reports, crime scene and autopsy photos, everything. I told him you'd drop by his office sometime tomorrow to introduce yourself."

"I'll go there in the morning." Hart settled back onto the couch. A question had nagged at him since he'd taken

Spence's phone call at the CPD's bomb squad. That and his conversation with Bonnie Brannigan had him wanting to clear the air.

"Why me, Spence? Why did you call *me?*"

"I view it as pure luck, since we lost contact with each other." He raised a shoulder. "I got a flyer for a criminal justice conference a few weeks ago and saw you named as a speaker on a bombing panel. I had no idea you lived in Chicago or were a cop, much less a bomb tech. But I figured there had to be only one O'Brien with the first name of Hart so I gave you a call."

Hart shook his head. "That's not what I mean. When I left Mission Creek, Zane Cooper accused me of stealing money from the golf shop. You and I worked together, I figured he must have told you I was thief. And I wondered if you believed I stole the money."

"Cooper never said a word about stolen money. No one else did, either." Spence's eyes widened. "Is that why you took off the way you did? Because Cooper accused you of being a thief?"

"That had a lot to do with it," Hart said through his teeth.

"Damn, Hart. That entire summer, whenever Zane Cooper looked at you all I saw was hate. Since Joan's the one who flirted up a storm with you while you kept your hands to yourself, his attitude was far from fair."

Hart drew in a slow breath. Spence didn't know he and Joan had spent a night together. At this late date, it didn't much matter.

"Think about it, Spence. I was the hired help from the trailer park. I don't have to tell you that Cooper had a thing about maintaining appearances."

"No, you don't. Look, for what it's worth, I felt lousy when you called a month or so after you left town and asked if I knew how you could contact Joan. Having to break the news that she'd run off to Dallas and married some lawyer didn't sit well."

"So, what happened?" Not that it mattered, Hart told himself. He didn't care about the man Joan had married. Didn't want to know any details of the life she shared with another man. *He didn't care.*

"What happened with what?"

"The lawyer. I ran into Joan this afternoon when I checked in. Her name tag says Cooper. She's not wearing a wedding ring."

Spence winced. "I've had so much on my mind lately that it didn't occur to me to tell you Joan manages the ladies' spa at the Lone Star. I guess you were surprised to see her."

"Yeah. I'm curious about her husband."

"His name was Thomas Dean."

"Was?"

"He died in a car wreck in Dallas not long after he and Joan got married."

For the past decade whenever he thought about Joan, Hart had forced himself to think of her as a wife. The mate of another man. A young woman who had freely given him her innocence, yet never intended to stay with him for longer than one night. He couldn't help but wonder what kind of man she had chosen over him. "You ever meet Dean?"

"No, just heard about him. Right after I set up my practice, Zane Cooper came to see me. He had decided to fund a trauma wing at the hospital in Dean's name and hired me to take care of the necessary legal documents. I remember Cooper mentioning his son-in-law's death happened so soon after he and Joan eloped that she hadn't had a chance to change her name on all her I.D. That's why she kept her maiden name."

"That had to have been rough on her," Hart murmured. "Her husband dying like that."

"Yeah. And it's a shame Dean's daughter never got to know her father."

Hart blinked. "Daughter?"

"Helena. You'll probably run into her, since she and Joan live in one of the Lone Star's employee suites. The kid's a real doll."

Joan was a widow, Hart thought. She had a daughter.

He sat in silence, wondering if there were other things about her life he didn't know.

Chapter 4

Hart spent a sleepless night in his suite's king-size bed, wrestling with ghosts of the past.

Around six-thirty he gave up and shoved back the vanilla-scented sheets he suspected had been ironed. The Lone Star had an outdoor jogging trail, and he was determined to run until he was too worn-out to think.

Why the hell had the few details Spence had told him about Joan clung like a burr in his head for the entire night? Why had he lost sleep thinking about her being a widow? A mother? Those facts meant nothing to him. *She* meant nothing to him.

Dammit, he had let her go.

But he had never forgotten her, he conceded as he yanked on running shorts and a black T-shirt bearing CPD's bomb squad logo. Not completely, anyway. Memories of her had lessened over time, but there were still instances when thoughts of her managed to slip uninvited into his mind.

Like every minute throughout the previous interminable night.

He grabbed a pair of white sport socks, then elbowed the drawer closed with more force than necessary. Fine, he thought. He had never forgotten her. It wasn't much of a mystery why a man might carry around the memory of a woman who'd cut out his heart.

He blew out a disgusted breath. Instead of focusing on the past, he needed to think about the present. He and Joan were different people than they'd been ten years ago. He doubted she still spent her days lobbing balls across one of the Lone Star's tennis courts. She was a business woman, the manager of a classy spa. A widow, raising a child. *He* no longer toiled as a country club groundskeeper, making sure everything looked presentable and ran smoothly for the cultured class. He was a cop, skilled in disarming explosive devices. All he and Joan had in common was the night they spent together. One night.

One night that had meant nothing to her.

"Dammit!" he muttered as he snagged his running shoes off the yawning expanse of closet floor. Before he'd met Joan Cooper he had never given away his heart. He damn sure hadn't felt the least bit tempted to risk giving it away since. That didn't mean he didn't want to. Someday.

Lately he'd caught himself feeling a twinge of envy when he attended the bomb squad's monthly cookouts and rubbed elbows with his co-workers' families. With increasing frequency he found himself wanting a real home, a wife and kids. Hart gave a derisive shake of his head. He couldn't exactly start down the path to getting those things when a casual conversation about a woman from his past had the power to make him toss and turn all night.

So, fine, that was an issue he needed to deal with.

Fate in the form of a bombing had brought him back to Mission Creek. He would consider that a sign, he decided while grabbing his watch and door card key off the nightstand. A sign that it was time to come to grips with all that had happened that long-ago summer. Time to put the past to rest so he could move on.

He was long overdue on letting Joan Cooper go.

He strode to the suite's door, unbolted it, then stepped into the cool quiet of the long, carpeted hallway. Pausing, he let the door drift shut behind him while he strapped on his watch. Catching movement out of the corner of his eye, he turned his head in time to see Joan appear from a doorway three rooms down.

She pulled the door closed with a soft click while giving an idle glance down the hallway. The instant she saw him, her chin came up and her shoulders stiffened.

Hart's eyes narrowed against an immediate stab of irritation. She had proven he meant nothing to her, so why did her nerves instantly go on alert each time she spotted him? Why the hell did she react to him at all?

When she reached behind her for the doorknob, he wondered if she might retreat back into the room until he disappeared down the carpeted hallway. Instead, she stood there, her fingers gripping the doorknob while they stared at each other across space. Across time.

He slicked his gaze down her trim, tidy turquoise suit, then on to those incredible legs that a blind man would have noticed. His eyes slowly resettled on her face. She looked elegant, classy with her dark hair pulled back in a smooth twist that emphasized the long, slender arch of her throat.

His hands fisted with the realization that after so long he still remembered the soft, warm taste of that flesh. Could again hear her raw, passionate moan when he took away her innocence and made her his.

Ten years ago, wanting her had been like a fever in his blood. In the space of a dozen heartbeats, he again felt something inside him stir. And realized it was the blood he'd let settle and cool over the years.

Don't go there, he warned, and took a mental step back. Don't go the hell near there.

The noise of the resort awakening around them slowly slid into his consciousness. A murmur of distant voices. The rattle of china on a room service cart. The far-off ding of an elevator. Finally Joan gave him a curt nod, turned and started down the hallway in the opposite direction, her long, wand-slim body flowing into the movement.

Hart hesitated. After the restless night he'd spent because of her—and the unsettling punch of lust he'd just experienced—it seemed wiser all the way around to keep his distance.

Hell, when it came to Joan Cooper he hadn't ever been wise.

"Morning, Texas," he said when he strolled up behind her at the bank of elevators.

She paused before turning, giving him an opportunity to skim his gaze down her back, over those long legs. "Good morning, Hart."

Close up, he saw the smudges of fatigue beneath her eyes that made him think she hadn't slept any better than he had. Although his ego would have preferred to think she'd lost sleep over him, common sense told him better.

Her glossed lips lifted slightly at the corners. "I hope you're enjoying your stay at the Lone Star. Be sure to let us know if you need anything."

The cool politeness in her voice had him raising a brow. "That the standard company line? Or did you just come up with it off the top of your head so we'd have something to chat about while we wait for the elevator?"

"You're our guest." Reaching, she pressed the elevator's already lit call button. "It's important to every employee that you have a pleasant stay."

He thought back to the sleepless hours he'd spent on a certain employee's account. "So far I wouldn't call my stay at the Lone Star pleasant."

The comment earned him a concerned look. "I hope

that's because of your business here. I can imagine how awful it must be having to view bombing scenes where people have died and been injured.''

He stared at her for a long moment. He wasn't complacent about his job. He couldn't be, not when he worked in a world where the unexpected always showed up and where the threat posed by each bomb builder changed as fast as technology advanced. Yet, what he did for a living had been the last thing on his mind this morning. He had thought of her. Only of her.

Now he forced his mind to the devastation he had seen the previous afternoon in the Men's Grill and the billiards room. Since Joan worked and lived at the Lone Star, the makeshift plywood wall with its padlocked door would no doubt serve as a constant reminder of how irreparably an explosion could change a person's world. ''You're right,'' he said, softening his voice. ''Working a bomb scene is one of the unpleasant aspects of my job.''

Nodding, she lifted a hand to her throat. ''It's hard knowing that the person who set the bomb is still free.'' Looking across her shoulder, she shifted her gaze down the hallway in the direction they'd come. ''I hope you find who did it, Hart.'' The sudden vulnerability that slid into her dark eyes sounded in her voice. ''I hope you find him soon before he has a chance to kill or injure someone else.''

Her child, he realized. Of course she wasn't concerned just for her own safety but that of her daughter.

''I'll do everything I can to make sure the person who made that bomb winds up behind bars.'' Pausing, he inclined his head toward the hallway. ''I take it the room I saw you walk out of is where you live? You and your daughter?''

Joan's hand slowly dropped from her throat. The vulnerability disappeared from her eyes, and her face took on a closed, blank look. ''Why do you ask?''

''Just wondering, is all. When I met with Spence last

night he mentioned that you're a widow. That you have a child and you live here.''

Her eyes were now as cool as her tone. "Why were you and the district attorney talking about me?"

"No real reason." He lifted a shoulder. "Your name came up in the conversation."

"What about you, Hart?"

"What about me?" he asked, aware that she had changed the subject before answering his question.

"Is there a Mrs. O'Brien waiting in Chicago for you to come home? Some little O'Briens?"

"No. Getting married and having kids is still on my to-do list."

"I see."

His gaze flicked to the small brass name tag above her left breast. He replayed Spence's explanation of why she still used her maiden name. Which, now that Hart thought about it, was odd since old man Cooper had endowed a wing at the hospital in his dead son-in-law's name. Wouldn't she want to be linked to something like that?

"Does your daughter go by Cooper, too?" he asked, just as an elevator chimed its arrival.

Something flickered in Joan's face, then was gone. "Yes." Very deliberately she turned and reached for one side of the double doors that slid apart, braced it open with her palm, then turned to face him. "I take it by the way you're dressed you're going jogging?" A thin smile accompanied the question.

"You've got a good grasp of the obvious."

She inclined her head in the opposite direction from the one they'd come. "If you take the flight of stairs at the end of the hallway to the ground level, the door you'll come to leads right out to the jogging trail."

"Thanks for the tip." Her blatant desire not to share an elevator with him had him taking a perverse step past her into the cab. "I'll ride down with you, if you don't mind," he said, trying to ignore the punch in the gut that came with a whiff of the warm, subtle scent of Chanel No. 5. He leaned against the wall opposite her, wishing to God she didn't look so beautiful, that just her presence didn't play so perfectly on his senses.

She hesitated before using a pink polished nail to press the button for the ground floor. "Of course I don't mind. You're a guest here, Hart. You can use whatever elevator you like."

"I'm also a cop, Texas." He crossed his arms over his chest. "Using a polite tone doesn't make it any easier to get a lie past me."

She turned to face him. "I wouldn't think for one minute that lying to a police officer would be easy."

"It's not. And it generally doesn't get you anywhere but into trouble, so you can drop the polite act." His mouth took on a sardonic curve as the door slid shut, closing them in. "The truth is, you mind like hell sharing this elevator with me."

He saw a muscle tighten in her jaw. "All right, Hart, since you won't let the matter alone, I'll forget my customer service training for a moment. You're right, I would rather not share this, or any other elevator with you. Does that make you happy?"

Her cool, even stare had the nasty mood he'd climbed out of bed with heat his temper all over again. "Yeah, it always makes me really happy when someone tells me the truth."

Turning toward the control panel, she restabbed the button for the ground floor. "In fact, since we're being honest with each other, why don't we take this a step further? Let's agree that we simply prefer to avoid each other." Looking back at him, she raised her chin. "Perhaps your stay at the Lone Star will be more pleasant for both of us if we have as little contact as possible."

With a faint hydraulic hum, the elevator reached the ground floor. The small chandelier that hung overhead tinkled with the movement.

Hart set his teeth. They had avoided each other for a decade, yet she still had the power to make him lose sleep. Make his blood stir while she stood only inches from him, looking as distant as the stars. She wanted space, he would give it to her. And while he was at it, he would somehow, some way sever those last connecting threads to her that had haunted him for so long.

Stepping toward the door, he halted inches from her, but didn't touch her.

"Now that you mention it, Texas, our having no contact sounds damn good to me."

Running into Hart that morning had, among other things, cut into Joan's schedule, causing her to reach the spa only moments before the wife of a Texas state senator arrived. After introducing the client to Britta, the six-foot, blond Swedish therapist, Joan held a meeting with several senior staff members, took calls from two European wholesalers who supplied the exclusive beauty products the spa carried, then welcomed a second new client who had flown in that morning on her private Lear jet for a week-long herbal detoxifying program. Joan had sandwiched in a goodbye kiss for Helena who had dashed into the spa before leaving to catch her ride to school.

Now, three hours into her workday, Joan paused in Body Perfect's opulent reception area, telling herself it was time to turn her attention to the paperwork in her office. A dozen pieces of correspondence sat on her desk awaiting her attention, as did several phone messages.

Still, she hesitated. She knew if she closed herself in her office that her mind would roam to Hart.

"Is there something I can help you with, Ms. Cooper?"

Joan turned toward the receptionist's sleek console, with its top-grade computer and phone system. Sonji Dunaway, blond and buxom, gave Joan an expectant look while soft, soothing music played around them, harmonizing with a small splashing fountain.

Joan shifted her gaze to the small gold clock on the console beside a crystal vase of yellow roses, their light scent perfuming the air. "I was wondering if Mrs. Zink had arrived yet for her shiatsu massage."

Sonji nodded. "She got here about ten minutes ago. I settled her into the therapy room with a cup of ginger-honey tea, then let Mariko know her client was waiting."

"Good. Let me know when Mrs. Zink's session is over. I have the information about the exercise regimen she asked me to put together."

The receptionist sent Joan the bright smile that had endeared her to the staff and clients. "Will do, Ms. Cooper. Anything else?"

"No." Joan gave the capable young woman an appreciative smile. "If you need me, I'll be in my office dealing with paperwork before my meeting with Miss Delarue."

Joan's heels sank into the thick carpet as she headed down the central corridor with spacious offices and therapy rooms opening to either side. Her own office was roomy and elegant, decorated in the same soothing pale-pink and cream tones as the reception area. Sonji had left a thermal carafe of tea on the mahogany desk that sat in the center of an Oriental rug. To one side of the carafe was a stack of the spa's signature-pink file folders. Documents awaiting Joan's attention were set squarely in front of her chair, arranged in order of priority.

Joan had just pulled off the jacket of her turquoise suit and settled behind her desk when the intercom line rang. "Yes, Sonji?"

"Miss Delarue is here."

Joan let out a breath. She and Maddie Delarue had scheduled the meeting to discuss the upcoming Pasta by the Pool dance. Yet, the Lone Star's event coordinator was also Joan's best friend and she knew the conversation she had put off having with Maddie would wind up squarely on Hart. "Send her in."

"Tell me there's more than one man in the world named

Hart O'Brien,'' Maddie stated when she swept through the office door. ''Tell me that the Chicago bomb tech who arrived here yesterday isn't *the* Hart O'Brien.''

Joan pursed her mouth. She had hoped they could get their business out of the way first. ''I take it you don't want to start out talking about Pasta by the Pool?''

''Hardly.''

Joan leaned back in her chair. ''I didn't think you would have heard yet about Hart being here.''

''So, it is him? *Him?*''

''Yes, it's *him.*''

''I was afraid of that.'' A few years Joan's senior—redhaired where Joan was dark; petite where Joan was willowy—Maddie dropped into one of the visitor chairs in front of Joan's desk. Dressed in a silk designer trouser suit in soft olive gray that complemented her voluptuous figure, Maddie looked her usual blue-blooded gorgeous. ''I had breakfast this morning with Bonnie to get the ball rolling on the mystery night gala that the club's sponsoring at the end of the summer. When she mentioned the bomb tech's name I just about choked on my omelette. Why didn't you call and tell me that *the* Hart O'Brien had shown up?''

''I planned to.'' Maddie's and Joan's families had been lifelong members of the Lone Star and a close friendship had developed between the girls early on. Now with Joan's mother dead and her father's memory destroyed by Alzheimer's, Maddie was the only other person who knew that Hart was Helena's father.

''Maddie, I had no idea Hart was the bomb tech Bonnie told us about in the staff meeting until I ran into him in the lobby yesterday afternoon. When I saw him I felt like I'd fallen into a black hole. Maybe I thought if I didn't call and tell you about seeing him that I would wake up this morning and discover it had all been a bad dream.''

''I guess that didn't happen.''

''No. I ran into Hart again this morning, and he's real.

Very real.'' She gnawed her lip, thinking about how as they'd stood inches apart in the elevator's intimate confines her heart had pounded hard enough to rock her body. She had always responded that way toward him—and she knew from her reaction this morning that the chemistry hadn't changed as far as she was concerned. It didn't matter how much time had passed or what else had gone on between them, she would always feel that thrumming, physical connection to Hart O'Brien.

Damn him.

Maddie ran a manicured hand up and down the thick gold links she wore around her neck. ''If Bonnie's description is accurate, the bomb tech is a real feast for the eyes.''

Joan pictured Hart as he'd looked a few hours ago, his mouth firm and unsmiling, his narrow, rawboned face made even more carelessly handsome by the dark stubble that shaded his jaw. And those inscrutable green eyes behind long, amber lashes. Just as they had ten years ago, his dark, go-to-hell looks had pulled at something deep inside her.

Feeling her throat go dry, Joan reached for the thermal carafe and poured two cups of steaming tea.

''For the record, Bonnie's description hits the target. But Hart's looks are the last thing on my mind.'' Joan handed Maddie a tea cup. ''Hart said he met with Spence last night, and for some reason, my name came up. Spence told Hart that I'm a widow and I live at the Lone Star with my daughter.'' Joan clenched her fingers, flexed them. ''I know it's just a fluke, but Bonnie put him in the executive suite three doors away from ours. Maddie, you know how Helena has the run of the Lone Star. With Hart staying here, in a room so close to ours, he's bound to at least catch a glimpse of her.''

Maddie's perfectly plucked eyebrows slid together in thought. ''His seeing her doesn't mean a thing. Unless...''

Sipping her tea, Joan met her friend's gaze over the rim of her cup. "Unless what?"

"I was at my cousin's in California the entire time Hart worked here, so I've never seen so much as a glimpse of him. Does Helena resemble him? Can you look at the two of them and tell they're father and daughter?"

"No, thank goodness. Hart's hair is lighter than Helena's and has a lot of auburn in it. Her eyes are brown, his are green." And this morning, those eyes had looked as dangerous as his job, Joan thought. "Helena has my build, too," she added. "Last night she and I went through some old photo albums for one of her Brownie projects. She looks exactly like I did when I was nine."

"That's something to be grateful for."

"About the only thing. Maddie, Hart is a police officer. He asks questions for a living. Conducts investigations." Joan sat her cup aside and rubbed at the headache building in her right temple. "He's already had an occasion to tell me that lying to a cop generally doesn't get you anywhere but into trouble. When he said that, I felt a premonition, like footsteps of the devil crawling up my spine."

Maddie gave her a wary look. "Why the heck did the subject of lying come up?"

"Because I told him I didn't mind sharing an elevator with him. He took exception to that. He was right, I did mind." And her nerves were still scrambling from the experience. "My stomach knots at just the thought of being around him."

"Considering your past, that's understandable. But you should look at things this way. You haven't lied to Hart about anything. In fact, *you* haven't really lied to anyone," Maddie pointed out. "The instant you told your parents you were pregnant they sent you packing to your aunt's in Dallas. It wasn't until you brought Helena back here to live two years later that you found out your parents made up the story about how you eloped with some fictional guy named Thomas Dean days before he died in a car wreck.''

"You're right, I didn't know. But when I found out about that story, I didn't do anything to change it or stop it, either.''

"Why would you? Hart O'Brien whispered sweet nothings in your ear, then rolled out of town like a tumbleweed in a tornado. Your parents wanted to protect you and their grandchild. So, instead of everyone looking at you like you were a woman scorned and your daughter illegitimate, you became a widow and your child avoided being labeled. What were you supposed to do at that point? Tell everybody in Mission Creek that your parents lied? That they made up Thomas Dean because you spent a night with a man who did a 'conceive and flee' on you?''

Joan couldn't help but smile at Maddie's term. "You're right, spreading the word that my parents had invented a combination husband for me and father for Helena wouldn't have accomplished anything.'' Even so, Joan had lost count of the nights she'd lain awake, smothering in guilt. Wondering if someday that lie might catch up to her and affect her relationship with Helena.

"And not only did your parents make up Thomas Dean,'' Maddie continued, "they went to considerable effort breathing life into him. Endowing a wing at the hospital in his name. A couple of stained glass windows in the church in his memory. The children's park. The artwork. They did all that to protect you and Helena.''

Joan knew those seemingly philanthropic acts were only part of her parents' motivation. They believed that their only child had thrown away her future by spending what they viewed as a sordid night with a groundskeeper at the country club. The shame of that had been almost more than her class-conscious parents could bear. Still, no matter the reasons behind Zane and Kathryn Cooper's subterfuge, in the end their actions had protected Helena.

Helena, who had changed everything. Nothing had prepared Joan for the love she felt for her daughter, something so deep and unfathomable it was undefinable. She would do anything for her child. Anything to shield Helena from harm. So, Joan had let her parents' lie live and breathe for ten years.

She glanced down at the pink file folders on her desk, many of which contained schedules for clients who had contracted for Body Perfect's services. People came to the spa to forget their responsibilities for a while. To forget the clock's ticking, forget that they had a life they had to get back to. For however long they were there, the spa was a place without time.

For Joan, Body Perfect represented just the opposite. Her responsibility to Helena had brought her here. The need to make a secure life for her daughter had forced the pampered country club girl, who had once dreamed of a life that included daily tennis matches and society lunches, to mature and transform almost overnight into a responsible parent.

A parent realistic enough to acknowledge that someday the time would come to tell Helena the truth.

"Maddie, you know that I've always planned on telling Helena about Hart," she reminded her friend quietly. "But not for years, not until she's old enough to understand. Right now she's just too young."

"No matter when you tell her, it won't be easy for her to figure out how her daddy gave you up." Maddie sipped her tea. "I sure can't."

"Hart didn't give me up. He never wanted me." Joan picked up a gold pen off her desk blotter, laid it back down. "His being here is such a shock because I never thought I would see him again. Never thought he would walk back into my life."

Maddie leaned forward, sat her teacup on the desk. "He hasn't exactly walked back into your life, has he? He came to the Lone Star because the D.A. brought him here to do a job. Hart O'Brien is here solely on business. When the bombing gets solved, he'll go back to Chicago. Maybe forever.''

Joan stared across the polished span of desk and saw compassion in her friend's blue eyes. Maddie was right. Hart hadn't come back for her. Motherhood and the passage of time had erased the yearning that he do so from Joan's heart. Yet, even now, she wondered what her life would have been like if Hart had remained in Mission Creek. If the loving words he had whispered against her heated flesh on that long-ago night had been true. If he hadn't chosen to stay away for nearly a third of her life.

Joan shoved away the thoughts that even now had the power to make her heart ache. What-ifs, might-have-beens, if-onlys—they had the power to drive a person crazy. Hart was, and could only ever be, a dream from her past. She needed to remember that, Joan thought, pulling her defenses more closely around her.

Now Helena was the only one who mattered. She was the one whose feelings had to be considered. If she knew Hart was her father, if he told her he wanted her, loved her, then turned his back on her, the safe, secure world she knew would shatter.

Because Joan intended to protect her child by holding tight to her own secrets, Hart would never know Helena was his daughter. He wouldn't get a shot at hurting her, of wounding her so deeply that her heart lay ripped open and bleeding for years.

Only Helena mattered.

Chapter 5

His muscles burning from an eight-mile run, Hart showered, ate breakfast, then phoned the Mission Creek Police Department to schedule a meeting with Chief Ben Stone.

"The chief will see you the minute you get here," a female clerk responded in a twanging Texas accent.

During his drive to the PD, Hart thought again about how Spence had assured him Stone welcomed his involvement in the investigation. The chief's agreeing to see him as soon as possible seemed to underscore that. Still, Hart knew that most law enforcement agencies didn't like outsiders stepping uninvited into an ongoing investigation. Since the district attorney, not the chief of police, had brought Hart in on the case, he wondered if Stone's welcome would be cordial only on the surface.

Shrugging, Hart figured he would find out soon enough whether Ben Stone and the members of the MCPD task force wanted him there.

The cop shop was in a well-maintained brick building

in the center of downtown. With the public parking spots in front occupied, Hart drove around to the building's rear.

He pulled into one of the slots and climbed out into the heavy, dry air that felt as though summer had arrived in March. As Hart strode across the lot, he noted that the parking space closest to the building was occupied by a city-owned Blazer with the gold badge of the chief of police on its door.

Following the clean-swept sidewalk around to the front of building, Hart walked in through the glassed entrance door to a lobby. The brown-carpeted space was furnished with sturdy-looking chairs and a counter behind which several people went about their jobs.

Hart took out his badge, flipped open the leather case. "Sergeant Hart O'Brien, Chicago PD," he said to the middle-aged reception sergeant. "I'm here to see Chief Stone."

The cop's gaze flicked to the badge. "Yeah, the chief's expecting you." As he spoke, the uniformed cop reached beneath the counter and buzzed open the door beside the counter. "I'll take you back to the chief's office."

"Thanks."

Sliding his badge into his pocket, Hart followed the cop into a suite of offices built around a common reception area furnished with a couch and matching chairs. The pristine upholstery and polished coffee tables created the atmosphere of an upscale business office.

A slim, attractive brunette sat at a neat desk in the center of the reception area, entering data on a computer keyboard.

"Missy, this is Sergeant O'Brien, Chicago PD," the sergeant said.

"Hi, Sergeant," the receptionist responded in the twangy voice Hart recognized from his phone call. Turning an impeccably made-up face in his direction, she gave him a bright smile. "I'll just buzz Chief Stone to let him know you're here."

''Appreciate it,'' Hart said. So far his reception at the MCPD couldn't have been warmer.

Nor could Chief Ben Stone have been more cordial when he waved Hart to one of the leather visitor chairs at the front of his desk. ''Good to meet you, Sergeant O'Brien. Looking forward to working with you.''

Stone stood well over six feet with the long limbs and strong shoulders of an athlete. He had tanned, craggy features, short, salt-and-pepper hair and probing, intelligent blue eyes. His dark-brown uniform shirt and matching pants had creases so sharp they could shave ice. As a sign of his rank, silver eagles nested on each collar point of his shirt. His spotless light-gray tie was speared midcenter by a small gold tie tack. His uniform brass was polished. An immaculate Sam Browne belt held a holstered .45 automatic Colt. Hart noted the gray Stetson hanging on the wood coatrack that stood in one corner of the office. He knew the Stetson was Texas's answer to the standard billed uniform hat issued by the majority of police departments.

''I'm looking forward to working with the MCPD, too,'' Hart replied as he settled into the chair Stone had indicated.

Stone sat in the tall, leather chair behind his cherrywood desk on which several file folders were neatly stacked beside a brass ashtray. The faint scent of rich leather and expensive cigars hung in the air.

''I take it the D.A. filled you in on my investigation?''

Hart caught Stone's use of *my*. ''Yes, I met with Spence Harrison last night.''

Got an earful, too, Hart silently added. He thought about the men with bags whom little Jake Anderson had mistaken for Santa's helpers. About the two cops who later kidnapped Jake and were now dead, one by suicide. Then there was Bobby J., the teenager beaten into a coma by two men he claimed were cops who belong to a secret group called the Lion's Den. Were those cops the same two who had later tried to kill Detective Molly French?

Hart didn't know. All he knew at this point was that the man currently studying him with intent blue eyes was ultimately responsible for the conduct of every sworn police officer in Mission Creek. The buck stopped with Ben Stone. The duty fell to him to ensure integrity within his department. If the problems that had become known were isolated incidents, that could mean there had been a few rotten apples around. However, if those men were indeed members of a larger gang of rogue cops, the entire department might be a rotten barrel.

If that was the case, Ben Stone could well be up to his neck in that barrel.

Time would tell, Hart thought. Meanwhile, the first thing he wanted to do was clear the air.

"Chief Stone, if I were a Mission Creek cop I wouldn't like having me around. Somebody with a badge from the outside sticking his nose in another jurisdiction's active investigation usually doesn't win a popularity award."

"True," Stone agreed. "I'd be lying if I said my troops cheered when they heard the D.A. called in a bomb expert. That news had the same effect as a slap in the face to every officer on my task force."

"Understandable, since I'm essentially looking for holes in the work they've done over the past ten weeks."

"Ten weeks is the point. My people have worked on this investigation for over two months and all we have are unprovable theories. No firm suspect. No overwhelming motive. No easy answers. I'm getting daily phone calls from the mayor, the city manager and the Lone Star's board of directors. Not to mention upset private citizens. Everybody's pressing me to get this case solved."

Pausing, Stone turned to the credenza behind his desk where a homey grouping of framed photographs of two elfin-faced young girls sat. He pulled a long, slender cigar and gold cigarette lighter from a drawer in the credenza's center. "If a cop from another jurisdiction can help solve this damn bombing, my people will just have to get over it," Stone added.

With a sharp thumb flick, a flame flared from the lighter. He touched the flame to the cigar's tip and puffed. Almost instantly the sharp scent of tobacco filled the air. "You let me know what you need, Sergeant O'Brien. I'll see you get it. And if any of my people give you grief, I damn well want to know."

"Let's hope that doesn't happen, Chief." The man's explanation that he'd opened the door on the investigation due to increasing pressure to close the case sounded on target. Still, talk was cheap and Hart preferred to take a wait-and-see attitude when it came to Mission Creek's top cop.

Lifting his chin, Stone blew out a stream of gray smoke. "Since you're a bomb expert, I expect that's the area you'll concentrate on?"

"At first. When I leave here, I plan to hit the lab and take a look at the bomb frag recovered. Later this afternoon I'll spend some time at the crime scene."

"I'll call the lab and make sure they know you've got carte blanche where this investigation is concerned."

"I appreciate that." Hart knew his bringing up the subject of corrupt cops would put Stone on the defensive, so he opted to tread around the issue. "Spence Harrison told me about the men Jake Anderson saw just before the bombing. The ones moving bags out of a back door at the Lone Star."

"Santa's helpers," Stone said around the cigar. "What about them?"

"I'm wondering about the club's security. Surveillance cameras specifically. I went jogging this morning and took a detour behind the clubhouse. I saw a couple of cameras aimed at the rear of the building. Surely one of them picked up the men Jake saw right before the bomb exploded."

"Those surveillance cameras weren't there ten weeks ago. The club had some cameras before the bombing—Yance Ingram can tell you exactly where. I know they were mostly in the areas where the members have access. The board had never seen a need to install surveillance cameras in out-of-the-way places like the back of the clubhouse."

"Too bad."

"You're telling me. The board placed a lot more cameras around the grounds after the bombing. Too little, too late for this investigation." Stone planted his forearms on the desk, his cigar clamped between two thick fingers while smoke curled slowly toward the ceiling. "Harrison said you used to live in Mission Creek. That you worked with him at the Lone Star."

"That's right." Hart wondered what Stone would say if he knew he and his mother had left town under threat of arrest.

"Then you've probably heard of the Mercado family."

"Also known as Mission Creek's answer to the Corleones."

Hart's comment earned a scowl. "I won't go into how I detest having an arm of the Texas mob operating around here. The Mercado group is like most every other Mafia family in this country. It's got someone smart at its helm. In this case that someone is Carmine Mercado. The old man is sharp of eye and brain—nothing gets by him. Anybody thinking of ratting what they know usually winds up in cement. For years the Mercados have run drugs and moved illegal weapons in and out of Mission Creek. I *know* that. Problem is, I can't prove it so I can't touch them."

Hart rested one ankle on the opposite knee. "I take it you brought up the Mercados because you think the men Jake Anderson saw with the bags work for the family?"

"I do, and I'm not alone in my thinking. Most of the cops on the task force believe there were weapons or drugs, maybe both in those bags. And that the bombing was some sort of gangland violence. Maybe even some up-and-coming Mafia guy wanting to make an impression on someone.''

"Do you have any idea who at the Lone Star needed impressing by a bomb?''

"That's the twenty-four-thousand-dollar question. Wish I knew the answer.'' Stone's mouth curved. "Maybe you'll have more luck getting to the truth than we've had so far.''

"Maybe.'' Hart glanced at this watch. He didn't want to overstay his welcome. "Chief, I'll check in daily with the task force to see if anything new comes up. As to what they've already got, I'd like copies of all crime incident reports and follow-ups. Also copies of all crime scene and autopsy photos.''

"Well now, it might take a little time for us to rustle up those copies.''

"Why is that?'' Hart wondered if he'd just run into the first wall of resistance.

"It'd be easier to show you why than to tell you.'' Ben stabbed his cigar out in the brass ashtray, then pushed back from his desk and rose. "Let's take a walk down the hall.''

"Sure.'' Hart stood and waited as Stone strode around the desk. Up close, Hart noted that the small gold tie tack in the center of Stone's tie was shaped like a lion.

Hart slid a hand into one pocket of his khaki slacks. Last night he'd seen Yance Ingram and Spence Harrison wearing the same type of pin. This morning while he ate breakfast in the Lone Star's Yellow Rose Café he'd spotted two men and a woman wearing the same lion-shaped pins. He couldn't help but wonder if it was more than just coincidence that the Mission Creek-sponsored civic award and an alleged group of rogue cops were both linked to a beast known for its courage and terrorizing ferocity.

"I headquartered the task force in our old lunch room,'' Stone explained as they walked out of the reception area and along a hallway. As they moved, the sounds of keyboards clicking, phones ringing and shoes scuffing along the tiled floor filled the air.

Stone led the way to a room with a piece of paper taped to the doorjamb that read: Stone's Group. Inside, three Formica-topped tables were jammed against the far wall in an edge-to-edge line. The table to the far left held a computer monitor, keyboard and a collection of disorganized photos, probably from the bombing scene. On the table in the middle sat a large black notebook that Hart suspected was the official case investigation log. Piles of loose papers avalanched around the notebook. The table on the right held a task force's most important piece of equipment: a coffeemaker. Nearby an American flag drooped on a pole topped by a brass eagle in midflight.

Two additional tables sat in the center of the room, butted side by side. Three officers, two in uniform and one in plainclothes sat around the tables. The plainclothes cop was in his shirtsleeves, his weapon and gold badge clipped to his belt. One of the uniforms talked on a telephone, the other jotted notes on a pad. Standing near the center table, another plainclothes cop with a burly build and dark hair going gray at the temples exchanged words with a younger, testosterone-pumped officer wearing a black pullover and slacks that emphasized his muscles.

"I've dug into Daniel Anderson's life so deep I can tell you the color of each pair of his boxer shorts," the burly cop said. "I've known virgins who were less pristine than that guy. Nobody had a reason to kill him. Or his wife, for that matter. They weren't the target of that bomb."

"Yeah?" the muscle-bound cop asked. "Can you prove it?"

"I don't have to *prove* who wasn't the intended victim, McCauley. I have to prove who was. And I say we're wasting time if we continue looking at either of the Andersons."

"Problem?" Stone asked quietly, moving to the head of the table. The discussion stopped.

"Talking strategy is all," the burly cop said.

"Any conclusions?" Stone asked, calmly, taking control.

"Nope," Mr. Muscle said, sliding his hands into the pockets of his slacks.

Stone pointed a hitchhiker-like thumb toward Hart. "This is Sergeant O'Brien, the Chicago PD bomb tech who the D.A. brought in to liaise. O'Brien's not here to step on our toes, so don't anybody get an attitude. He'll work by himself, parallel to this investigation. I've given him access to everything we've got. Maybe he can tell us something about that bomb that'll give us a solid lead on who built it."

"A solid lead," the burly officer mumbled. "That'd be a change of pace."

Ignoring the comment, Stone met Hart's gaze. "Let me introduce Detectives Gannon, McCauley and Hasselman, and officers Stanton and Reece."

The cops either nodded or raised a hand as their names were called. The uniforms schooled their expression to blank masks; the burly detective, Gannon, gazed at Hart with curiosity.

A woman walked into the room carrying a stack of file folders, her low heels snapping against the linoleum floor. Stone nodded in her direction. "And this is Detective French. She looks happy because this is her first day back from her honeymoon."

One of the uniform cops at the table made a disparaging sound in his throat. Stone silenced him with a stern look.

Spence Harrison's contact, Hart thought as he watched Molly French's shoulders go knife-blade stiff. She was the only officer on the MCPD who had the district attorney's complete trust.

Shifting the files into the crook of her left elbow, she walked to Hart and offered her hand. She was petite, young—late twenties to early thirties—with dark-brown curly hair and green eyes. She wore a tailored navy-blue jacket and slacks, a white shirt and a long, mannish red necktie.

"Good to meet you, Sergeant."

"Same here, Detective."

Stone walked over to them. "Molly, Sergeant O'Brien has requested copies of all our reports and photos. Considering how behind we got on our filing while you were off, I told him it might take a while to rustle up those copies." He sent a pointed look at the tables strewn with unorganized stacks of loose papers and photographs. "See what you can do about getting him those copies. Then make sure things get organized the way you had them before you left."

"Of course, Chief, I'm a whiz at clerical work." She paused, closed her eyes, then looked at Hart. "Nothing personal. I'll make sure you get the copies you want. Where are you staying so I can deliver them?"

"At the Lone Star. If it's out of your way to bring them by, call me and I'll pick them up."

"I can save you both a trip," Ben said, then shifted his gaze back to Molly. "I'm having dinner with Joan tonight. Leave the copies in my office. I'll drop them at the Lone Star when I pick up Joan."

Hart felt his jaw lock in reflex. Irrational as he knew it was, the fact that Joan had dinner plans with Ben Stone sent a surprising snake of envy curling through his gut. Irritation followed close on its heels. He didn't care if she had a man in her life. And he damn well wasn't going to examine why he found it disturbing that she did.

Molly French glanced at her watch. "I'll have the copies ready before my shift's over, Chief." Giving Hart a curt nod, she walked away, found a spot at the table and went to work.

Hart offered Stone his hand. "Thanks, Chief. I'm on my way to the lab."

Stone returned the handshake with decisive, impressive strength. "Let me know if you come up with anything there. And call me if you need something else from this end."

"I will."

Hart headed for the door, his mood darkening with each step. He didn't want to think about Stone tangling those strong, thick fingers into Joan's dark hair as he drew her mouth to his. Didn't want to think about her pulse pounding in response. Didn't want to think about her long, lean body, slick with sweat from the man's touch.

Dammit, he didn't want to think at all about the woman who'd left him bleeding and wounded.

Ben Stone's narrowed gaze tracked Hart as he strode out of the task force room. Ben detested having the Chicago cop nosing around the bombing investigation. Unfortunately, Ben couldn't do anything about that. If he protested, Spence Harrison would want to know why. Ben didn't need the D.A. breathing down his back more than he already was.

Shifting his stance, Ben met Paulie McCauley's waiting gaze. Ben gave the muscular detective a slight nod before heading back to his office.

Five minutes later McCauley settled into one of the chairs across from Ben's desk. "You need something, boss?"

Ben blew a stream of smoke from around the cigar clenched between his teeth. "You working security at the Lone Star tonight?"

"Hasselman and I are working our usual shift, five to midnight." Detective Paulie McCauley was young, bright and fueled by cool, rock-hard ambition that didn't discriminate between right and wrong. Ben valued those qualities. As he did McCauley's stint in Vice where he had learned the fine art of installing telephone taps, legal and otherwise.

"O'Brien's already snooped around the back of the clubhouse, looking at the surveillance camera setup. That tells me he's not planning to limit his view of our investigation to just the bomb angle. We've got safeguards in place. We've cleared out the security office at the Lone Star, but I'm not leaving anything to chance. I want O'Brien watched *and* listened to."

"No problem. You need me to tell Captain Ingram what you want?"

"No, I'll talk to Yance. You just make sure the first thing you do when you get to the club is head for the telephone room. I want the tap on the phone in O'Brien's suite installed as soon as possible. That, along with the hidden surveillance cameras, will help us keep tabs on the bastard. He gets too nosy, we put him out of commission."

"Say the word." McCauley had a short fuse and possessed no qualms about using his impressive strength to force people to do what he wanted. Those traits had made him a shoo-in for membership in the Lion's Den.

Ben leaned forward. "If I do 'say the word,' I'll want things done fast and clean. No loose ends."

"Don't I always deliver what you want, Chief?" Grinning perfect white teeth against a tanned face, McCauley rose and headed for the door.

Alone, Ben swiveled his chair toward the credenza behind his desk. Through a haze of cigar smoke he studied the framed photos of his two daughters. His chest tightened as he thought about how much he missed Olivia and Rebecca, wanted to see them, hold them. He knew they would have grown much taller and had most likely changed almost totally in looks during the three years since he'd seen them.

Three years, he thought with bitter resentment. Three years since Irene decided she no longer wanted to be his wife. She had hired a divorce lawyer who had seen that Ben paid heart-stopping monthly amounts for alimony and child support. All he'd wound up with was their mortgaged-up-to-the-eyeballs house and visitation rights. Those rights didn't do him a hell of a lot of good since the judge had allowed Irene to move his daughters to northern California. He had fought for them, spent a fortune to get his girls back. By the time his appeal went to court, Irene had turned his girls against him and they didn't want anything to do with him. They had a stepfather now who'd taken his place.

Back then, before his life went to hell he had been a good cop. An exemplary one who'd never even once considered stepping over the line. The divorce and subsequent pyramid scheme in which he'd lost the remainder of his money had left him depressed, vulnerable and ripe for picking.

Even to this day Ben had no clue how El Jefe's people knew the right time to approach him. He pictured the tall, swarthy Latino who had stepped out of a shadowy corner of his front porch on the night Ben planned to eat his gun. In a thick accent El Jefe's emissary explained that law enforcement had tightened its hold on the border town of Laredo. His organization needed a new American clearing house for drug money. All Ben had to do was provide a secure place to store that money, then launder it. For his work he had been guaranteed a percentage of all the money he handled. A percentage of millions.

Ben hadn't liked stepping into crime's dark side, but complete destitution had left him little choice. He needed money to survive. Now he had amassed enough capital that he had several offshore bank accounts, each worth millions. He knew he could take the money, disappear and live in comfort the rest of his life. The thing was, he had discovered he *liked* operating on the other side of the badge. Liked it almost as much as the fortune he'd amassed.

And he damn well wasn't going to let a sharp-eyed Chicago bomb tech screw up his finely tuned life.

Unconsciously Ben fingered his gold tie-tack. He had

modeled the Lion's Den after an elite secret fraternity, entry by invitation only. *His* invitation. And just like in a fraternity, Ben issued pins to members of the Lion's Den. Pins he had fashioned to look almost like the ones the city handed out as a reward for civic service. Almost, but not quite.

Leaning back, Ben tapped a finger against his bottom lip. He had seen O'Brien's gaze drop to his gold tie-tack, sensed the bomb tech taking note. Molly French knew about the Lion's Den—she had tipped her hand when two of Ben's cops tried to take her out. The only reason she was still alive was because she couldn't prove the group of rogue cops Ben had quietly and covertly established over time actually existed. Still, Ben wondered how many people she had voiced her suspicions to. And who those people were.

Blowing out a last stream of smoke, he stabbed out his cigar in the ashtray. He hoped the tap on the phone in O'Brien's suite would provide quick answers to those questions.

Those weren't the only questions Ben had. He had several of a more personal nature. The most pressing: why had O'Brien's eyes gone a shade darker when he'd heard Ben was having dinner that night with Joan Cooper? The cop's response had been subtle, then instantly hidden, but Ben had caught it. And he damn well wanted to know the reason for that reaction.

Had O'Brien and Joan known each other years ago? Ben wondered. Was there some sort of history between them? Some emotion that still lingered?

O'Brien's reaction to Joan's name concerned Ben almost as much as the thought of the Chicago cop conducting his own investigation into the bombing. Ben had worked hard over the past months to establish a friendship with Joan. Although she was clearly hesitant to take their relationship to a physical level, he had every intention of doing so. Just as he intended to someday make Joan his wife. And Helena the replacement for the daughters he desperately missed.

Hart spent the rest of the morning and part of the afternoon at the MCPD's lab. From the bomb fragments found in the rubble, he knew that the bomber had used a mechanical timer—an antique pocket watch—as the device that detonated the bomb. That meant the bomb had not been radio controlled, which would have required the bomber to be within a certain range of his device in order to set it off. Hart knew of several instances where a bomber using a radio-controlled detonator had been recorded in the act by hidden security cameras.

Unfortunately, the Lone Star bomber didn't need to worry about getting caught in the act. First, there hadn't been any security cameras in or near the Men's Grill. Second, by using a mechanical timer all the Lone Star bomber had to do on that fateful morning was plant his package near the rear wall in the Men's Grill, then get the hell out of Mission Creek.

After he finished at the lab, Hart returned to his room at the Lone Star where he changed into worn jeans and a denim workshirt. He carried his field kit downstairs where he used the key Bonnie Brannigan had given him to open the padlock on the makeshift plywood door.

Hours later he was still busy amid the blackened heaps of rubble in the center of the Men's Grill. The portable lights he'd moved from beside the doorway gave the smoke-scented air an eerie cast. Wearing his steel-soled boots, he had walked the blast site several times, trying to get the feel of the place, looking for any additional pieces of bomb frag the lab techs might have missed. So far, he had found nothing.

Leaving his field kit open on the floor, he sidestepped a grouping of tables crisscrossed with pieces of charred ceiling, insulation and boards. He walked past the bomb's shallow crater, moving to the jagged, gaping hole in what was left of the restaurant's rear wall. With the lights aimed in that direction, he peered beyond the hole into what had been the billiards room where the worst of the fire had raged. Exposed two-by-fours were charcoal black, their surfaces crazed into dozens of shiny, tile-size squares that glinted in the light's reflection. From scenes he'd worked, Hart knew "alligatoring" was the term the fire cops used for the phenomenon.

He shifted his gaze to the area where the janitor's closet had been sandwiched between the Men's Grill and the billiards room. Again, he wondered if Willie Pogue, the maintenance man who'd stashed paint and thinner in the closet, had the expertise—and motive—to build the dynamite bomb. Despite Yance Ingram's assurances that the maintenance man was innocent, Hart intended to check out the guy for himself.

Hart's stomach suddenly sent out a low, protesting rumble, a reminder he had skipped lunch. Angling his watch toward the light, he saw it was after five. Deciding he'd done all he could for the day, he walked back toward the center of the room.

Crouching beside his open field kit, he had one latex glove peeled off when he glanced up toward the grouping of tables covered with charred insulation and boards. His gaze narrowed on what looked like part of a singed piece of paper lodged between two pieces of insulation.

Pulling a penlight out of his kit, he aimed the beam upward while he took two crab-like steps toward the tables. Tilting his head, he saw that the paper had at least one column of numbers handwritten in dark ink. Still crouched, he reached for the Polaroid camera from his kit, snapped several photos of the paper. The instant Hart rose, the paper was out of his line of sight. If he hadn't left his field kit in the exact spot he had—then crouched to pull off his glove—he would never have seen the paper. That was no doubt why the lab techs had overlooked it.

Pulling on a replacement glove, he moved several

burned boards that had once been a part of the ceiling. Next, he shifted aside the top piece of insulation. Sandwiched between them were two pieces of paper.

Holding the penlight between his teeth, Hart carefully turned the papers over. Each piece had the name Esmeralda hand-written across the top. Below the name were columns of dates and figures written in black ink. The Polaroid hummed as Hart snapped pictures.

Brow furrowed, he slid the pictures and pages into separate plastic evidence envelopes. He suspected what the columns of dates and figures represented, but didn't want to get ahead of himself. He needed to examine the pages closer in far better light before he formed any conclusions.

That was the thing about starting an investigation, he mused as he replaced the penlight, Polaroid and envelopes in his field kit. The beginning was like walking into a dense fog. All you could do was grope your way along. You didn't know what you might find ahead, behind or to the sides of you. Didn't know what you might miss if you didn't ask the right question. Or look in the right spot at the right time.

Which is what he may very well have just done.

After switching off the bank of portable lights, he hefted the field kit and headed toward the plywood door.

The hallway with its pink granite floor and glittering lights was a vivid contrast from the bomb site's murky gloom. He hadn't realized how stale the air was he'd been breathing until he inhaled the sweet scent of fresh flowers that floated down the long hallway.

Settling the field kit on the floor, he secured the padlock, vaguely aware of the high-pitched squeak of tennis shoes rushing over granite.

The shoes screeched to a halt behind him.

"Only policemen are supposed to go in there, mister."

Turning, Hart flicked his gaze downward. Standing in front of him was a young girl, her dark eyes reflecting the stern tone he'd heard in her adolescent voice. Her long black hair was pulled back from her face, flowing around her shoulders like satin ribbons to her slim hips. Her limbs were lanky and long, promising willowy height one day.

He matched her solemn expression. "I am a policeman, miss."

Her dark, measuring gaze contrasted with her bright red dress, red tights and high-topped tennis shoes with gold-threaded double strings. She carried a neon-blue backpack slung over one shoulder. "If you're a policeman, you're supposed to have a badge."

"You're right. I do have a badge."

"Can I look at it?"

Hart resisted the urge to ask the mini storm trooper if she was assigned to Yance Ingram's security force. "Sure."

He tugged the badge case from the snug front pocket of his jeans. "My commission card with my photo is in there, too," he said, holding back a smile.

When she reached for the case, he saw that her short, oval fingernails were painted the same fire-engine red as her dress. With her hair streaming across her thin shoulders, she took her time studying the badge, then the commission card.

"Your first name's Hart?" she asked finally.

"That's right."

Her forehead furrowed. "Why is it spelled funny?"

He liked the way she seemed to seriously consider things. "I guess spelling wasn't my mother's best subject."

"Are you a police chief, too?"

Hooking a thumb in the front pocket of his jeans, Hart wondered if she asked the question because she knew Ben Stone. "No, I'm a sergeant."

Her dark eyes skimmed from his face downward. "If you're a policeman, why are you wearing fireman boots?"

"Sometimes on my job I have to walk around places that have a lot of broken glass and other sharp stuff lying around. These boots have steel plates in the soles. When I wear them I don't have to worry about what I step on.''

"Okay.'' Apparently satisfied that his credentials were genuine, she handed the badge case back. "Why do you have a suitcase?''

He fought a smile. "Has anyone ever told you that you ask a lot of questions?''

She nodded matter-of-factly. "My mom says the only way to learn something is to ask.''

"Your mom's right.'' He gestured toward the floor. "That's not exactly a suitcase. It's called a field kit. I use it when I collect evidence at a bomb scene.''

She sent a leery look at the plywood wall behind him. "I was packing my clothes in my suitcase when the bomb went off in there. It was real loud—I heard it all the way in my room upstairs. And the whole building shook. It caught on fire in there, too. A little boy got hurt really bad and his mom and dad died. It was scary.''

"I can imagine.'' The leftover fear in her expressive face had Hart veering away from the subject. "So, why were you packing your suitcase? Did you go on a trip?''

She shook her head. "I spent that night with my best friend, Ceci. Her mom and dad run the riding stables here. Do you ride horses, Mr. Hart?'' As she chattered, she shoved her long hair behind her shoulders. Hart's gaze went to the official brass Lone Star name tag pinned to her dress. The tag read: Helena Cooper.

He felt a sudden, jagged jolt to his nerves. *Joan's daughter.*

It took real effort for him to speak around the word-trapping lump that mysteriously filled his throat. "I've never been on a horse in my life.''

"Ceci and I ride all the time. If you want to learn to ride, you can take lessons here. I dance, too, and ride my bike.''

Easing out a breath, he forced back emotion and tried to keep up. "You know, I think I saw you riding your bike in the far corner of the parking lot when I got here yesterday.''

She smiled. ''That was me and Ceci. We can ride on that side of the parking lot when no delivery trucks are scheduled.''

Hart paused. She might be part tomboy, but she didn't have that look. ''You said you're a dancer. What kind?''

''Ballet.''

She would be a natural, he thought, with her long, thin legs and build veering toward willowy. Just like her mother's. And just like her mother, Helena would someday be a true beauty.

Although he wasn't sure why he felt the need, Hart decided to ask some questions of his own. ''Does your wearing a Lone Star name tag mean you work here?''

''When I get home from school I sometimes help out with some things.'' She rolled her eyes—dark eyes so much like her mother's that Hart's throat went dry. ''I have to do *all* my homework first, though.''

''Where do you help out?''

''I stuff envelopes in the main office. I can roll silverware in the kitchen as long as I stay away from where they cook. My favorite thing is helping my aunt Maddie. She does all the events here. When I help out in her office I get to see the wedding stuff.''

''Do you ever help your mom in the spa?''

Helena's eyes widened. ''Do you know my mom?''

''Yes.''

She scrunched her nose. ''If you know my mom, how come *I* don't know you?''

''I worked here one summer a long time ago. Before you were born. I met your mom then. I moved to Chicago after that.''

''Did you use to date her or something?''

''No,'' he countered instantly, trying not to think about the ''or something'' that had haunted him for the past ten years. ''We were just friends.''

Tilting her head, Helena eyed him for a moment, then gave him a bright smile. In the dusky rose of her cheeks, dimples flashed, elusive and charming. "Mom's taking me swimming tonight after we get back from dinner at Chief Ben's house. You could come to the pool, too. I know it would be okay with mom."

Helena's casual reference to "Chief Ben" had Hart's shoulders tightening. He had no reason to think Stone was anything other than the forthright cop he seemed to be. So why did the idea of his cozying up to Joan and her daughter have Hart's stomach twisting and his cop's sixth sense stirring restlessly?

"Thanks for the invitation." He had planned to abide by the agreement he and Joan had made that morning to avoid all contact. However, if the pages he found at the bomb site represented what he suspected they did, he might have to renege on that agreement.

The thought of the evidence now in his field kit had him glancing at his watch and mentally calculating the time change between Mission Creek and Denver. He needed to call his FBI contact there before the man left his office.

Hart shifted his attention back to the child who so closely resembled the woman he had once loved with an almost scorching intensity. He took a slow, deep breath, then crouched to look Helena in the eye. "I expect I've kept you long enough. It's nice to meet you."

She surprised him by extending her hand. "Since you're my mom's friend can I call you Hart instead of Mr. Hart?"

"If it's okay with your mom." Just touching her hand— so small, her fingers thin, her palm soft—tightened his chest.

"Okay. See you."

Hart rose slowly. He felt a tiny catch in his heart as he watched Joan's outgoing, gorgeous little girl skip off down the hallway, her tennis shoes squeaking against pink granite.

Chapter 6

Helena bounded into the living room when Joan arrived home from work. Returning her daughter's bright smile, Joan assumed the anticipation sparkling in Helena's eyes was due to their upcoming dinner with Ben Stone. The young girl had developed an affection for the police chief who took the time to regale her with stories about his work, always calling the bad guys "crooks" and the police officers "good guys."

"Hey, kiddo. You look happy."

"Mom, I met your friend Hart. He said he knew you before I was ever born. Did you know he's staying here?"

Because it was a sure indicator of how Helena felt about a person, Joan had always given her leeway in how she addressed adults. Helena's referring to Hart by his first name meant she'd taken an instant liking to him.

Great.

"Yes, I know he's staying here," Joan replied. With unease creeping up her spine, she slid a palm down Helena's long, dark hair, savored its familiar softness.

"Sweetheart, I need to change clothes. Chief Stone will be here to pick us up for dinner in less than a half hour."

"Okay. I saw Hart coming out of the bomb site," Helena persisted as she trailed Joan into her bedroom. "Everybody keeps telling me that only policemen can go in there. So, I thought I'd better tell him in case he didn't know. Then I made him show me his badge since he said he's a policeman."

"Helena, I don't want you confronting an adult about what they're doing." Sending the child a look as stern as her voice, Joan unbuttoned the jacket of her turquoise suit, then pulled it off. "I've told you before if you see something you think is wrong, you're to come and tell me. If I'm not around, go to Mrs. Brannigan or Captain Ingram or one of the other security officers. Understand?"

"Uh-huh." Fingering the tidy and expansive array of decorative bottles filled with scents and creams on the marble-topped dresser, Helena lifted a shoulder. "But, Mom, it was okay for me to talk to Hart because he's a policeman. You always say it's okay for me to talk to policemen."

"It is. But you didn't know he was a police officer when you first spoke to him, did you?"

"No." Sprawling stomach-down on the bed, Helena propped her chin on her hands and swung her tennis shoe-clad feet in the air. While Joan changed clothes, Helena chattered about Hart's badge, commission card, soot-covered fireman boots, and his field kit that looked like a suitcase.

By the time Ben Stone arrived to pick them up for dinner, a headache throbbed in the center of Joan's forehead. Although she tried to hide her discomfort, she couldn't miss the concerned way Ben studied her throughout the evening. Still, Mission Creek's police chief was the perfect host, chatting amiably with Joan while Helena raced around his backyard tossing a Frisbee to his golden retriever, Warrant. The steaks and mushrooms Ben grilled were excellent, the homemade chocolate ice cream delectable. He even accepted with good grace Joan's explanation that she needed to cut their evening short because Helena's friend, Ceci, had invited Helena and two other friends for a prebedtime swim in one of the Lone Star's pools.

It wasn't until after the girls were happily skimming through the water like dolphins that Helena remembered to mention she had invited Hart to join them. The announcement had notched Joan's headache into sledgehammer zone.

A half hour after she and Helena had returned to their suite, Joan stood in her bathroom with its gleaming white tiles and sparkling fixtures while she washed down two double-strength aspirins. The fact that Hart hadn't shown up at the pool had done nothing to ease the throb in her head. How could it? How could she relax when she sensed the first encounter between father and daughter would not be the last?

Wings of panic fluttered in her stomach. Clenching her fists, she fought the urge to grab Helena and run as fast as she could away from Hart, away from the past, away from the truth that had lain dormant for so long.

Fighting off a shiver, Joan stared at her reflection in the wide mirror ringed by bright lights. Hart had been in Mission Creek for a short time, yet the strain she felt already showed in the smudged shadows beneath her eyes. She had the skill to camouflage the smudges with makeup, so no one would notice. What people would notice was if she and Helena suddenly left town. For Hart—a man who made a living asking questions and, no doubt, getting answers—their leaving would surely draw his attention. And, perhaps, his suspicion.

She and Helena *had* to stay in Mission Creek, Joan resolved as she aligned a thick, white towel on one of the bathroom's heated racks. All she could do was pray that Hart finished his work there soon. Pray that when he returned to Chicago he would do so without discovering the truth about Helena.

The doorbell chimed. Instantly Helena raced out of her bedroom bellowing, "I'll get it!"

Even before Joan reached the living room, the dread that tightened her chest told her Hart was the person on the other side of the door.

She was right.

"Hi, Hart!" Helena, dressed in a knee-skimming purple and green nightshirt, smiled brightly as she swept the door open. "I told Mom I met you today. Did you forget we'd be at the swimming pool tonight?"

"No." Although Helena held the door wide open in obvious invitation, Hart remained in the hallway. The warm smile he sent the young girl made his carelessly handsome face even more handsome. "Some business came up and I couldn't get away."

"That happens to Mom a lot at the office." As she spoke, Helena waved him inside. "We go swimming a lot at night, so you can come anytime."

"I might do that." As he stepped through the doorway, his gaze met Joan's over Helena's head. "Sorry to drop by so late. I need to talk to you."

Joan schooled her expression to cool and impersonal. "I was just about to remind Helena that it's her bedtime."

"Mom, do I have to?" her daughter objected as she closed the door behind Hart. "Can't I stay up and talk to Hart? He just got here! And since he's a policeman he could maybe tell me some good-guy stories just like Chief Ben does."

"Not tonight, kiddo. You have a lot to do tomorrow."

She saw something dark come and go in Hart's gaze as he slid his hands into the pockets of his khaki slacks. "Helena, what sort of good-guy stories does Chief Ben tell you?"

"Well…things like how the police always track down the crooks. Then they put handcuffs on them and take them to jail. Just like on TV.'' She angled her chin, sending her still-damp dark hair sliding across her shoulders. ''Do you have any good stories?''

''I imagine I can come up with a few. When it's not so late.''

''Okay.'' Helena pressed her lips together, seemingly acquiescent. ''I guess I have to go to bed now.''

''Looks that way.''

''Don't forget to brush your teeth after you dry your hair,'' Joan reminded her.

Helena eased out a sigh. ''I won't. Night, Mom. Night, Hart.''

''Good night.'' That she and Hart had spoken the words in unison sent a prickle up Joan's spine.

Her stomach roiling, she waited to speak until she heard Helena's bedroom door click shut. ''Hart, we agreed this morning to avoid each other.''

''Something's come up,'' he countered evenly. ''It's important, or I wouldn't be here.''

''Do you have a problem with your suite? Or with something else about the Lone Star?'' On unsteady legs she moved to where the phone sat on the end table beside the couch. ''I'll be happy to call the appropriate staff member to help you.''

Eyes flashing like stormy jade, he strode to where she stood. ''Do me a favor and cut the garbage,'' he said, keeping his voice low. ''If I've got a problem with my damn room—or anything else—I'll deal with it. I'm here because you're the only person I can talk to about this.''

Pressure dropped onto her chest, leaden weights of panic. Was Helena the important topic he could discuss with only her? Had he somehow found out he had a daughter?

A muscle jerked in his jaw as he studied her with a cop's intensity. ''Why is it every time I get close to you I see little flashes of panic in your eyes?''

Logic told her if he had to ask, he didn't know.

She forced a thin smile. "Perhaps you're mistaking panic for annoyance?"

He stared down at her, stretching out the silence. "Yeah, maybe," he said finally.

Shifting his stance, he swept his gaze around the living room. With the same narrow focus with which he had studied her, he took in the deep-cushioned furniture, tidy accessories and bookshelves that framed the dark fireplace.

Joan had the uneasy feeling that Sergeant Hart O'Brien didn't miss much.

"Nice place," he commented. "Looks like you have the same floor plan as the suite I'm in."

He was standing closer than she would have liked, but she refused to let herself cringe away. "I do, except Helena and I each have our own bedroom."

"Speaking of Helena, she's one reason I'm here. I wanted you to know I met your daughter. I wasn't sure she would mention it. Apparently, she did."

Your daughter, not *our* daughter. Joan wrapped her arms around her waist. The feel of silk against her palms had her suddenly remembering she was wearing only her long white robe with its matching filmy chemise underneath. She put a hand to the robe's closure. "Helena told me about meeting you the minute I got home from work."

"You've got a great kid, Texas."

"Thank you." She unbent enough to smile. "Sometimes I think she forgets she's a kid. It sounds like she did that today when she confronted you coming out of the bomb site. She likes to ask questions. I guess you found that out."

"No kidding." Hart grinned. "The Chicago PD could use her as an interrogator."

The grin was the one Joan remembered from ten years ago. The first time she had seen Hart, he'd been digging a flower bed near the Lone Star's tennis courts. She had halted midswing, her fingers clenched on her racket, her gaze glued in his direction. Riveted, she watched him labor beneath the Texas sun, his auburn hair damp, his tanned, rippling muscles shimmering with sweat. He'd been the most desirable man she had ever seen. As she stood staring, he paused from his digging, wiped a forearm across his brow, then looked up and sent her a slow, devastating grin.

Joan, young, pampered and filled with the belief that she could snap her fingers and have whatever she wanted, instantly lost her heart to that grin.

A grin much like the one he was giving her now.

She wavered, suddenly desperate for space, desperate to distance herself from the man who still had a way of sneaking past her defenses. She moved toward the dark fireplace at the far end of the room while she worked on steadying her breathing. She didn't want this. Didn't want Hart's presence to mean anything. Dammit, he had torn her heart out by the roots, yet he could still lure her with a grin. *One grin.*

She turned, her arms clenched around her waist. "Why did you want to make sure Helena told me she met you?"

Hart's face sobered. "She's a gutsy, friendly kid, and I like that. It also concerns me. Considering what I've already turned up in my investigation, it's not a good idea for her to go around the Lone Star talking to strangers. Asking them questions. You need to make sure she stops."

His obvious concern for Helena had Joan's heart sticking in her throat. "Is it unsafe for her to be here? Hart, do I need to take Helena away from the Lone Star?"

"That's not what I'm saying." He rubbed a hand across the back of his neck. "When I conduct an investigation it's like piecing together a puzzle. Even if I have only a few pieces, I try to envision the entire picture. That's all I'm doing now. Anticipating something that might, or might not, happen down the line. I just wanted to make you aware."

"Thank you. I appreciate you telling me. I'll remind

Helena again in the morning that she's not to confront anyone.''

He nodded. "There's another angle to what I've turned up in my investigation. I need to talk to you about that, too."

She frowned. "Me?"

"You," he said, meeting her gaze levelly. "This may take a while. Mind if we sit down?"

Joan eyed the plush sofa and chairs that formed a cozy grouping around the fireplace. *Too cozy.*

"We can talk in the kitchen." Barefoot, she padded past him, gesturing toward the long-legged stools on one side of the slate-blue counter that separated the living room from the kitchen. "Have a seat."

She walked into the kitchen as Hart settled onto a stool. Facing him, she tried not to notice how his thick, auburn hair glistened beneath the bright lights, tried not to think about the hard, sinewy muscles beneath his black shirt. Tried not to think about the night when her flesh pressed against those dense, hot muscles, melting like wax against a flame.

"Would you like a drink?" Her voice sounded far steadier than she felt.

"Do you have scotch?"

"Yes. Rocks?"

"Neat."

With an unsteady hand, she reached for a glass. The emotion she felt stirring inside her didn't matter, she reminded herself. What mattered was the child in the room down the hallway getting ready for bed. Joan knew better than anyone how compelling Hart O'Brien's presence could be. And dangerous. He had proven that by professing his love, then leaving her alone, deserted and pregnant. She would never again trust him. Never risk the steady balance of her perfect, beautiful daughter's life.

After pouring his scotch, Joan walked around the counter and slid onto a stool, leaving an empty one between them. "Hart, as I said, I appreciate your concern for Helena. But I don't understand why you want to talk to me about your investigation. I don't know anything about the bombing, other than what I've heard secondhand or read in the newspaper."

"The bombing isn't what I need to talk to you about." Swiveling his stool to face hers, he sipped his scotch while studying her over the rim of the glass. "Before I get into things, I need to ask you not to repeat what I tell you."

"All right."

"Do you know who Jake Anderson is? The little boy who lost his parents in the blast?"

Joan nodded. "Jake's adoptive mother, Tracy Collins, is a friend of mine. She's also the pediatric burn specialist who treated Jake after the bombing."

Hart swirled his scotch. "Does she practice at the same hospital where your family funded a trauma wing in your late husband's name?"

The reference to Thomas Dean had Joan hesitating. Was Hart just making conversation? Or had he found a reason to dig into the man her parents had invented as her husband and Helena's father?

"Yes, it's the same hospital," she said carefully.

"I guess it's no secret a Mission Creek cop kidnapped Jake and Dr. Collins. And during a struggle while rescuing them, the man Tracy later married killed another cop."

"The story headlined the news for days. The police officer who did the actual kidnapping committed suicide shortly after his arrest. As far as I know, no one has found out why the two officers did what they did." Joan furrowed her brow, trying to anticipate where Hart was headed. "Have you found out why the officers kidnapped Jake and Tracy?"

"Not yet. I do know that it's possible both dead cops belonged to a group called the Lion's Den. Ever hear of it? Hear someone mention it?"

"The Lion's Den," Joan repeated. "No, I don't think so."

"Did Dr. Collins tell you about the men Jake saw behind the clubhouse before the bomb exploded?"

"Yes. She said two men were hauling bulging bags out a door and loading them into a car. Jake called them Santa's helpers with bags of toys."

Hart leaned forward. "I found two pieces of paper when I went over the blast site this afternoon. They were sandwiched between lengths of charred insulation and mostly hidden from view. I've faxed the pages to a contact at the FBI to look at. He's tied up on a big investigation and won't be able to get back to me for a couple of days. Even without hearing his opinion, I'm almost certain the information written on those pieces of paper means that the bags Jake saw were filled with money."

"Money?" Joan arched a brow. "From where?"

"From somewhere inside this club. The fact the two men were moving the bags out of the back door and stashing them into a private vehicle puts an illegal spin on things."

Joan nodded slowly. "What was written on the papers you found at the bomb site?"

"Columns of dollar amounts. Dates. Numbers that could be codes for bank accounts." While he spoke, Hart ran a finger around the rim of his glass. "I worked a case where one gang bombed another's money laundering operation. I learned then that it's customary for people who wash money to keep detailed records to protect themselves. Most verge on obsessive when it comes to documenting the collection and disbursement of funds. That's because their records provide proof to whomever they answer to that they properly channeled all of the cash. If things don't add up, someone's in big trouble." He took a sip, then frowned into his glass. As if deciding he no longer had a taste for scotch, he sat the glass aside. "The name Esmeralda was printed across the top of both pieces of paper.''

"Who's Esmeralda?"

"I was hoping you could tell me. Do you know if anyone by that first or last name works at the Lone Star? Or ever worked here? Is, or was, a club member?"

Joan thought for a moment. "I don't recognize the name. Bonnie Brannigan can run Esmeralda through the computer. She'll be able to tell you for sure."

"I don't want to ask the general manager to run the check," Hart said quietly. "I'm asking you."

Joan's eyes widened. "Surely you don't suspect Bonnie of running a money laundering operation inside the club?"

"This investigation is like any other—I suspect everyone until I find a reason not to." He raised a palm. "My gut tells me I'm looking at what's known as a *prima facie* case. That's when you've got a piece of evidence at one end and another piece at the other end. Together, the two pieces lead to a reasonable assumption of what's in between. I've got mystery men hauling bulging bags out of the back door of the Lone Star. And records that could be from a money laundering operation floating down from the ceiling in a room where a bomb exploded."

"Do you think the bombing and money laundering are connected?"

"Anything's possible. All I'm sure of right now is that an operation like that couldn't be headquartered here without someone high up in the club knowing about it. Hell, maybe it's still going on." Hart pursed his mouth. "They'd need a room, a secure place away from prying eyes to keep the cash until it's processed."

"A storage room?"

"Storage room, mechanical room, something like that. But secure. A place with controlled access."

"There's plenty of storage and equipment rooms at the Lone Star. I just don't know where they all are. Or who all has access to them. The only way to find out is to ask around. But it sounds like that's not what you want to do.''

''You're right, I don't. Until I know more, I don't want to tip off anyone with ties to the Lone Star by making noises about money laundering, secure storage rooms or Esmeralda.''

''I have ties to the club,'' Joan reminded him quietly. ''You're asking me.''

''I'm asking because I know you, Texas. Know the type of person you are.'' He rose, carried his glass into the kitchen and sat it beside the sink. Turning, he met her gaze across the counter. ''Never in a million years would the pampered, country club princess I knew get involved in a money laundering operation. That's just not you. Not your style.''

She took no offense to his description of her because that's exactly what she had been—spoiled, pampered and full of herself. The summer she met Hart she'd had two primary goals: perfecting her tennis serve and getting her hands on the handsome, muscled groundskeeper. She'd accomplished both.

And rocketed her life in an entirely different direction than she had dreamed possible.

''Time passes, Hart. That foolish young girl no longer exists. I'm not the same person I was ten years ago.''

''No?'' He retraced his steps, pausing beside her stool to brace a hand on the counter. ''Are you telling me that sometime over the past decade you turned to crime?''

''Of course not.'' She stared down at his lean, tanned fingers splayed against blue ceramic tiles. The jolting memory of the feel of those firm, calloused fingers cupping her breasts, curving possessively against her heat, claiming her had her spine going stiff.

''What is it?'' he asked quietly as he put a finger beneath her chin, nudged it up. ''Where did you just go?''

Into the past. Into your arms. ''Nowhere.'' Batting his hand aside, she surged off the stool. When she realized the movement had boxed her between his body and the counter, her breathing shallowed. It was as if his nearness had somehow sucked out most of the oxygen in the room.

"I'm simply pointing out that time passes," she managed. "I'm not the spoiled eighteen-year-old girl I once was." Eighteen and wildly in love with you.

She curled her hands against her thighs while Hart's scent slid around her, into her, breathing life into memories that had lain dormant for so long. Something trembled inside her—part fear, part longing. She wanted neither.

She set her teeth. "It's hard for me to accept that someone with ties to the Lone Star might be involved in money laundering. It's also difficult for me to believe someone had reason to explode a bomb inside the Men's Grill. But, they did. I lie in bed at night worrying that person will set another bomb. Then another. I live in fear for everyone's safety, especially Helena's."

"I'm going to find the scum who planted that bomb," Hart said evenly. "It may take a while, but I'll find him."

"If my running Esmeralda through the computer will help you, I'll do it."

"It will help. Thank you."

"I'll do the run first thing in the morning."

When she started to slide past him, he dropped a hand on her shoulder, staying her steps. "I agree with you, Texas."

Feeling the hard firmness of his hand through silk had her swallowing hard. "About what?"

"You've changed." His voice deepened, brushing across her flesh like heated velvet. "In some ways."

She could have jerked away. But she didn't. Something in his face pulled at her, kept her rooted to the spot. "In all ways."

"No, your eyes are the same. The very same. So is your mouth." He slicked a fingertip across her bottom lip. "It feels the same. If I kissed you, I imagine you'd taste the same."

A storm of age-old longings pounded in her blood. "That's not going to happen," she said, even as desire weakened her resolve.

His free hand cupped the side of her throat. "Your heart is pounding, Texas. I can practically hear it."

"It does that when—"

He dipped his head, caught her bottom lip between his teeth. "When what?" he asked against her mouth, then deepened the kiss before her brain could register the order to snap away.

Her body quivered once—in surprise, in defense, in response.

Her hands, still fisted at her sides, barely resisted the urge to grab onto the man who had once left her torn to shreds. Even while she struggled to hold something back, her mouth surrendered to the assault and answered his.

The world narrowed to the scrape of his tongue against hers, the greed of his lips, the feel of his body as he wrapped an arm around her waist and tugged her against him. Her nipples peaked beneath the silk chemise; need spiked through her, strong and fierce, awakening the pulse between her legs.

How was it possible, she thought through a haze, to be swept away so quickly? To want so desperately what you knew you shouldn't have? Couldn't have.

The heat of his kiss seared through her, breathing life into carefully buried needs that fought their way up, so that she answered greed with greed. She felt his arousal against her belly, knew he wanted as badly as she.

Wanted her for that moment. That instant. Until he walked away.

With this man there would be no way to completely block out the past. No sinking totally into oblivion. Those ten years had happened, she reminded herself dimly. Proof of them was the child they had created. The wonderful, loving child whom she would do anything—everything—

to protect. Protect against a man whom she could never again trust.

Joan pressed her fists against his chest. She might as well have tried to shove back a brick wall. "Hart, stop," she managed against his mouth.

He responded by changing the angle of the kiss, intensifying the heat and hunger, passion and promise.

She nearly whimpered with need before she jerked her head back. "I said stop."

"All right." His arm remained locked around her waist as he gazed down at her, his eyes looking like smoky emeralds. "Give me a minute."

"No." She pulled away, sidestepped around him, desperate for air, for distance. "That shouldn't have happened," she said, even as frustrated desire twisted inside her. Her voice wasn't as cool as she wanted, but it was rigid enough to make his mouth tighten.

"Maybe it shouldn't have, but it did." He looked away, muttering an oath as he shoved a hand through his hair. "There I was, thinking I'd gotten you out of my system."

"I don't want to be in your system." She took another step back. "I don't want you in mine." Her palms were sweaty, and her lungs needed more oxygen than she could suck in. "What happened between us was a long time ago. I don't want it to happen again. I'm not the same person I was then. Nothing's the same." Turning, she walked to the door, pulled it open. "Go. Just go."

"That's probably a damn good idea." He strode to the door, pausing when he reached her. As if he'd flicked off a switch inside him, his eyes were steady now, level, unreadable. "There's one more thing you ought to know, Texas."

She tightened her grip on the door knob. "What?"

"You taste the same. Exactly the same."

Hart decided he was destined to spend his mornings while in Mission Creek jogging off his sexual frustration, compliments of Ms. Joan Cooper.

Attempting to jog it off, anyway.

Having decided to distance himself from the Lone Star, he had veered off the jogging trail a few miles back. Now he pounded along a cobblestone street, passing sprawling mansions with vast, jewel-like grounds that boasted swimming pools, cabanas and an occasional tennis court.

It was nearing six-thirty; the rising sun had transformed the sky into a charcoal haze. The already-warm morning air was thick with humidity and smelled of the flowers blooming in well-tended beds on either side of the street. Keeping his pace steady, Hart gripped one end of the towel he'd hooked around his neck and scrubbed it over his sweat-soaked face.

Nearly an hour of running hadn't relieved his basic frustration. He had jogged religiously for years—had discovered the therapeutic effect of letting his mind go free while his muscles strained and burned. He often made a point to run during a difficult case when he had both mental and physical knots to untie. Jogging worked equally well when he had personal problems to work out, which included those dealing with females.

Not this time.

Dammit, why the hell had he kissed her?

"You're…an…idiot," he answered, forcing the words past his heaving lungs.

The kiss had been unfinished business. Period. *Unplanned* business, enacted on a sudden impulse. He had stood near her while the remembered scent of Chanel No. 5 whirled in his head, and decided he wanted to taste her again. *Had* to taste her.

So he did.

As if summoned by a seductive phantom, he again felt her lush body straining against his, her flesh heating, softening like warm honey. In that long hover of time while his mouth joined with hers he had wanted her, craved her with the same searing intensity he'd felt ten years ago.

He'd spent a decade trying to convince himself he was over her. A decade of dating other women, sleeping with them, all the while telling himself that if he just kept looking he would find the right fit. The right woman.

The right woman. Hadn't he thought he'd found her a long time ago? Found her, then lost her because all Joan Cooper had wanted was a fling. Hell, maybe she'd viewed losing her virginity to a dirt-poor groundskeeper as some perverse status symbol of the cultured class. After all, she'd jumped from him to Thomas Dean. Taking Helena into account, Joan hadn't waited long to make that jump.

The short, high-pitched whoop of a siren coming from behind him nearly sent Hart out of his running shoes.

He jerked around. A brown sedan that had the unmistakable look of an unmarked detective cruiser crept behind.

"Jesus." His breathing choppy, he rested his hands on his thighs while the cruiser braked abreast of him. With a soft hum, the passenger window slid down.

"Detective French," Hart said when the driver came into view.

"Sergeant O'Brien."

Stepping forward, he rested a forearm in the cruiser's open window. "Was I speeding?"

Her mouth curved. "Not quite." This morning she had her curly brown hair piled on top of her head. The mannish navy pantsuit she'd worn the previous day in the task force room had been replaced with a man's white dress shirt tucked into a pair of jeans. "Do you know where the hospital is?"

He nodded. "Sneak up on me again like that, I'll need to go there."

"You need to go there, anyway." She glanced at her watch. "Can you meet me there in an hour?"

"Yeah." He pulled the towel from around his neck and mopped his face. "Is someone sick?"

"A kid named Bobby J." As she spoke, Molly shifted her gaze out the windshield, then to the car's rearview mirror. Hart wondered if it was from ingrained habit, or if she was checking for a tail.

He pulled in deep breaths while waiting for his pulse to steady. Bobby J. was the teen from the rec center who'd been beaten into a coma by two men he claimed were MCPD cops. Cops who allegedly belonged to the secret group known as the Lion's Den.

"Spence Harrison mentioned Bobby J.," Hart said. "The D.A. also said you're the one officer on the MCPD he's sure he can trust."

A shadow slid over her eyes. "My job's the same as yours, O'Brien. I look for bad guys." She glanced again in the rearview mirror, then remet his gaze. "Problem is, around here the bad guys wear badges, too. And one of those guys might have rigged the bomb."

Chapter 7

After Detective Molly French interrupted his morning jog, Hart went back to the Lone Star, cleaned up, then drove to the hospital. An hour later he and the MCPD detective stood beside a bed separated from others by a gauzy privacy curtain.

With the heavy smell of disinfectant seeping into his lungs, Hart gazed down at Bobby J.'s gaunt body. The teenager lay motionless, his face as pale as the white sheet that covered him. A stand holding an IV bag was positioned near the head of the bed; a softly beeping wall monitor displayed green lines that represented the comatose boy's vital signs.

"How long has he been in the coma?" Hart asked in the hushed tones that all hospitals seemed to demand.

"A couple of weeks." Placing a hand on the boy's rail-thin shoulder, the detective turned a face taut with worry Hart's way. "We can go downstairs to talk. I wanted you to see Bobby first. See what they did to him."

Hart stared into her furiously glittering eyes. "Do you know for sure who 'they' are?"

"I have a good idea. There's a coffee shop off the lobby. Let's go there." Patting the boy's shoulder, she leaned in and crooned, "See you later, handsome."

As they walked along a corridor busy with medical personnel and patients, Hart noted the detective's gaze flick into each room they passed. Again, he wondered if her acute awareness of her surroundings was merely her cop's sixth sense at work, or if she had reason to think she was being watched.

They took the elevator to the first floor, stepped into the lobby, then veered down a hallway and entered the almost deserted coffee shop. After going through the service line, he and Molly carried steaming mugs of coffee to a table at the room's rear. As was the ingrained habit for most cops, both angled their chairs to place their backs to the wall and their eyes on the entrance.

Hart sipped his coffee, finding it only slightly less acidic than that brewed in the Chicago PD's bomb squad office.

"Spence gave me an overview of what's happened with a few of your fellow officers," Hart began. "He didn't go into detail, but it sounds like the MCPD has serious problems."

"It does." Molly wrapped a hand, adorned by a thin gold wedding band, around her coffee mug. "I want you to understand that I don't like looking at our own people for wrongdoing—I wear the same badge they do. But too much has gone on...*is* going on for me to turn a blind eye." She paused, then added, "The D.A. brought you here not only to try to solve the bombing but to look at what's happening inside the department. Harrison said I should tell you what I know. What I suspect. A lot of that is based on gut instinct."

"Why don't you start at the beginning and go from there?"

"Okay." As if gathering her thoughts, she leaned back

in her chair. "Ten weeks ago I was assigned to patrol, working nights. I was out running errands the morning the bomb went off, and I heard the call on my radio. I went to the scene in case whoever snagged the call needed help. By the time I got there, about nine-tenths of the department had shown up."

"It was a major emergency."

"That's what I kept telling myself. Still, something didn't sit right—there were too many cops too fast. I got the sense some of them had an *interest* in what was happening at the bomb site that went beyond their jobs." She shook her head. "It sounds weird and I can't explain it. It's just a feeling I had. Still have. That's the first time I thought something inside the PD wasn't quite right."

Hart knew all about the almost undefinable instinct cops developed on the job. His own sixth sense had saved his butt more than a couple of times during his career. "Go ahead," he prodded.

"I transferred to Mission Creek from the Laredo PD and lost a chunk of seniority. I volunteered for the country club bombing task force because it looked like a way for me to work up the ranks a little faster. Chief Stone turned me down, said he couldn't spare the manpower by taking me off the street." She raised a shoulder. "I kept asking, he kept saying no. He finally said I could work on the task force without pay during the day if I did my regular shift at night."

"That must have made for some long hours."

"Headaches, too." Her mouth tightened. "The guys on the task force didn't like me being there. It didn't seem to matter I'd logged a couple of years of street time on the Laredo PD—they thought I should start over in Mission Creek. Plus, my working without pay made them suspicious that I had some hidden agenda. Although I'm a detective now and assigned to the task force, not much has changed. Of the cops you met yesterday, only Joe Gannon has given me a chance."

"The burly older plainclothes cop? The one trying to convince Mr. Muscle that Jake Anderson's parents were too clean to have been the bomber's intended target?"

"Yeah, Mr. Muscle," Molly repeated, her mouth curving. "Good name for Paulie McCauley, since he likes to try to force his opinion on others." She nodded, the dark curls shoved on top of her head bouncing. "I'm sure you figured out I'm the only one who does anything about keeping the reports and photos organized. Plus, Frank Hasselman is supposed to be a whiz with computers. You can't tell it by his performance on the task force because ours has crashed about three times."

"I haven't had a chance to read any of the reports Stone dropped off for me last night, so I don't know if the task force has made a lot of progress. What do you think?"

"I don't know. The chief runs things and doesn't share information. With me, anyway." She eased out a breath. "Stone's given me the dog work."

"The clerical stuff?"

"That, and he's assigned me to check every complaint the Lone Star has ever received, just in case the bomber is some disgruntled club member. I spend my time following up complaints about golf course divots and dents made by parking valets. I've talked to enough members of Mission Creek's snooty set that I want to hurl."

Hart held back a smile. "I suppose those complaints have to be looked into. Still, I doubt anyone would blow up the Men's Grill because of a divot or a dent."

"Tell me about it."

He angled his chin. "So, you first suspected something was not quite right with the department when so many cops showed up at the bomb scene. What happened next?"

"Ed Bancroft and Kyle Malloy happened. They're the cops who kidnapped Jake Anderson and his adoptive mom. Malloy died during a struggle and Bancroft was taken into custody. I went to the jail hoping to get him to tell me why he and Malloy snatched Jake. Ed was a family man, he had kids—his kidnapping Jake was totally out of character.''

"Did he talk to you?"

"He couldn't. I found him swinging by the neck in his holding cell from an overhead fixture, courtesy of his own belt."

"His own belt? The jailers didn't confiscate it when they booked him?"

"They took the belt and his shoelaces. Between the time Ed got booked and I arrived, his belt wound up in the cell with him." Molly held up a hand. "Before you ask, whoever gave him the belt didn't sign in because Beau Maguire—the cop manning the jail desk—claimed he stepped away for a few minutes. Chief Stone gave Maguire a couple of days on the ground without pay, but the punishment was the equivalent of a slap on the wrist."

"Did any of the other prisoners have a view of Bancroft's holding cell?"

"No, it was isolated from the others."

"So both cops died, Bancroft perhaps conveniently, without explaining their motive for kidnapping Jake?"

"Correct."

"How does Bobby J. play into this?"

"I work with kids at the city's rec center, try to keep them on an even keel. Bobby is…was one of those kids. I've got a good rapport with a few of them, so they confide in me. That's how I found out Bobby needed money to keep him, his mother and three sisters afloat. To get that money he'd gotten involved in some sort of activity that wasn't on the up-and-up."

"What sort of activity?"

"I don't know. All I could find out was that Bobby had gone to work for some really bad guys. Danny and I suspected it was the Mercado mob."

"Spence said the rec center hired a basketball coach, an ex-con by the name of Danny Gates. That the same Danny?"

"Yeah." Molly held up her left hand, wiggled her fingers. "My husband, Danny."

"I see."

"Look, O'Brien, I know what you're thinking. The cop got conned by the ex-con. That's not the way it is. When he was young, Danny made a mistake by going to work for Carmine Mercado. When he decided to go straight he told Carmine he wanted out. The mob's response was to set up Danny to take the fall for an armed robbery. He served ten years for a crime he didn't commit."

"Why did Mercado go to the trouble of setting him up? Why not just kill him?"

"Because Danny grew up best friends with Carmine's nephew, Ricky. He reminded his uncle that Danny saved Carmine's life when Danny worked for him. Ricky got the old man to agree that if Danny kept his mouth shut, he'd let him live. All Danny wants now is to help the kids at the center."

"Like Bobby J."

"Yes."

"Spence mentioned Bobby claimed the two men who beat him were cops. Cops who belong to a secret group called the Lion's Den. Do you believe the kid's accusations?"

"It sounds bizarre, but Bobby didn't have a reason to lie," Molly answered quietly. "The night he was beaten, I tried to find out if he said anything to the cops who answered the assault call. When I talked to Neely and Evans, they flat-out told me to leave things alone, that Bobby was a delinquent headed for prison."

"Not too helpful."

"No. And I got the impression my fellow officers would have liked for me to crawl into a hole and disappear."

"Spence said two cops and a nurse tried to kill you. One of those cops and the nurse are sitting in jail, keeping their mouths shut while the other cop is on the lam."

"Larry Higgins and Beau Maguire are the cops you're

talking about. Maguire's the one running. The nurse is his girlfriend.'' Molly gave Hart a rueful look. ''Not too popular, am I?''

''Doesn't sound like you're a contender for the Miss Congeniality award.'' Hart frowned. ''Wasn't Maguire the cop who left the jail desk when the belt wound up in Bancroft's cell?''

''The same. To make a long story short, Maguire and his girlfriend drugged me. When I came to, Maguire and his partner, Higgins, had me inside the bomb crime scene at the Lone Star where they both worked as security when they were off duty. Maguire drew a gun on me. He said I'd stuck my nose where it didn't belong once too often. I had to do something to buy time so I blurted that I knew about the Lion's Den. They looked like I'd hit them between the eyes with a sledgehammer.''

''What happened next?''

''Maguire dialed a number on his cell phone, asked for some extension that I couldn't hear and repeated what I'd said about the Lion's Den. Whoever he talked to told him to hurt me, then kill me. Higgins did a number on my shoulder. Luckily, Danny crashed in and tackled him. I collared Maguire, but blacked out from my injury. When I came to, he was gone. Higgins claimed I was obsessed with solving the bombing and I'd sneaked into the site to plant evidence so I could get credit for closing the case.''

''What evidence?''

Molly sent Hart a thin smile. ''That's one of many questions he refuses to answer.''

''What about Maguire's cell phone? Did the records show who he called?''

''Sure did. He dialed the MCPD dispatch nonemergency phone number. A big drug bust had gone down that night so there was a lot of activity on the street, and dispatch was a zoo. None of the dispatchers remembers for sure answering the call. Since it came in on the nonemergency line, the call wasn't recorded.''

"The fact it was made to the PD is proof that Higgins and Maguire worked with or for some other cop. And that the Lion's Den counts cops in its membership." Hart finished his coffee, set the mug aside. "Bottom line is, Ben Stone has a rogue group inside his department. What's he doing about that?"

"Nothing, unless there's some internal investigation going on that I haven't caught wind of."

Hart knew if Stone had turned a blind eye to the recent actions of several of his officers, then he was guilty of ineptness…and possibly a whole lot more. However, Molly might be right—Stone could be conducting an internal investigation off the books that only a few key people knew about. Which, Hart conceded, would be the smart thing for Stone to do.

The now-familiar sense of wariness that came with thoughts of Ben Stone tightened Hart's gut. He wondered again if the fact that Stone had some sort of personal relationship with Joan was clouding his opinion of the chief. Hart couldn't exactly blame Stone for being attracted to her. After all, she was a beautiful brunette with legs up to her ears. Long, silky legs that, on a long-ago summer night, had tangled with his while she claimed she loved him. Needed him. Vowed she wanted a life with him. Only him.

Hart blew out a breath. Working a case was like working on a bomb. You had to keep your focus. You had to have a clear objective and work to that end, even when you were drinking sweat. Dammit, he needed to keep his mind off Joan and concentrate on the reason he'd come to Mission Creek.

"What about Stone?" he asked.

"What about him?"

"What's your gut tell you? Could he be involved in the Lion's Den?"

"Uh, I've done some checking on the boss. Unofficial, you understand."

Hart slid her a look. "I understand that whatever you're about to tell me, I didn't hear from you."

"One night I found myself inside the PD's personnel office. I figure I wound up there because I'd been sleep-walking. Anyway, since I *was* there, I decided to get a better background picture of some of my fellow officers. You know, so I could maybe get along better?"

"Mmm-hmm." Hart was beginning to like Molly French immensely. "What did you discover while you were in this self-improvement mode?"

"That a large chunk of Stone's salary is being auto-matically sent to the probation department."

"*Probation* department?"

"Don't get excited. I found out that probation has a division that handles all matters of child support and ali-mony. The judge on Stone's divorce walloped him with big child-support and alimony payments. She put the chief in the system to make sure the money got automatically transferred from his paycheck to his ex's account each month."

"Did Stone's file give you any hint he might be con-nected to something not on the up-and-up?"

"Not his file." Molly paused. "Last year I answered a call where a woman accused a patrol cop of rape. I took the report, then transported her to the hospital to have a rape kit done. Since the suspect was a cop, I informed my sergeant. He advised the chief. The next day the victim recanted her story."

"You think someone paid her off? Maybe threatened her?"

"I'm not sure what I think. The victim was married and her husband was out of town when the incident occurred. I know for sure she had sex with a man other than her husband. Pretty rough sex, considering her busted lip and bruises. It's possible the sex was consensual, then she got scared and decided to yell rape to protect her marriage."

"Who was the patrol cop she accused?"

"Paulie McCauley. Mr. Muscle."

"Who now works under Stone on the bomb task force."

"Right." Molly shifted in her chair. "So, O'Brien, what do you think about all of this?"

"You've got two cops dead, another sitting in jail keeping his mouth shut and one on the lam. A teenager beaten into a coma by men he claims are cops who belong to a secret group called the Lion's Den." Hart shook his head. "There're a lot of questions that need answers. A lot of knots that have to be untied before the truth can come out."

"I'm not sure I'm going to be much help untying those knots," Molly said. "I don't have many people I can trust to watch my back, so I have to be careful. Real careful."

"You can add me to the list of people you can count on to watch your back."

"Thanks. And you can add me to yours."

"Deal." Hart took out a business card, jotted a number on its back. "That's my cell phone. Call if you need anything." He handed Molly the card, accepted the one she gave him.

They rose, retraced their steps down the spotless corridor that led to the lobby. When they veered toward the exit, Hart noted an entire wall devoted to a listing of individuals and businesses who'd made significant financial contributions to the hospital. Zane and Kathryn Cooper's names were engraved as benefactors under the heading Thomas Garrick Dean Trauma Wing.

Hart's shoulders tensed. Damn Zane Cooper. Damn him and his cursed lie that Hart had stolen money. A lie made up to keep the dirt-poor groundskeeper away from his precious, pampered daughter.

What would have happened, Hart wondered, if he had stayed in Mission Creek? If he'd been there, would Joan have still wound up marrying Thomas Dean?

"Something wrong, O'Brien?" Molly asked.

Hart tamped back the mix of anger and frustration that

seeing the wall of hospital benefactors had settled in his gut. He'd learned years ago that all the what-ifs were a waste of time. He *had* left Mission Creek. Joan *had* jumped into Thomas Dean's bed.

He looked at Molly. "Is there a gym somewhere I can spend a couple of hours beating the hell out of a punching bag?"

Five days and four sleepless nights after she'd let Hart O'Brien kiss her senseless, the experience still weighed on Joan like lead.

Even now, as she stepped out of Bonnie Brannigan's office after a two-hour meeting, the primary thought on Joan's mind was the possibility of running into Hart. Which she had done in various locations throughout the club's grounds for the past five days.

Giving her head a disgusted shake, she crossed the elegant reception area that guarded what she thought of as the Lone Star's inner sanctum of management, sales and catering offices and conference rooms. Instead of thinking about Hart, she should have her mind on the late-afternoon meeting with the club's general manager that had proven so beneficial. Bonnie had not only conveyed the board's approval of Joan's request to hire a massage therapist who was expert in the ancient Chinese healing art of Tuina, she had also received the go-ahead to expand the spa's reflexology program.

Shifting her leather portfolio into the crook of one arm, she mentally added her new responsibilities to her to-do list. Those new items, along with her promise to help Maddie Delarue with the upcoming Pasta by the Pool dance would keep Joan busy.

Not too busy, though, to prevent her thoughts from straying to Hart. And that damn kiss. Then, there were the subsequent nights she'd spent tossing and turning.

Camouflaging her increasing fatigue with carefully applied makeup, she had performed her workday and personal duties while wishing she could go ten minutes without the man creeping into her mind. Ten minutes without remembering the feel of his mouth on hers, the hot fire of his kiss, the hard, luring press of his body against hers. She had not felt those sensations for a very long time—not since the last time she and Hart were together. The night they had conceived a child. The night Joan had lain in Hart's arms while he swore he loved her, would do whatever it took to keep her in his life.

Lies, Joan reminded herself. Years ago she had forced herself to accept that every soft, silky word Hart had whispered to her on that life-changing night had been a lie. And yet, knowing that, she'd let him take her into his arms five nights ago. Let him kiss her until her eyes rolled back in her head. How could a man who had lied to her, deserted her, still make everything inside her yearn so quickly? So easily.

As she moved along a corridor where the thick carpet muffled her footsteps, Joan pressed a hand to her stomach. Dammit, Hart had no right. No right to bring everything back. No right to stroll into her life when just his presence threatened her daughter's safe, secure world.

Their daughter's world.

The thought had Joan clamping down on a hard tug of guilt. Hart was Helena's father. As much as she longed to deny that fact, it was the truth. A glaring truth when held up against the lie about Thomas Dean that her parents had fabricated, then breathed life into. A lie that Joan had never denied. A lie that she had always planned to someday expose to her child.

Just the thought of telling Helena had wings of panic fluttering in Joan's chest. Dear Lord, how could she possibly explain all of the circumstances so that Helena would understand? How could she justify the lies, even though she'd created them with the intention to protect?

It had been one thing to keep Helena ignorant of Hart's existence when Joan had no idea where he'd disappeared to. No clue if he was even alive—moot points, now that Hart had shown up again at the Lone Star.

Over the past five days he had made a habit of spending his afternoons sitting outside on one of the sun-drenched patios while he read through volumes of police reports. Despite her best intentions not to, Joan had begun watching for him, covertly studying his profile, the sexy, angular lines of it. Over the years she had yearned for him, desperately, impossibly. Now that he was back, that yearning bloomed inside her like a flame she'd never been able to extinguish.

Just as Hart drew the mother, he drew the child. Helena now made a beeline for the patio each day when she arrived home from school. Tossing aside her neon-blue backpack, she would drag a chair beside Hart's and seemingly bask in the attention of the man who not only asked her questions but appeared genuinely interested in her answers.

With an increasingly sickening clarity, Joan knew she would someday have to explain why she'd continued to withhold the truth about Helena's father after Hart had arrived on the scene. All she could do was pray Helena would accept that Joan had wanted to protect her from a man who had proven himself capable of lying, then walking away and never looking back.

Dread, like the ticking of a clock, pounded in Joan's brain as she continued along the carpeted hallway. Try as she might, she couldn't shake the feeling that her world was about to spin irrevocably out of her control.

Just as she was about to turn down the short corridor that led to the bank of elevators reserved for the staff's use, a deep voice stated, "Look, we don't know if there's anything to the run or not. Could be a coincidence."

Although she couldn't see him, Joan knew the voice belonged to Yance Ingram, the retired police captain who headed the Lone Star's security operation. The unfamiliar edge of steel in Ingram's voice had her pausing, unwilling to step around the corner into Ingram's line of sight.

"Coincidence, my ass," another man hissed. "I check for runs on the Lone Star's computer network each week to make sure nothing's going on that we need to know about. This is the first time anything like this has popped up. There's no way in hell you can convince me that her running *this* search the other morning just happened. You been retired so long that you've forgotten cops don't believe in coincidence?"

"I remember," Ingram shot back as the elevator dinged its arrival. "Coincidence or not, at this point all you can do is keep an eye open. If she uses her computer to make another run on emerald—or anything else that raises a red flag—you let me know. Me and the boss will deal with it."

A knot tightened Joan's throat as she inched forward and peered around the corner. The tall, lanky man following Ingram onto the elevator was dressed in the same navy blazer and gray slacks that all the Lone Star security officers wore. When the man turned to press the call button, Joan saw the same hostility in his expression that she'd heard in his voice. She didn't know the man's name, but she recognized him as one of the MCPD cops who had worked off-duty security at the Lone Star for several months.

When the elevator door slid shut, she leaned a shoulder against the wall and expelled a slow breath while thinking about Ingram's use of the word *emerald*. She had specifically run *Esmeralda* through the computer, not emerald. Yet, she remembered just enough from her high school foreign language class to know that the Spanish translation for emerald was esmeralda.

Had Ingram and the other officer been talking about the run she did for Hart days ago? The run that had seemed a dead end, since she had found no former or current employees or club members with the name Esmeralda.

She didn't know, she thought as an instinctive fear sneaked up to tickle the back of her throat. All she knew was that she needed to find Hart.

Chapter 8

"**I** wonder where Hart is?" Helena asked that evening while a harried hostess guided her and Joan to a booth inside the Lone Star's filled-to-capacity Yellow Rose Café. Helena, wearing a long yellow T-shirt over black leggings and red high-top tennis shoes, paused to stash her neon-blue backpack beneath the booth before sliding onto the seat opposite her mother. "I couldn't find him anywhere when I got home from school."

Nor could Joan locate Hart after she overheard the conversation between Yance Ingram and the other security officer. She'd checked the club's numerous outdoor patios, the area around the three swimming pools, had called Hart's suite, even knocked on the plywood door to the walled-off bomb site in case he was working inside. Deciding he was nowhere on the resort's premises, she left a message at the front desk saying she needed to see him. She'd then hurried back to the spa in time to make a late-afternoon appointment with the governor's wife.

"Sergeant O'Brien isn't like most of the Lone Star's

guests who are here on vacation," Joan reminded her daughter, whose mouth had settled into a petulant sulk. "All those afternoons you've seen him sitting out on one of the patios he's been working—reading reports on the bombing. Maybe he got through all the reports and now has to work at the police station."

"I guess," Helena said glumly. Using a red-polished fingernail, she traced the squares on the yellow gingham tablecloth that covered the booth. "Do you think he found the bad man who set the bomb? Then checked out? Would Hart leave us without saying goodbye?"

If Helena was despairing over Hart leaving now, what would it do to her if she knew he was her father? Could she handle the pain if he walked away after her feelings for him deepened?

Joan thought of the overwhelming devastation she had felt when Hart disappeared from her life. Even after so long the memories still had the power to sneak up like a phantom, squeezing her heart in its agonizing grip.

Like now.

Needing a minute to let her emotions settle, she shifted her gaze to where a planter ablaze with the riotous colors of marigolds, petunias and snapdragons separated a small bar from the café. Like most evenings, the bar was cluttered with people and full of noise.

"Mom? Do you think something happened to make Hart leave without telling us goodbye?" Helena repeated.

Wanting to prepare her daughter in case Hart did just that, Joan searched for the right words. "Sweetheart, you remember the last vacation you went on with Grandpa Zane and Grandma Kathryn?

"You were really excited about leaving, but by the end of the two weeks you called me and said you were having fun but you missed me and were ready to come home."

Helena considered for a moment. "I guess I got homesick."

"That's right. The same thing could happen to Hart.

When his work is done here, he'll be anxious to get home to Chicago. He might not have time to say goodbye.''

"But I like him and he likes me, too," Helena persisted firmly. "'N he's your friend from a long time ago. Don't you think he'd feel bad if he didn't see us before he left?''

"What I think is that you don't need to worry about Hart having already left Mission Creek. He won't do that at least until after they solve the bombing. If someone had been arrested for that recently we would have heard.''

Helena shrugged. "I guess so," she said while nudging her unused menu to the edge of the table. "Mom, I don't like Cole Callaway anymore. He acted like a creep in school today.''

Accustomed to her daughter's mind-bending changes of subject, Joan had no problem keeping up. "What did Cole do?''

"We were supposed to be studying our spelling words, but Cole played with a couple of quarters instead, spinning them on top of his desk. Mr. Young heard it and asked him what he was doing. And you won't believe what Cole said!'' Helena announced. Not waiting for a response, she blurted, "Cole said that he dropped some money and was just picking it up. I think Mr. Young *knew* Cole was playing, but he didn't even do anything.''

"Nothing?''

"He just gave Cole one of his mean looks and said to put the quarters back in his pocket. He let Cole get away with it.'' Sitting up straight, Helena wrapped her thin arms around her chest. "Cole lied, Mom. And last week he pushed Jeffrey down at recess, then said he didn't. I've decided I'm not going to play with Cole anymore. If he lies about those things, who knows what else he'd lie about?''

Joan felt a reflexive spurt of pride at Helena's sense of conviction, then realization hit.

Oh, God, she thought. Like every other responsible parent she had taught Helena the difference between right and wrong, good and bad, truth and lies. Made sure her child understood what was acceptable and what wasn't. In Helena's mind—which lately sometimes veered toward more adult-like thoughts than those of a child—lies were wrong. All lies.

Even those told to protect. To shield.

Joan reached for the glass of ice water a waitress had placed in front of her. Helena was too young to understand why her beloved grandparents had chosen to invent a father for her who had never existed. Too young to comprehend why her mother had done nothing about righting that lie when she'd found out about it. Too young to look at both sides. If Helena learned the truth now, what would her reaction be? How far would her disappointment in them go? Would she wind up forever hating her grandparents? Her own mother?

Planting her elbows on the table, Helena rested her chin on her fists. "I looked for Hart when I got home from school to tell him about creepy Cole Callaway. I think Hart should be able to give him a ticket or something."

Knowing Helena had looked for Hart instead of making a beeline for the spa to share the story with *her* had Joan sensing again that the control she held over her world was slipping like sand through her fingertips.

Helena glanced across the café and her expression turned instantly sunny. "Look, Mom, there's Hart now!"

Joan glanced over her shoulder. Hart stood in the café's doorway looking tall and gorgeous, dressed in black slacks and a heather-gray shirt. Over the past days his tan had deepened so that his green eyes now seemed to blaze in his carelessly handsome face. She couldn't help but notice that the appreciative gazes of several women diners had zeroed in on him, as well. Nor could she fault them. The way Hart lingered in the doorway while his eyes slowly swept the crowded café and bar reminded her of a hunter searching for prey. Dangerous. Menacing. Desirable. Watching him, she felt her heart jolt, just as it had on the day she'd first laid eyes on him.

That age-old attraction drew her, even as it set off alarms. "He can eat dinner with us, can't he?"

Joan knew if she said no, her daughter would ask why. And Joan would be forced to lie. Some words, she thought, were best not spoken. "If he wants to."

Helena scrambled out of the booth and charged around yellow-gingham-covered tables toward the café's entrance.

With a bittersweet, undeniable longing for what might have been, Joan watched father and daughter exchange grins as Helena grabbed hold of one of Hart's hands and tugged.

Why couldn't you have loved me? Joan thought. If you hadn't cut me out of your life you would have known that beautiful little girl was yours. Ours. You could have watched her grow up. Loved her.

"It's fajita night," Helena was explaining as she and Hart arrived at the booth. "Mom and I eat at the Yellow Rose every fajita night. And we get sopapillas with honey for dessert."

Joan gave silent thanks when Helena scooted in beside her, leaving the opposite seat vacant for Hart.

Pausing, he looked down at her with those sinfully green eyes. "I've received an invitation to join you for dinner. Is that okay with you?"

"Of course."

"When I got home from school I looked for you," Helena said while Hart settled into the booth. She then launched into a repeat of the story about Cole Callaway and the quarters.

As if hanging on her every word, Hart gave her his full attention, nodding on occasion. "I expect Callaway will be sorry he lied, once he finds out it cost him your friendship," Hart observed solemnly after Helena finished her story.

"I just don't like liars."

"Neither do I," Hart said.

The quick, instinctive fear of a cornered victim had Joan balling her hands into fists.

Just then the waitress dropped off the iced tea Joan and Helena had ordered when they first arrived. Pulling out her pencil and pad, the woman focused on Helena. "What'll you have this evening, young lady?" After jotting orders for three fajita specials, the woman scurried away.

Helena turned her attention back to Hart. "So, where were you this afternoon? Why weren't you working on the patio like you usually do?"

"Helena." Joan laid her hand on her daughter's. "That isn't any of your business."

"It's okay," Hart said with a shrug. "I had some people I needed to interview. Then I went by the police station to see if the task force has gotten any new leads in the case."

"Me n' Mom went to the police station," Helena stated while peeling the paper off a straw then stabbing it into her glass.

"Mom and I," Joan corrected automatically.

"Mom and I," Helena amended while rolling her dark eyes at Hart. "We went to see Chief Ben's office. Is your office in Chicago like his?"

Joan noted a tightening around Hart's mouth at the mention of Ben Stone. "Nothing like it," he replied. "In fact, the bomb squad's office isn't even in the same building as the rest of the police department."

Helena angled her chin. "Why not?"

"Because of the type of work we do." Hart leaned in as if sharing a secret. "Everybody on the Chicago PD calls the bomb squad office the Bat Cave."

Helena's eyes widened. "Is it in a secret place? In a cave like Batman's?"

"No, its location isn't secret and the building doesn't look anything like a cave. It's just not like a typical office.

We have to have a big workshop with a lot of benches and tools. That's because after a bomb explodes we collect the pieces left and try to put them back together.''

"Why do you do that?"

"Depending on the type of bomb and materials used we can sometimes get a lead on the person who built the bomb. Then we can track him down and arrest him." Hart smiled. "We even have a dog who has her own house at the Bat Cave."

"What kind of dog?"

"A German shepherd named Red Wire. She can smell a bomb."

Helena pursed her mouth. "Where'd she get the name Red Wire?"

"There's a saying among bomb techs—never *ever* cut the red wire."

"How can a dog smell a bomb?"

"A dog's sense of smell is about one thousand times better than a human's."

"But Red Wire's a dog, so she can't talk," Helena said around sips. "How does she let you know when she smells a bomb?"

"She went to school to learn to do that. Anytime Red Wire smells explosives, she sits and stays really still until her trainer tells her she can move."

Grinning, Hart reached across the booth, skimmed a finger down Helena's nose. "I'll bet my pension you wind up working as an investigative reporter. Or a cop who's awesome at interrogations. You don't leave any rock unturned."

"Does that mean I ask a lot of questions?"

Hart chuckled. "You got it."

"Mom says there are no dumb questions, so if I want to know something I should ask."

Joan brushed her daughter's long, dark hair behind her shoulder. "It seems my words have come back to haunt me."

The conversation she'd just witnessed made Joan realize the easy camaraderie that had developed between Hart and Helena over the past days. The totally natural way father and daughter responded to each other made Joan's heart ache for what might have been. For what was.

The waitress arrived at the booth with a tray loaded with sizzling platters of fajitas.

Joan knew the three of them looked like a family out enjoying a meal. That, after all, was what they were. A mother, a father and their child. Except two of the people were ignorant of that small fact. *Hart, you have a daughter. Helena, he's your father.* Each word viewed separately was simple. Easy. Together they were words Joan didn't dare utter. If she did, Hart and Helena would both hate her.

The food that had smelled so enticing to Joan when she and Helena walked into the café now turned to tasteless sand in her mouth.

Neither Helena nor Hart seemed to notice Joan picking at her food while Helena dominated the conversation with stories about school and the type of knots her Brownie leader had taught the troop to tie during their last meeting.

Helena had popped the last bite of a sopapilla into her mouth when blond-haired, blue-eyed Ceci Underwood appeared in the café's doorway and began waving anxiously.

"There's Ceci," Helena said. "Her dad must be ready to take us to get the stuff for our science project."

"What sort of project?" Hart asked.

"We have to pour different colors of dye in jars of water and put one white flower with a long stem in each jar. Then we have to watch the flowers and write down where the color goes inside them, and how long it takes. Ceci's dad is driving us to the store so we can pick out the flowers and the dye ourselves."

"Sounds like you've got an interesting project ahead of you," Hart commented as he plucked up the check the waitress had left.

Helena looked at her mother. "Can I be excused?"

"May I," Joan automatically corrected. "And, yes, you may."

"Bye!" Scooting off the seat, she snagged her backpack from under the table before zipping away.

Joan watched Hart as he pulled money out of his billfold. "I don't want you buying our dinner."

"Let me. You and Helena saved me from eating alone. I do that enough as it is."

Because she had wondered countless times, she couldn't help but ask, "Don't you have someone in your life back home?"

"Someone, meaning a woman?" He flicked her a look as he dropped bills on top of the check. "Are you curious enough about me to want to know if I'm involved in a relationship?"

She didn't want to be, but she was. "I'm just making conversation, Hart. You don't have to answer—"

"There's been a lot of someones in and out of my life over the past ten years. For some reason none of those relationships worked. I hope I'll find the right person someday. Get married. Have kids." Green eyes behind thick amber lashes locked with hers. "Like you did. I've told you this before, Texas. You've got a great little girl."

"Thank you." Joan forced a smile. "It's...obvious that she's fond of you."

"The feeling's mutual." His forehead furrowed. "I've wondered if I've done things right where Helena's concerned."

"What sort of things?"

"The only kids I've really ever been around are the children of the guys on the bomb squad. That's only for short periods when we have family get-togethers." He raised a shoulder. "I work in a business where information is power, so I think it's great Helena is gutsy enough to ask so many questions. I always give her an answer, but I never know for sure if what I say is the right thing. Like talking about my job. She knows I'm a bomb tech, but I don't want to keep reminding her about the bomb that exploded here. Bombs are easy things to have nightmares over.''

The fact that he'd given so much thought to Helena's feelings caught Joan off guard. For years she had ached for this man, needed him, wept for him and finally managed to close her heart to him. Now his concern over the words he spoke to a child put a burning in Joan's throat.

''From…what I've seen, you're doing a fine job,'' she managed, then took a long sip of tea in a vain attempt to quell that burning. ''With kids you never know what's going to happen next. Or, in Helena's case, what her next question will be. All you can do is go with the flow and hope for the best.''

''Thanks for the advice. Now, tell me what's wrong.''

His change of subject had her hesitating. ''What do you mean?''

''You picked at your food. Hardly ate anything. Didn't have a lot to say.'' He settled one of his hands on the gingham cloth inches from hers. ''What's bothering you, Texas?''

You are, she thought. Over the years she had dated, had even had a serious relationship with one man who had loved her and Helena. Joan had known he would have made a wonderful husband and father. She had tried to open her heart to him. Had *wanted* to love him. Yet, she couldn't. Because always, always her unresolved feelings for Hart had stood in her way.

Now, sitting across the booth from him, she was acutely aware of his physical presence, the power of his shoulders beneath his shirt, the seductive curve of his wide mouth, the intensity of his green eyes. How many times since he walked out of her life had she tried to understand what there was about this one man that had drawn her so compellingly?

That drew her still.

Don't go there. The voice blaring in her head warned that her heart wasn't the only thing at risk where this man was concerned. She had to think of Helena. Protect her child.

Needing distance, Joan slid her hand away from his and leaned back in the booth. If she didn't need to tell Hart about the conversation she'd overheard she would have suggested they go their separate ways. As soon as they talked, she promised herself.

"Did you get the message I left for you at the front desk?"

"No. I missed lunch, so I came here the minute I got back. What message?"

At that instant Joan glimpsed Yance Ingram and Paulie McCauley following the café's hostess to a nearby table. McCauley was a MCPD cop who worked security at the club during off-duty hours. Both men were clad in the blue blazer, white shirt and gray slacks worn by all the Lone Star security detail.

The uneasiness she had felt that afternoon when she'd overheard the conversation between Yance Ingram and the security officer whose name she didn't know returned full force.

She realized the tenseness she felt had settled in her face when Hart asked, "What's wrong?"

When she turned her head, she saw his gaze had followed hers and was now focused on the two men.

"I need to tell you about something I heard this afternoon. Overheard, to be exact. I think it has to do with the computer search I ran for you."

Just then, Ingram glanced across the café, his gaze locking with Joan's. He studied her with a steady intensity before his mouth curved and he gave her nod.

She forced a smile for the security chief, then picked up her tea and sipped.

Hart looked back at her. "What did you overhear?" His

eyes had hardened, even though his expression seemed relaxed.

She glanced at Ingram. He had risen from his chair and was walking toward the café's door while he punched in a number on his cell phone. Even though she had no real reason to think his call had anything to do with her, Joan suppressed a shiver.

"I don't want to talk about it here."

"All right, Texas," Hart said levelly. "Let's go find someplace where we can talk."

"'Atta boy, Warrant." Chuckling, Ben Stone wrestled a tooth-pocked Frisbee from the jaws of his two-year-old golden retriever. "One more throw, then I'll go in and rustle us both up some grub."

Under the pale light of the moon, Ben's tidy backyard was subdued shades of gray and black, with occasional patches of white. The fragrance of night-blooming flowers hung in the air. The roomy workshop Ben had proudly built himself from the ground up squatted in the shadows in the yard's far corner.

With the retriever jumping in frantic circles around him, Ben flicked his wrist and sent the Frisbee sailing. Warrant vaulted after it. Just as the dog clamped its powerful jaws onto the Frisbee, Ben's cell phone rang.

"Never off the clock," he muttered before answering.

"Ingram here. Guess what I just saw."

"That'd be a hard thing to do, Yance, since I don't even know where you are."

"At the Lone Star. I'm just walking into the security office."

"That doesn't give me much of a clue." When Ben joined the MCPD, Yance Ingram had served as his mentor. The older cop had shown Ben the ropes and protected him from the political potholes that could have sidelined Ben's rise up the ranks. After Ingram's wife died of a long illness that wiped out their savings, Ben had taken care of his former mentor by offering the then-retired MCPD captain a cut of El Jefe's action. When a vacancy occurred for the director of the Lone Star's security operation, Ben had sent the board a glowing recommendation that had assured Ingram the job. In exchange, the retired cop ran things at the Lone Star the way Ben wanted. Everything had gone smooth until the day the bomb went off.

"I give up, Yance," Ben said as Warrant dropped the Frisbee onto the toe of one of his uniform boots. "What did you just see?"

"Your girlfriend and O'Brien. They're eating dinner together at the Yellow Rose Café."

Ben thought again about O'Brien's reaction to the mention of Joan's name days ago in the task force room. Then there was the report Ingram had given him about the run on Esmeralda made on the computer in Joan's office at the spa. Despite the name's glaring connection to El Jefe, Ben had wanted to believe that had been innocent on Joan's part. He had told himself that Esmeralda could be a brand of pricey beauty products sold in the spa. Or the name of some foreign masseuse Joan planned to hire to tend to wealthy, pampered clients. More than anything, Ben had wanted no connection to exist between Joan and Hart O'Brien.

He had managed to keep that hope alive until last night when the tap on the phone in O'Brien's suite recorded the conversation between the bomb tech and an FBI agent based in Denver. From what was said during the call, it was obvious O'Brien had found papers that had been overlooked at the bomb site. Papers documenting the money laundering operation that had once run like a well-oiled machine. Papers that Ingram had routinely secreted in the drop-down ceiling inside the club's security office. Papers obviously dislodged by the bomb's blast.

"Anybody else with Joan and O'Brien?" Stone asked.

"Her kid was, but she took off with the Underwood

girl. I hate to tell you this, Ben, but the three of them looked like a cozy little family.''

Ben closed his eyes.

''I don't think we can just sit back and ignore what's going on,'' Ingram continued. ''First, Joan makes the run on Esmeralda. Second, we hear yesterday's conversation between O'Brien and the FBI guy. Third, Joan and the cop eat dinner together. Seeing them like that proves what we suspected. She made that run for him, or she let him use her computer to do it. From the way they were looking at each other tonight, I'm here to tell you there's more than just business between them. If we don't do something fast, El Jefe will be on us like stink on road-kill.''

Ben's teeth locked hard enough to crack fillings. Joan was his. Dammit, she and Helena were his.

''So, boss, how do you want things handled?'' Ingram asked.

''I want that idiot Willie Pogue blown to hell,'' Ben ordered, referring to the Lone Star's maintenance man who had stored cans of paint and thinner in the closet between the Men's Grill and the billiards room. When Ben planted the bomb, he hadn't known the combustibles were in the nearby closet. The bomb's detonation ignited the paint and thinner. The resulting fire had spread within feet of the Lone Star's security office. The moonlighting cops on duty had barely managed to keep the flames from devouring over a hundred thousand dollars in unlaundered cash. And they'd had one hell of a time keeping things hidden from the firefighters who insisted on entering the security office to check for hot spots.

''You want Pogue blown to hell?'' Ingram asked.

''Nothing wrong with your hearing, Yance.'' The instant Ben had heard the taped conversation during which the Fed verified to O'Brien that the papers he'd found were from a money laundering operation, Ben had started making plans.

He pulled a cigar from the pocket of his uniform shirt,

lit up and reviewed those plans again in his mind. Yes, he decided, they would work. Drawing in smoke, he expelled it in a thin blue cloud.

"Here's the deal, Yance. From the questions O'Brien asked about Pogue the night you showed him the bomb scene, offing Pogue is the perfect solution for us," Ben explained. "O'Brien's already wondering if Pogue stuffed that closet full of accelerants because he knew a bomb was going to go off only a few feet from there the next day and he wanted as much collateral damage as possible. If we make it look like Pogue's the bomber, our problems are solved. The D.A. gets off my back and the bomb tech hightails it back to Chicago." Away from Joan. "We can get back to business as usual."

"Sounds like a plan to me. You want to help me build this next baby, too?"

Ben thought for a moment. "Yes, the bomb that kills Pogue has to be identical to the one that exploded in the Men's Grill." Ben glanced at the dark workshop on the far side of the yard. Everything they needed to build another bomb was inside. "Get over here as soon as you can. I want this thing over with."

"Ten-four, boss." Ingram paused. "While we're taking care of loose threads, what about Higgins?"

"What about him?"

"He's sitting in the county jail, keeping his mouth shut about why he tried to deep-six Molly French. I think it's time we show him we're men of our word and take care of his problem. If she's not around to testify against him, his problem goes away."

"All right. Is McCauley working security at the club tonight?"

"Sure is. In fact, I'm going to have to call him on his cell phone and tell him he just lost his dinner date."

"Tell him to make plans to deal with French. I don't care how he does it as long as it looks like an accident."

Ingram chuckled. "You know Paulie, he's got a real creative mind."

Ben clicked off his phone and stood motionless in the still, night air. Warrant, apparently having given up on any further tosses of the Frisbee, now scurried around the yard from one point of canine interest to another.

"Dammit," Ben hissed around his cigar. He thought about how Joan had held him at arm's length for months. About how he'd let her. He'd convinced himself his being patient would bring her around. She was so beautiful. So perfect. She wouldn't walk out on him like Irene had. If Joan were his, he would treat her like an angel. Her and her little girl.

Not *if,* Ben amended. *When.* Joan and Helena would be his. Since the night El Jefe's representative stepped out of the shadows on Ben's porch, he'd been playing the odds. He'd had yet to lose. More to the point, he didn't intend to lose this time. *Ever* lose. He had the intelligence and ability to deal with whatever came along.

He would use any means to get what he wanted. Any means at all.

Chapter 9

After the waitress delivered his change to the booth, Hart followed Joan's winding path around gingham-covered tables toward the door of the Yellow Rose Café. He didn't have to look in the direction of the table where Officer Paulie McCauley sat to know that the MCPD cop's gaze tracked their progress. What Hart did wonder about was what sort of civic deed the cop had done to earn the small gold lion pin affixed to the lapel of his navy blazer.

The instant they cleared the door of thc café, Hart snagged Joan's elbow and turned her to face him. Her eyes were huge and dark in the pallor of her face. He could almost feel the uneasy tension that gripped her. Tension that had settled inside her the minute Yance Ingram and Paulie McCauley strolled into the Yellow Rose.

Logic told him that whatever she overheard earlier that day involved either Ingram or McCauley, or both. Studying her face, Hart frowned. He didn't like seeing the paleness that had settled in her cheeks. Nor did he like thinking her uneasiness had something to do with the computer check he'd asked her to run on Esmeralda.

"Where's a good place to talk?" he asked.

Easing out a breath, she gestured toward a pair of French doors that led to a trellised walkway behind the clubhouse. "On the other side of the adult pool there's a new terrace that the grounds people just put the finishing touches on. It has hedges and some benches tucked into arbors. It's private."

Hart glanced back toward the entrance to the Yellow Rose. Yance Ingram had yet to return to the café after leaving in what looked like a hurry with his cell phone plastered to his ear. Hart knew that Ingram had made the call the instant he'd spotted Joan and himself sharing a booth. Who the hell had Ingram called? Hart wondered. And why?

He looked back at Joan. "The terrace sounds good." Because he savored the feel of her skin against his—had always savored it—he held on to her elbow an instant longer before dropping his hand. "Lead the way."

A nearly full moon rode a sky crowded by hot stars as they moved along the trellised walkway. The flowering plants and bushes in nearby planters and well-tended beds filled the air with perfume.

Minutes later they reached one of the many patios that dotted the Lone Star's grounds. In a move that Hart told himself was simply reflex, he placed a hand at the small of her back while they passed tables topped by colorful umbrellas at which members of the wait staff served drinks to patrons taking advantage of the warm, moonlit night.

Leaving the crowded patio behind they continued along a cobblestone path. As she moved, the hem of Joan's yellow sundress swirled around her long legs. Hart felt the heat of her body against his palm, the compelling sway of her trim hips. Setting his jaw, he tried to ignore the sheer sexual frustration eating at his gut.

It suddenly occurred to him that the long-ago night they

spent together had been much the same as this one, with the moon and stars blazing overhead. One night that had haunted him for a decade. One woman he'd never quite gotten out of his system. Nor had he forgotten that she'd whispered she loved him, then had fallen into bed with another man, become his wife and borne him a child.

That Hart still felt a drag of hurt over their past had his mood darkening like the shadows around them. Dropping his hand from the hollow of her spine, he bit back a curse at the thought of how, moments before, he had sat across from her in the café's cozy booth, thinking how much he wanted to kiss her again. And again.

He could try to convince himself that the need he felt for her was just physical. Problem was, he knew better. Although he couldn't look at her and not want her, that need went way beyond just the itch to touch her. He wanted more.

With her, he always wanted more.

When had she gotten inside him again? he wondered. How the hell had he let it happen? And what was he going to do about it?

"The terrace is that way," she said when the cobblestone path split and angled off in opposite directions.

Hart nodded as they veered toward the right. He wasn't into self-deception—he and Joan weren't out for a romantic stroll in the moonlight. The only reason she was with him right now was because of his investigation. Which was exactly what he needed to focus on.

Their footsteps echoing against the stones, they followed the path's lazy curve that took them toward the adult swimming pool. Lights beneath the water's surface picked up a shifting web of emerald green that somehow made the pool look endlessly deep.

On the far side of the Olympic-size pool sat a darkened cabana with red-and-white-striped awnings.

Hart shifted his gaze past the cabana to a terrace bordered by neat hedges interspaced by high latticed arbors.

Lights concealed at the base of the hedges cast the area in soft, dim hues and shadows. "I take it that's where you want to talk?"

"Yes."

There, Joan settled on a wrought-iron bench nesting beneath one of the arbors. Hart saw what she meant about privacy—if he hadn't been directly in front of her, she would be hidden from his view. He chose to remain standing, angled so he could see anyone coming along the path in either direction.

"Tell me what you overheard," he said quietly.

"Okay." She pressed a hand to her temple as if trying to get her thoughts in order. "I had a meeting this afternoon with Bonnie Brannigan. I had just left her office and was almost to the end of the hallway that leads to the staff elevators when I heard a man talking. I couldn't see him, but I knew the voice. It was Yance Ingram's."

"What did he say?" Hart prodded when she paused.

"That *they* didn't know if there was anything to the run, or not. Maybe it was just a coincidence. Another man whose voice I didn't recognize told Ingram that he checks periodically for activity on the Lone Star's computer network just to make sure nothing goes on that they need to know. This run they discussed was apparently the first thing that had sent up a red flag."

"They didn't say what run?"

"Not at that point. The second man commented that there's no way *her* running *this* search the other morning just happened. Then he asked Ingram if he'd been retired from the department so long that he'd forgotten cops don't believe in coincidence."

Hart swept his gaze from one end of the shadowy cobblestone walk to the other. "How did Ingram respond?"

"He told the man to keep an eye open. Ingram then said if she uses her computer to make another run on emerald—or anything else that sounds an alarm—for the other man to let him know. If that happens, Ingram will take it up the ladder, and he and the boss will deal with it.''

"Emerald," Hart repeated, meeting her gaze. "What makes you think they were talking about the run I asked you to do?"

"Do you speak Spanish?"

"I picked up some street Spanish when I rode a black-and-white." His mouth lifted at the edges. "Most of which I can't repeat in mixed company."

"I don't remember a lot of the Spanish I learned in high school, but I do know that the translation for emerald is esmeralda."

Hart narrowed his eyes. The nameless man Ingram had been speaking to was right—cops didn't believe in coincidence. "Did they say anything else?"

"No. Right then the elevator arrived."

"Did you get a look at the man with Ingram?"

Joan nodded. "I peeked around the corner as they stepped into the elevator. He's tall and lanky with short brown hair. I've seen him here—he's one of the MCPD cops who works security on the evening shift. I just don't know his name."

"He runs computer checks," Hart said thoughtfully.

"Yes. Do you know who he is?"

"A detective assigned to the bomb task force matches that description. Name's Frank Hasselman. Molly French—another task force cop—says Hasselman's a whiz on computers."

"I guess Hasselman is who I saw," Joan observed. "It's obvious he keeps an eye on the club's computers and tells Ingram whatever he finds."

"And since Ingram referred to 'the boss,' that means there's at least three big brothers." Hart paused, his mind analyzing this new information. "What does the Lone Star's organization chart look like? Does Ingram work for Bonnie Brannigan or does he report directly to the board of directors?"

"He reports to Bonnie, just like I do. The same goes for all the other division managers."

"Who does Bonnie report to?"

"The club's board. Flynt Carson is this year's president, so he and Bonnie meet weekly."

Hart nodded grimly. "My contact at the FBI finally called back. He confirmed the pages I found at the bomb site are from a money laundering operation. A pretty big one, taking into account the dollar amounts listed."

Joan rose from the bench, wrapping her arms around her waist as if to ward off a chill. "The other night you said you thought you had a certain type of case. Where you have a piece of evidence at one end and another at the other end." She furrowed her forehead. In the moonlight her face was a study of silver light and shadows. "I can't remember what you called it."

"*Prima facie.* Together, the two pieces of evidence lead to a reasonable assumption of what's in between."

"Doesn't the same thing apply here? You find papers from a money laundering operation at the bomb site with the name Esmeralda written across the top. I run that name on the computer in my office and come up with nothing. Yet, it's almost certain what I did sent up a red flag with certain members of the club's security team. Can't we reasonably assume that those men have something to do with money laundering? That they're possibly even the men Jake Anderson saw loading bulging bags that maybe contained money out of a back door of the clubhouse right before the bomb went off?"

Hart slid his hands into the pockets of his slacks. "I like the way your mind works, Texas. Anytime you want to sign on as my partner, you let me know."

She arched a brow. "I have a feeling you've already reached the same conclusion."

"Doesn't matter. I'm still impressed. Is it possible Ingram or the other guy saw you? That maybe they know you overheard their conversation?"

"No. I'm positive they didn't see me."

"Even so, they know you ran Esmeralda. In case they ask you why, we need to come up with a logical reason that has nothing to do with the papers I found." Hart shoved a hand through his hair. "You've already said you don't know anyone named Esmeralda. Is there some sort of product with that name?"

"Actually, there is someone. I didn't make the connection the other night when you asked me to run the name because you wanted employees or members of the Lone Star. But I attended a conference for spa managers last year in New York. One of the vendors there was a woman named Esmeralda. She designs costume jewelry. Her style is way too offbeat for Texas, so I didn't order any of her pieces to carry in the boutique at Body Perfect."

"This is good." Hart pursed his mouth. "Just because you don't carry any of Esmeralda's stuff in the spa now doesn't mean you're not considering ordering some. If that's the case, is there a reason you'd run her name through the computer?"

"Yes. I would have to check to see if the gift shop or the other boutiques here have ever carried any of her jewelry. If so, we would already have a vendor number for her. I would have to use that same number if I placed an order with Esmeralda."

"So, suppose someone asks why you ran the name? Is it a reasonable explanation that you hit a few wrong computer keys and ran Esmeralda through the employee and member databases instead of the vendor database?"

"Totally reasonable."

"Good." Hart figured the explanation covered Joan; still, he needed to be sure. "Can you pull it off? If Ingram or Hasselman—or anyone else—asks why you ran Esmeralda, can you make what we've come up with sound convincing?"

"I think so."

He met her gaze. "I was wrong to ask you to do that run."

"You didn't force me. I could have said no."

"True, but I should have thought about the Lone Star's computers being networked. And the possibility that someone might monitor them for all activity."

"Someone, being the security force, meaning police officers." Joan paced to the edge of the terrace, then back again. "Two police officers kidnapped Jake Anderson," she continued. The anger that had settled in her voice sparked in her eyes. "And two others tried to kill a female detective. Now, it looks like still other police officers are involved in money laundering." She shook her head. "Hart, what the hell is going on?"

"I don't know. Not yet. But I plan to find out." He took a step toward her. "You're seeing Ben Stone."

"Yes." Her chin slowly rose. "Are you saying Ben's involved in any of this?"

"Nothing points that way. Still, like you said, something's going on with the Mission Creek cops. Stone's their boss. It's something to consider, is all."

She narrowed her eyes. "I'm fond of Ben, as is my daughter. I need to know if you have any evidence that suggests he's done something wrong. *Any evidence.*"

How fond? Hart wondered. "You can relax. There's zero evidence against Stone."

The look of immense relief that spread across her face tightened Hart's jaw.

"I'm glad," she said. "Very glad—"

"Yeah, I can see that."

She tilted her head. "You don't like the fact I'm glad there's no evidence against Ben?"

"What I don't like is knowing the guy can put his hands on you." As he spoke, Hart closed the distance between them. "I don't like that one bit, because that's what I want to do."

"Hart, I…" She looked away. Her mouth, full and naked in the moonlight, lured him. "It's best that you don't put your hands on me."

"Like this?" Settling his palms on her bare upper arms, he pulled her gaze back to his. Her flesh felt like warm, rich cream beneath his stroking fingers. "Is it *best* I don't touch you like this?"

"Yes." Closing her eyes, she made no move to step from his touch.

"Best for whom?"

"Me." She pressed her lips together. "You." Her voice had lowered, and it now seemed liquid enough to slide over his skin. "Both of us."

"Dammit, Texas, I *want* my hands on you. All over you."

"Hart—"

He dipped his head, nibbled her lower lip. He watched her lashes flutter, reveled in the sound of her breath catching with pleasure. "Every time I kiss you, you taste better."

"So do you." Fisting her hands in his hair, she dragged his mouth to hers.

Swamped by memories and needs, he wrapped an arm around her, drawing her closer, savoring the flavor of her, the scent, the feel. As he deepened the kiss, the memories of the past and the reality of now twined together until he could almost forget there had been time between.

He felt her body softening, felt her heart beating against his, quick and unsteady.

As unsteady as his own.

His hand slid up her spine, fingers spreading until they tangled in her hair. It was insane to want her this way, he told himself hazily. Crazy to hold on to the eternal, unending need for this one woman that had continued to ache inside him over the years like a raw, deep wound. He had a wild, desperate thought to drag her off behind one of the trim hedges and—

"Well, y'all will have to excuse us for barging in."

Hart felt Joan jolt, then spring out of his hold like a startled rabbit.

"Bonnie. C.J." Joan shoved her fingers through her tousled hair, looking like a kid caught dipping both hands into the cookie jar. "I…we didn't hear you."

"That's an understatement." Bonnie Brannigan, wearing a teal-blue suit styled as perfectly as her blond hair, sent a knowing look to the burly, gray-haired man whose arm she had linked with her own. "C.J. and I met some friends at the Empire Room for dinner. Since I need to check to make sure some equipment got delivered by the pool we decided to take a stroll."

Nodding, Joan slid her hands into the pockets of her sundress. "It's a pleasant night for a stroll."

"That it is," the Lone Star's general manager agreed, then locked her gaze with Hart's. It wasn't disapproval he saw in her blue eyes, but something close. "I guess we're not the only couple who decided to take advantage of this moonlight."

"That's right, you're not." Hart took a step forward, offering a hand to Bonnie's powerfully built escort. "Hart O'Brien."

"C.J. Stuckey," the man said, returning the handshake.

"I apologize for not introducing the two of you." Bonnie flipped a wrist, sending the charms on her gold bracelet tinkling. "It didn't occur to me you hadn't crossed paths."

"Haven't had the pleasure." Hart's gaze flicked to the small gold lion pin on the lapel of the man's suit coat. "But I've heard a lot of people say that C.J. Stuckey is the lucky man who put that huge diamond on Bonnie Brannigan's finger."

"That I am," C.J. said, beaming a proud smile. "I thought I'd take advantage of this moonlight to try to talk this little lady into moving up our wedding date. It gets lonely out there on the ranch."

"We might just have to think about that." Smiling, Bonnie shifted her gaze to Joan. "Now, honey, tell me what Helena and Ceci Underwood are up to with all those white roses.''

Joan blinked. "Roses?"

Bonnie nodded. "Just a couple of minutes ago we spotted the girls skipping in from the parking lot, each carrying a bundle of white roses in the crook of their arm like they'd won a beauty pageant. Mr. Underwood was right behind them, lugging two grocery sacks."

"Oh, no," Joan groaned. "Helena and Ceci are working on a science project. Mr. Underwood took them to the store. They were supposed to buy white carnations."

Bonnie laughed. "Well, that just goes to prove if you send a man shopping there's no telling what he'll come home with."

"I have a feeling I'd better go see if I can help with the project," Joan said. "Or at least try to get things back in control."

"Probably a good idea," Bonnie murmured as she turned to her fiancé. "C.J., why don't you walk Joan to the Underwood's suite, then wait for me in the bar? I haven't had a chance to talk to Hart in a couple of days about his investigation. While he and I are discussing business, we can walk over to the pool and check on that equipment."

C.J. dropped a kiss on her temple. "Anything for you, darling." He turned to Joan. "My late wife and I raised three daughters. I seem to remember how those science projects can get out of hand. How about we go see if the Underwoods need some backup?"

"An excellent idea." Joan hesitated, then met Hart's gaze for the first time since she'd bolted from his arms. She looked flushed and tousled and so damn desirable. "I... Well, good evening, Hart."

"See you around, Texas." He watched her walk away on C.J. Stuckey's arm, wanting her with such intensity that he ached.

"I should apologize for interrupting."

"Only if you mean it," Hart said, shifting his gaze back to Bonnie. "Something tells me you wouldn't."

She dipped her head. "You're right."

"I also don't think you wanted to get me alone to talk about my investigation."

"Of course not. I reckon if there's something going on that I need to know, you'd have told me."

"That's right, I would have." At this point he had good reason to suspect some of the members of the Lone Star's security force were involved in a money laundering operation. Whether the club's general manager was also up to her neck in illegal activity, he didn't know. And he damn well wasn't going to tip his hand until he did know.

"Well." Stepping forward, Bonnie slipped her arm through his. "Come on, handsome, let's walk and talk at the same time."

He glanced down at her as they left the terrace behind. "Why do I feel like I'm in for a lecture?"

"Because you are." She patted his arm. "And it's nothing personal. It's just that I love Joan like she was one of my own girls, so I've got this mile-wide protective streak where she's concerned. I'm not one of those mothers who can sit back and keep my mouth shut when I know one of my girls has got herself tangled up with a dangerous man."

Hart raised a brow. "You think I'm dangerous?"

"Good Lord, yes," Bonnie chuckled as they made their way along the cobblestone walk. "To a woman, a man with your charm and good looks is just as dangerous as a bomb with a lit fuse. There's a lot of potential to get hurt."

Hart wondered what Bonnie would say if she knew his and Joan's history. That he'd been the one who'd taken the brunt of that explosion. Since he didn't want to get into it, he said, "I'm not looking to hurt her."

"Of course you're not. And I didn't mean to imply that." As she spoke, she gestured in the direction of the dark cabana near the Olympic-size pool. "The equipment

I need to check on should be on the other side of the cabana.''

"Let's take a look," Hart said. Seconds later he paused, taking in the mammoth stack of wooden crates. "What's in all these?"

"Italy."

"Italy?"

"The Lone Star's throwing a party. Pasta by the Pool. All of the resort's guests and members are invited. The maid should have left an invitation in your suite."

"I saw it." He remembered raising an eyebrow at the gold embossed lettering on what was obviously expensive card stock.

Bonnie gestured to a grassy area beyond the pool. "Soon this whole place will resemble a town square in a small Italian village. Quaint. Personable. Maddie Delarue—she's our events coordinator—is flying in an Italian chef to oversee the food preparation. We'll serve wines from the most prestigious Italian vineyards. You should make a point to attend." Bonnie sent him a charming smile. "If you do, be sure to save me a dance."

"A dance?"

"That's right. We're bringing in musicians. The Italians have the most romantic music in the world."

He raised a shoulder. "Sounds like a lot of fuss to make over pasta, vino and a few love songs."

"For what our guests and members pay, they deserve to have a fuss made over them."

"Good point." He glanced back at the crates. "Is everything here?"

"As far as I can tell." Bonnie slid her arm back through his. "Now, I know you're not looking to hurt Joan," she said, deftly picking up the thread of conversation where she'd left it. "But you could, without ever intending to."

He glanced down as they walked back in the direction of the clubhouse. "I thought the lecture had ended."

"Not yet."

He eased out a breath. "Like I said, I don't plan to hurt her."

"You're going back to Chicago, right?"

"That's where I live. And work."

"Exactly. Hon, Joan's had a rough time, what with Thomas Dean dying and making her a widow so young. And that sweet Helena never knowing her father is a tragedy in itself. Now that Joan and Helena are both building a relationship with Ben Stone, it'd be a shame for anything to get them sidetracked."

"Namely me," Hart shot back, feeling his temper build. For reasons he didn't want to examine too closely, he was getting damn tired of hearing Ben Stone's name linked with Joan's.

"Namely you," Bonnie agreed. "And don't think for one minute I think any less of you or Joan for being attracted to each other. She's a beautiful woman. And with a handsome devil like you after her, what else can she do? But, there's some other things you need to consider."

"Such as?"

"Helena. I've noticed how she makes a beeline for you every afternoon when she gets home from school. With kids, actions speak louder than words, and it's obvious she's crazy about you. What's it going to do to that darling little girl when you leave here?"

Hart wanted to counter that he hadn't thought about that. But he had. And he knew he would miss Helena fiercely after he returned to Chicago. "What you're saying is, I'm in Ben Stone's way. And you're advising me to step back."

"I'm saying I care about everyone involved. That includes you. A lot of feelings are at risk here, and I'm trying to make things easier." Bonnie squeezed his arm. "I've seen Ben look at Joan and I can tell his emotions where she's concerned run deep. And he's nuts about Helena. He's already talked to me about having a surprise party in May for her tenth birthday. Joan doesn't even know about it because Ben wants to surprise her, too. That ought to tell you that there are genuine feelings involved—''

Bonnie went on talking, but Hart stopped listening. He damned near stopped breathing. *May.* Helena would be ten years old in May.

Hart did the math, counting back the months. Which meant she had been conceived sometime during the month of August. Born exactly nine months after he and Joan had made love.

He continued walking at Bonnie's side even though he felt as if a fist had just slammed into his gut. He couldn't seem to grab a breath of air.

Slow down, O'Brien, he told himself. Think. He had been the first man Joan had been with—that he was sure about. But that was all. She might have dated Thomas Dean the entire summer Hart had worked at the Lone Star. Dated him, but just hadn't slept with him until after the night she and Hart spent together. Hell, she could have slept with Dean the *next* night. And there was always the possibility Helena had been premature. Considering what Joan had been through, losing her husband, an early delivery could have easily happened.

Hart pictured Helena, his mind searching her features. She had Joan's dark eyes and hair, the promise of her mother's true beauty in her face. Joan's build, too—long, lanky limbs and an already willowy height. Hart didn't think there was anything of himself in Helena's physical appearance, but what about Thomas Dean? Did her face mirror the shape of the man's? Her mouth? Her nose? Hart knew he couldn't exactly go around asking people those questions without raising eyebrows. The only way for him to get the kind of answers he needed was to see a picture of Thomas Dean.

Hart felt the muscles in his jaw work as he and Bonnie neared the clubhouse. He didn't like the little questions rolling through his mind. Questions that had no ready answers.

Frowning, he reminded himself that there was no way for him to predict where the answers to his questions would lead. Not yet. He had worked enough investigations to know that jumping to conclusions could land him in trouble. Big trouble. So he wouldn't jump. He would bide his time, look at each separate piece until he had all the answers.

When he and Bonnie reached the French doors beneath the trellised walkway, he paused and faced her. "You care about Joan and Helena and you don't want them hurt. I get your message, Bonnie, loud and clear."

She smiled. "I hope you aren't upset with me."

"I'm not. In fact, you may have done me a favor. Knowing how things stand is always better than not knowing."

He would find out exactly how things stood, Hart promised himself. He intended to get the ball rolling first thing in the morning with a phone call to a bomb tech on the Dallas PD who owed him a favor.

The next morning Hart's plan to make that call got waylaid when the phone on his nightstand rang just after five o'clock.

"Yeah?" he asked groggily as he pushed himself up in bed.

"Ben Stone, here. Looks like we found the bomber."

"Who?"

"Willy Pogue. He's the Lone Star's maintenance guy who stacked all the paint and thinner in the closet between the Men's Grill and the billiards room."

Frowning, Hart scrubbed a hand over his stubbled jaw. He had interviewed Pogue, had been relatively certain the man had nothing to do with the bombing. "Why do you think he's the bomber?"

"Because our 911 center lit up like a Christmas tree a

few minutes after an explosion ripped through Pogue's garage. There must have been some gasoline involved because the blast started a small fire. It's still too hot for my men to go in, but one of the fire guys said it looks like Pogue was building a bomb on his workbench. From the sound of things, the medical examiner will have to spend some time picking up pieces of the bastard. I'm headed to the scene. Thought you'd like to meet me there.''

''Yeah, I appreciate the call, Chief.'' Hart reached for the pen and paper on the nightstand. ''What's the address?''

Stone relayed the information, then added, ''Think about it, O'Brien, we may have this case wrapped up by tonight. You could be back in Chicago tomorrow, sleeping in your own bed. Bet that would make you happy.''

Hart thought of Joan. Of Helena. Of all the questions still roiling in his mind.

He wasn't going anywhere until he had the answers to those questions.

Chapter 10

Twenty minutes later Hart steered his rental car onto the street where Willie Pogue had lived and died.

In the chalky dawn light, Hart noted the series of look-alike one-story row houses that lined both sides of the street. At the end of a cul-de-sac sat the usual knot of emergency vehicles, their strobe lights pulsing blue and red across the faces of the nearby houses.

Hart pulled in behind the ME's long black station wagon. Climbing out into the cool morning air, he smelled the acrid stench of smoke.

He skirted around a group of Pogue's neighbors clustered behind a police barricade. Most in the group wore robes and slippers. Some had a vague, stunned look that came from having had a bomb blast rouse them from sleep.

Flashing his badge, Hart identified himself to the patrol cop maintaining the crime scene log. That done, he ducked beneath a stretch of yellow tape that ringed the yard's perimeter.

The Mission Creek Fire Department had the fire out, and firefighters still dressed in full, yellow turnout gear were in the process of cranking up their canvas hoses. The garage and the back side of the small house still vented steam, but some evidence techs were already headed up the driveway, toting their field kits.

Chief Ben Stone, D.A. Spence Harrison, Detectives Molly French and Paulie McCauley stood in a loose circle in the center of the front yard. All nodded to Hart when he joined them.

Meeting McCauley's gaze, Hart thought back to the previous night and the way the cop had tracked him and Joan when they left the Yellow Rose Café. He wondered if McCauley had reason to be as concerned about the computer run Joan had done on Esmeralda as Yance Ingram and Frank Hasselman apparently were.

"We've only got the one body," Ben Stone began. The chief, Hart noted, had taken time to shave and dress in one of his sharp-pressed brown uniforms before he came to the scene. Everyone else in the circle was dressed like Hart in T-shirts and jeans.

Hart glanced at the house's front porch where a small pink swing sat. "I interviewed Pogue last week. He mentioned his wife and kid. Where are they?"

"The hose jockeys checked and they're not inside," Stone replied. "One of the neighbors said Pogue's wife took their kid to Austin a couple of days ago to visit her mother. The neighbor didn't know how long Mrs. Pogue planned to stay, but is sure she hasn't come back yet. We figure that's right, since her car isn't parked in the garage or anywhere along the street. We're trying to find someone who knows how to contact her in Austin."

A high-pitched squeak had everyone looking toward the top of the driveway. Two morgue attendants stepped into view, pushing a gurney with wheels in need of a good oiling. Lying on the gurney was a black plastic body bag. The bag was misshapen and wet.

A balding man with a waist the size of an inner tube and wearing a black windbreaker marked ME's Assistant trailed the gurney. When Stone gestured, the man cut across the lawn toward the group.

"What have we got, George?"

"A real mess, Chief." The man used his tongue to shift the toothpick stuck in one corner of his mouth to the other side. "As you can imagine, the body was badly dislocated. Lots of blood everywhere. Course, what do you expect when a bomb goes off while somebody's holding it?"

"You think Pogue was actually holding the bomb?" Hart asked.

George turned his head and focused his small, dark eyes. "Who're you?"

Spence stepped in. "Sergeant O'Brien is with the Chicago PD's bomb squad. He represents my office on the bombing task force."

"Okay." George pulled the toothpick out of his mouth, slid it into the pocket of his windbreaker. "Judging from the way the guy came apart, I'd say he had the bomb on his workbench and was basically right on top of the thing. His legs are fine except for the wood fragments they caught. Most of the damage is to his chest and abdomen. *Severe* damage. To my way of thinking, he had the device near his stomach when it went off."

Stone nodded. "Sounds reasonable. Have you released the scene to my evidence guys?"

"Yeah, they're already working it." George checked his watch. "The ME'll probably do the autopsy first thing after he gets in this morning. You better call, though, to make sure before you send someone over to observe."

"Will do." Ben looked at Molly French. "You get that honor, Detective."

Molly shoved her corkscrew brown curls away from one cheek. "I'll be there."

"Sure you can handle that assignment, French?" McCauley asked, leering at his fellow detective. With his

T-shirt clinging to his bulging muscles, McCauley looked like he could bench-press the SWAT team without breaking a sweat. "I'd hate to hear about you fainting in the middle of what's left of the stiff."

Molly's chin angled like a sword. "I can handle anything that comes along, McCauley. You'd do well to remember that."

McCauley looped a thumb into his waistband beside his badge and holstered automatic. "I guess time will tell."

"Knock it off, both of you," Stone ordered. "We've got work to do." He gestured toward the house's garage. "Let's take a look at the scene."

Hart fell in at the back of the group. As he crossed the yard the water from the fire hoses squished up around his shoes. On the driveway firemen were moving in teams around a faded blue Chevy going to rust, gathering their remaining equipment.

He noted the garage's aluminum overhead door had been pulled out of its frame. It was apparent the door had been down at the time of the detonation by the way the aluminum panels were bowed outward. The fire guys would have wanted to raise the door to get water on the flames, but the bowing would have made that impossible. So they'd used what was probably grappling hooks to pull the door away from the frame.

Inside the garage, evidence techs were busy sifting and photographing the debris exactly as Hart had done at hundreds of bomb scenes. The air inside the garage was damp, and heavy with the scent of burned wood. A workbench sat against the wall nearest the house; a pegboard that held a meager collection of hand tools hung above the bench. Stacks of cardboard boxes lined both sides of the garage, front to back.

Because the damage inside the garage was less severe than what had occurred in the Men's Grill, Hart knew that a much smaller amount of explosive had been involved in this incident.

Stone raised a hand when a tech with a thatch of bright red hair looked up from his camera and narrowed his eyes.

"We're not here to screw up the scene," Stone assured him. "We just want a look at what we've got."

"You're the boss, Chief," the tech said. "Just don't touch anything unless you ask first." He went back to snapping photos of a charred gas can.

Hart moved toward the front of the garage where the blast had occurred. A jagged half-moon had been blown out of Pogue's workbench. Wooden shrapnel sprouted like porcupine quills from the nearby sections of the walls and cardboard boxes. Much of the bench was charred from the fire. Red smears covered the walls and boxes. On the floor in front of the workbench a crimson puddle was well on its way to the coagulation stage.

Hart instantly felt a headache start at the base of his skull. Without asking, he knew Pogue's choice of explosive had been nitroglycerine-based dynamite. Same as the person who had built the bomb that exploded inside the Men's Grill. Hart wondered if Pogue had used the identical type of device—an antique pocket watch—as a timer.

If Pogue had indeed built both bombs, where had he intended to plant the one that had accidentally killed him? Hart wondered. And where the hell had the guy who worked on a maintenance crew learned to build bombs? Hart had run a background check on Pogue before he'd interviewed the man. He had no criminal history. No military service or membership in any militia group, during which time he might have gotten experience with explosives.

Still, Hart knew that anyone could go to the library or log onto the Internet and find instructions on bomb building. Pogue might have done just that, then practiced in the secrecy of his garage until he gained some level of skill.

Hoping fresh air would ease the ache in his head, Hart moved to the gaping hole in the side of the wall where the garage's walk-through door had blown out into the backyard. There he waited for the red-haired tech to finish snapping photos, then gestured to the man. After identifying himself, Hart asked, "Did you see the body before the ME bagged it?"

"Yeah. I took photos for the task force."

"What about Pogue's hands?"

"What about 'em?"

"Were they there? Were they intact?"

"Yeah." The tech furrowed his forehead. "The hands had some lacerations and tissue loss, but they were both still attached to his arms."

"Thanks."

When Hart walked back out onto the driveway, Spence followed, his dark eyes somber. "Care to suggest a scenario on what might have happened in there?" the D.A. asked.

"It's possible Pogue was setting the leg wires into the detonator and he caught a spark." Hart lifted a shoulder. "It's hard to imagine anyone stupid enough to wire a charge with the batteries connected, but it happens. Especially if the person building the bomb is self-taught."

"You don't sound convinced that's what happened."

"I'm not. Pogue's hands were still attached to his arms."

Spence winced. "I was tempted to whip through a drive-through and grab breakfast on the way here. Now, I'm damn glad I didn't. What's the significance about Pogue's hands?"

Hart held out his own hands to demonstrate. "If he was leaning over the workbench like this, seating a detonator in the charge and the explosive went off accidentally, his hands would be the first to go."

"You're sure they're still intact?"

"Yes. I asked the evidence tech who photographed the body. He said Pogue's hands were still there. And not all that badly damaged."

"Okay." Spence raked his fingers through his dark hair. "So, what does that mean?"

"I'm not sure. Because his chest and stomach area caught most of the blast, we know he was facing the workbench when the bomb exploded. What he was doing with his hands at the time is anybody's guess. All I know is, they weren't near the bomb."

"Speaking of the bomb, it would be damn nice to know why Pogue was building it. And where he intended to plant it."

"Keep in mind most bombs are messages. Problem is, we're still not sure who was the intended recipient of the bomb that went off at the Lone Star."

Spence looked back at the garage, then leaned in. "If it was meant to kill my former marine commander, Phillip Westin, then it's logical to think the terrorist group, El Jefe, was behind that bomb. After all, Westin was headed to Mezcaya to join a mission to take down El Jefe. Killing Westin could have been the cartel's way of warning everyone what was in store if they tried to screw with them."

"True. But we can't forget about Daniel and Meg Anderson," Hart said. "I don't think they were the intended target, but I can't prove that. So, if they *were,* what the hell message did the bomber send by killing Mr. and Mrs. America?"

"You got me. And don't forget the theory that Stone and most of the task force favor."

"The Mercados," Hart said, rubbing at the ache that lingered at the base of his neck.

"Now that you've had time to read through all the task force's reports, what's your opinion? Do you think the Texas mob could be behind the bombing?"

"Hell, it's possible. Mobsters send a lot of messages with bombs—in the criminal world of Chicago, I see a lot of that. When the mob uses a bomb, it's not just sending a message to whoever they blow up, but to everybody else in the organization."

"So, if the Mercado mob planted that bomb at the Lone Star, what was their message?"

"Your guess is as good as mine." Hart thought about the pieces of paper from the money laundering operation he'd recovered at the bomb site. Money laundering operations were a favorite activity of mob-related organizations. Hart had previously told Spence about the papers, but he hadn't yet had a chance to apprise the D.A. about the conversation Joan had overheard the previous afternoon.

Hart leaned in. "Something came up last night that I need to brief you on."

"Okay." The D.A. angled his head. "No offense, pal, but you look like hell. Did the something that came up last night keep you from getting your beauty sleep?"

"A couple of somethings did that." Hart's thoughts darted to Helena, then just as quickly he shoved away the possibilities that preyed on his mind. He refused to jump to conclusions. As with any investigation, he would check facts, details, dig until he had the truth.

"I'll be in court all day," Spence stated. "Why don't you drop by my house this evening?"

"Fine. I'll call before I come."

Just then, Ben Stone stepped out of the garage door and summoned them back inside. "Both of you need to see what Detective French found."

Wearing latex gloves, Molly French stood beside one of the cardboard boxes. With wooden splinters from Pogue's workbench sticking out one side, the box resembled a porcupine.

Molly met Hart's gaze as he and Spence walked toward her. "Bags," she said, gesturing toward the box's gaping top. "Canvas bags. And there's money, too."

"How much?" Spence asked.

"Too much to count right here," Stone said, and smiled. "Looks to me like we not only found our bomber, but those bags mean Pogue's probably one of the Santa's helpers little Jake Anderson saw. I didn't know the guy, but considering Pogue held a maintenance job at the Lone Star, I figure he was no rocket scientist. That means he took orders from someone. My guess is the Mercados." As he spoke, Stone shifted his gaze to McCauley. "Go by and pick up Hasselman. The two of you get with the vice boys and brief them on what we've found here. Have vice spread the word on the street about Pogue. We need to find out if anybody knew him and who he worked for. We find that, we'll know who paid the bastard to build and plant his bombs."

"I'm on it, Chief," McCauley said, then strode out of the garage.

Spence crossed his arms over his chest. "Chief Stone, this is just a reminder so we don't have problems on evidence down the line. Make sure you have a search warrant in hand before your people step foot inside Pogue's house."

"I'm already on it," Stone replied. "The minute I saw those bags and the money inside that box, I called Joe Gannon. He's working on the warrant now."

"Good." Spence glanced at his watch. "I'd better head home and get cleaned up for court. Keep me posted."

"Will do," Stone said, then looked at Hart. "What's your plan?"

Sliding a thumb into the front pocket of his jeans, Hart glanced at the dead man's damaged workbench. For bomb cranks, building explosive devices was a way of life. It was their passion, and they inevitably had a place where they built their bombs, the same way hobbyists had hobby rooms.

"I want to go through the drawers on Pogue's workbench, see what sort of supplies and tools he kept around to build bombs," Hart replied. "After your techs log the evidence from here into the lab, I'll head there and take a look at it. If we've got the same type of frag recovered from the Lone Star scene, that'll go a long way in linking the bombs.''

"My bet is the frag will be the same," Stone said, resting a hand on the butt of his holstered Colt. "I've got a gut feeling this case is close to getting wrapped up. About damn time, too. I'm sick of explaining to everyone in Mission Creek why my people haven't found the murdering bastard who set the bomb at the Lone Star." Stone's mouth curved as he met Hart's gaze. "I expect you'll head back to Chicago soon."

"Maybe," Hart said. Everything depended on the answers he got to questions he had yet begun to ask. "Then again, maybe not."

After sharing the mind-numbing kiss with Hart three nights ago, nerves had continued to ooze from every pore on Joan's body. A firm believer that there was nothing like a good, sweaty workout to get the jitters out of one's system, she had decided to spend this evening doing just that.

With Helena out riding her bike with Ceci Underwood, Joan had put in a phone call to Maddie Delarue. The Lone Star's events manager had agreed to join Joan in the spa's otherwise deserted exercise room.

Now, an hour later, Joan's black headband and red leotard were damp with sweat. That didn't stop her from increasing the speed on the treadmill and jogging even more furiously. Panting like a woman in the throes of childbirth, she hoped to hell this evening's workout would not only calm her nerves but wear her out to the extent that she would later fall into an exhausted sleep.

"Slow down, will you? You're making me perspire just watching you." On the next treadmill, Maddie walked at a moderate pace. With her long red hair piled carelessly on top of her head and her eye-catching curves clad in snug purple spandex with zigzagging green stripes, she looked as if she belonged on the cover of a glossy exercise magazine.

Joan shook her head and kept up the frantic pace. "If I slow down, I'll explode," she said, breathing heavily. "Just like that bomb did."

"Oh-oh." With a stab of a manicured finger, Maddie turned off her own treadmill, then reached for the control panel on Joan's and did the same. "I *knew* tonight wasn't about exercise," she said while both machines ground to a halt. "Sounds like we need to talk. It's either that or sweat. I can't do both at the same time."

Without waiting for Joan's replay, Maddie stepped off her treadmill. She sauntered to a nearby padded slant board next to a rack holding various free weights. Leaning back against the board, she said, "So, talk, girlfriend."

"Okay." Joan dropped onto an exercise mat that covered a portion of the spa's glossily polished parquet floor. Every muscle in her body was weeping. "It's Hart," she huffed, then reached for the gym bag she'd left nearby. Pulling out a hand towel, she mopped her soaking face and throat. "I don't know...what to do...about Hart."

"Hmm." As if studying the high ceiling painted with streamlined art deco figures, Maddie tipped her head back and sipped elegantly from a purple plastic water bottle that matched her outfit. "A couple afternoons in a row I spotted Helena out on one of the patios, talking to the same man. I figured it must be O'Brien, but I wasn't sure. So, one day when he was alone I just sashayed on up and introduced myself. It was him, all right." Maddie arched a finely plucked brow. "Girlfriend, that is one sinfully handsome man."

"I agree."

"And he's got that charmer's grin, to boot," Maddie continued. "Very compelling with an edge of danger to it. If I hadn't had the misfortune of being in California with my cousin when Hart O'Brien worked here ten years ago, you wouldn't have been the only female flirting with him.''

"Maddie, I'm in trouble." Joan pulled a water bottle from her own bag and drank in deep, greedy gulps. "Big trouble.''

"When a woman says that about a man, it usually means something physical has, or is about to happen. Which is it?''

"We've kissed. A couple of times. I'm not sure how that happens." Joan let her gaze slide across the spa's impressive array of exercise equipment that stretched around the entire room. "We just wind up...together.''

"I don't have to ask if the attraction is still there.''

"It's just like before. Sometimes it almost seems as if the past ten years never happened. The other night Hart and I walked out to the new terrace. We went there to talk. Only talk. There were stars and moonlight and we just...'' Joan pressed a hand to her stomach were the memory of Hart's kisses brought an answering tug of longing. "It's crazy. Considering our past, he's the last man I should have anything to do with. But somehow I wound up in his arms. If Bonnie and C.J. hadn't come along when they did, I don't think I would have said no if Hart had asked me to sleep with him.''

"Wow. You do have it bad.''

"Then there's Helena.''

Maddie's blue eyes turned solemn. "Oh, honey, don't tell me Hart's found out he's her father?''

"No, he doesn't know." Joan looped the towel around her neck, keeping her hands clenched on its ends. She had hoped the punishing workout would purge some of the guilt and frustration she'd dealt with over the past days. Wrong. "He doesn't know. Yet. I'm thinking about telling him.''

"You're not serious." Leaning away from the board, Maddie studied her friend's face. "Oh, my sweet Lord, you are.''

"Like you said, Helena makes a point to talk to Hart every day after school. One afternoon he wasn't around when she looked for him and she sulked for hours. That same night the three of us ate dinner together."

"The three of you?"

"Hart just showed up at the Yellow Rose when Helena and I were there. She asked if she could invite him to join us. It would have been awkward to try to get out of it," Joan said with a dismissive wave of her hand. "The point is, it was the first time I'd really seen Helena and Hart together. Listened to them talk. It's clear that they've become close during all those afternoon chats. And the feelings aren't just on Helena's part—it's evident Hart cares for her, too. He even told me he worries when he answers her questions about his job. He's afraid he'll give her nightmares. Maddie, it's like...well, they've formed some sort of bond."

"In addition to the blood bond that's already between them."

"Yes," Joan agreed quietly. "Helena never missed having a real father because my dad was always around for her. He and my mother took her on vacations, Dad taught her to play baseball, to fish. Now, it breaks my heart when Helena and I visit him at Sunny Acres. I've tried to make her understand that even though he no longer remembers who she is, deep down her grandpa Zane still loves her."

"I know that can't be easy for either of you."

"Especially Helena. Yesterday she came home from her Brownie meeting with a flyer about this year's father-daughter banquet. Dad's always taken her. He'd show up with flowers and candy—that made it an even more special night for them. When Helena gave me the flyer, she said she guessed she couldn't go this year because she doesn't have a grandpa or a daddy."

"But she does have a daddy," Maddie said softly. "And he's here."

"Yes." Joan's voice hitched as a tide of guilt rose into

her throat. "If Hart didn't care about her, if he didn't bother giving her the time of day, I wouldn't consider telling him. But he *does* have feelings for her." Joan blinked back tears. "All of Helena's life, I had no idea where Hart was. No clue if he was even still alive. So, letting Helena live the lie my parents dreamed up about Thomas Dean didn't seem so bad. Now that she knows Hart, cares about him, it does."

"Oh, honey." Maddie pushed away from the slant board and settled on the padded mat beside Joan. "Are you sure telling them the truth is the right thing to do?" she asked, clenching Joan's hands in her own. "When we talked about this before, you said you couldn't trust Hart not to do the same thing to Helena he did to you. What if you tell him and history repeats itself? What will it do to her if he tells her he loves her, that he wants her in his life, then he up and disappears for the next ten years?"

"I've spent hours agonizing over that." Joan took a deep breath. "The truth is, Hart didn't care about me, not the way I wanted him to. All he wanted was one night. With Hart, it's different where Helena's concerned. It shows in his eyes how much he's come to care for her. If he knew the truth, I don't think he could walk away from her."

"You don't think. But you don't know."

"You'd agree with me, Maddie. If you saw the way they've connected, you'd agree."

"Maybe. But you also told me you don't think Helena is old enough to understand what happened between you and Hart. You can't tell him the truth and not her."

"You're right, I can't."

"So, has your thinking changed? Have you decided she's old enough to understand?"

"No." Just the thought of trying to explain things to Helena twisted Joan's insides into a cold knot. "I just know that whether I tell Helena the truth now, or wait until she's older, one of the primary things she's going to ask me is why I lied to her about the identity of her father. Letting more time pass isn't going to make that lie any easier for her to understand. Or accept. Or make her think any better of me for telling the lie in the first place.''

"I suppose not. But then, she's got to come to understand that you were protecting her.''

"I hope so, Maddie. God, I hope so.''

As Joan mopped the towel across her face, the cellular phone clipped to her gym bag buzzed. She reached for the phone, answered it.

"Ms. Cooper, this is Frank Hasselman. I'm on the security staff here at the Lone Star.''

Her shoulders stiffened. Hasselman was the man she'd overheard talking to Yance Ingram about the computer run she'd made on Esmeralda. Was he calling to ask about that run?

"What can I do for you Officer Hasselman?''

"Your daughter's had an accident. I need you to get out here to the parking lot as soon as you can.''

Joan felt the blood drain from her face. "Helena?'' Grabbing Maddie's arm, Joan dragged her friend up and off the floor with her. "Is Helena— How badly is she hurt?''

"Oh, God,'' Maddie gasped as they bolted for the door.

"Her left wrist is hurt and her knees are scraped up pretty bad,'' Hasselman reported in a monotone voice. "Other than that, she seems fine. Can't say the same about her bike, though.''

Looking back, Joan had no memory of the wild, frantic dash she and Maddie made down flights of stairs, through the Lone Star's basement and out across the manicured grounds. All Joan knew was that her child was hurt. As she ran, she sent up unending silent prayers that Helena would be all right.

By the time Joan and Maddie sprinted toward the far corner of the parking lot, several people had gathered there. Panic gripped Joan by the throat when she spotted

Helena's bicycle a few feet beyond the grouping of people. The bike lay on its side, the back wheel bent and mangled.

As she raced closer, Joan heard a man's reassuring voice. Hart's voice.

"I think you'll live," he said.

"What about my bike?" Helena asked with a soft sniffle.

"It's in a lot worse shape than you. But a bike can be replaced. You can't."

Joan shot into the circle, Maddie right on her heels.

Helena sat on the pavement, her knees scraped and bleeding, her left arm cradled to her chest. Hart was crouched beside her, one of his arms wrapped around her shoulders.

"Helena!" Joan knelt, tears welling in her eyes. It was all she could do not to wrap herself around her daughter, but she held off. Pulling Helena into a tight embrace could injure her worse.

"Mama." Using her good arm, Helena grabbed Joan's hand. Helena's mouth curved, but her lips twitched and the intended smile turned into a trembling wince.

Joan's shaking fingers brushed her daughter's long, dark hair away from her cheeks. "Honey, are you hurt anywhere else but your wrist?"

"I asked that, too," Hart said quietly. "She says her knees are the only other casualties."

"Mama, that van came right out of nowhere. Ceci and I were riding in the parking lot since there weren't any deliveries scheduled," she added in her and her friend's defense. Tears welled in her eyes, slid down her cheeks. "It just appeared and I couldn't get out of the way quick enough."

Terror dug claws into Joan's throat. "Sweetheart, are you saying a van hit you?"

"It came speeding out of nowhere," Helena sobbed. "I tried to get out of the way, but it slammed into the back of my bike. It wasn't my fault, Mama. Honest."

"My God." Joan cupped Helena's pale, tear-damp cheek while exchanging a look with Hart. The grimness in his face told her that he, too, knew Helena could have been injured much worse than she was. Maybe even killed.

With a sick dread roiling in her stomach, Joan's gaze swept the parking lot around them. "Where's the van now?"

"It drove off right after it hit my bike," Helena whimpered through her tears.

"The driver didn't stop? He hit you and didn't stop?"

"That's right, Ms. Cooper." Frank Hasselman, dressed in the Lone Star's requisite navy blazer and gray slacks stepped through the growing crowd. "It wasn't your daughter's fault. I'm in the process of interviewing her friend, Ceci Underwood. She confirms the story. Luckily Ceci caught a good enough look at the van so that we know it was white with some damage to one of its rear doors."

Keeping his arm around Helena's shoulders, Hart sent Hasselman a flat, cold look. "What are you doing about finding the van, Detective?"

Hasselman held up a two-way radio. "Well, Sergeant, I've notified MCPD dispatch and issued an APB for a hit-and-run vehicle. Every patrol cop on the street has their eyes open for the van. If the driver hasn't gotten it hidden in some garage by now, we'll find it."

"I want to know if you do." As Hart spoke, Joan saw a measure of his control slip, showing the heat and fury in his green eyes.

Hasselman angled his chin. "This incident isn't under the jurisdiction of the bombing task force, O'Brien. It's MCPD business. Our people will deal with it."

"For now," Hart said under his breath, then met Joan's gaze. "I got back here a few minutes after this happened," he said, his voice low. Calm. "When I spotted Helena's bike, I drove over."

"She needs her wrist X-rayed."

Hart dipped his head. "My car's right there. The engine's still running. Driving her to the E.R. will be faster than waiting for an ambulance."

"I agree."

Looking down, he thumbed the tears off Helena's cheeks. "In Chicago, anytime a kid gets hurt and has to go to the hospital, she gets to go for ice cream after that. I think it's a law. Does the same go for Mission Creek?"

"I think so." Helena pressed her face against her mother's shoulder. "My wrist hurts, Mama."

"I know, sweetheart," Joan replied quietly. "Ready to go get it X-rayed and all fixed up?"

"Ready," Helena said as Hart and Joan helped her to her feet. Helena took one limping step then expelled a whimpering breath.

"Honey, what is it?" Joan asked. She was terrified Helena had sustained some sort of internal injury when the van knocked her off the bike. "What else hurts?"

"Just my knees. It hurts to bend them." Her shoulders sagging, she gave Hart a plaintive look through tear-reddened eyes. "Can you carry me?"

"My pleasure." He scooped her into his arms. "My carriage awaits," he added, striding toward a dark car that sat idling, its driver's door gaping open.

The sight of Hart holding his child for the first time tightened the already constricting band around Joan's chest. Just then, Maddie slipped up and curled an arm around her friend's waist. "Need me to go with you?"

"No, thanks." Joan put an unsteady hand to her throat. "I didn't see Ceci's parents in the crowd. Hassleman's interviewing her and she's probably really scared so you might see about her. Then give her a hug and walk her home. Make sure she knows that Helena will be okay."

"Consider it done." As they neared the car, Maddie inclined her head in Hart's direction. "I see what you mean—he's crazy about her. That thing he came up with about the ice cream was so sweet it put a lump in my throat.'' Maddie shook her head. ''I sure wouldn't want to be the driver of that van when Hart O'Brien catches up with him.''

''He left, Maddie.'' Now that the shock was subsiding, the thought that Helena could have been killed had fury pounding through her. ''He hit her, then drove off. I'd like to get my hands on that damn driver myself.''

''Me, too.'' Maddie leaned in. ''And I think you're right.''

''About the driver?''

''Hart and Helena. After seeing them together, I think you're right. You should tell them the truth.''

Chapter 11

Unnoticed by Joan and Helena, Hart stood in the hospital corridor, gazing through the open door into the small treatment room. With one shoulder propped against the wall, he watched the poignant sight of mother and daughter sitting side by side on the exam table while they waited for a nurse. Helena leaned heavily against Joan, who spoke soothing words while stroking her child's long, dark hair.

Her child.

Hart scrubbed a hand across the back of his neck. He had promised himself not to jump to conclusions. Swore he would wait for answers—which he had yet to receive. Still, when he'd driven up and seen Helena lying in that parking lot writhing in pain, white-hot fear had burned through his belly. Fear that she'd been badly hurt. Maybe even near death.

He had experienced horror often—a man didn't work intimately with bombs and not have personal knowledge that the devil walked the face of the earth. Yet the terrorizing fear for Helena that had gripped him seemed far worse than anything he had felt before.

Step back, O'Brien, he cautioned himself. The chances were almost nil Helena was his child. After all, he and Joan had spent only one night together. Another man had been in the picture during that same time or immediately after. Hart was well aware he currently stood right around the corner from the trauma wing funded in that man's memory. Thomas Dean, whom everyone in Mission Creek acknowledged was Helena Cooper's late father.

Hart focused his gaze on Joan and studied her profile beneath the treatment room's bright lights. A black headband held back her sleek, dark ponytail; the snug red leotard she wore clung to seductive dips and curves that had haunted his dreams for years.

Sipping the coffee he'd snagged from a vending machine, he forced his thoughts off the woman and onto the mother. She was good, he thought as he watched her coax a smile from her injured child. A natural. Years ago, it had never occurred to him that the pampered, self-possessed country club girl who'd flirted with him incessantly could possess such deep, maternal instincts.

She would have told him, he assured himself. No matter that all Joan had wanted from him was a one-night fling, if there'd been a chance Helena was his, she wouldn't have—*couldn't have*—passed off his child as belonging to another man. She'd have told him the truth. And it was almost beyond belief that the concerned, coddling mother he now watched would lie to her child about her parentage.

So, yeah, he concluded. No way was Helena his. He might as well call his buddy on the Dallas PD bomb squad and tell him not to bother getting his hands on a picture of Thomas Dean. Case closed.

The squeak of crepe-soled shoes on tile pulled Hart's attention down the hallway to a nurse who approached at a bustling speed. The chubby woman with a cheerful expression entered the small treatment room, a clipboard propped in the crook of one arm.

Joan slid off the exam table while the nurse gathered supplies. Seconds later the woman settled on a stool and began tending to Helena's skinned knees while engaging the young girl in an ongoing conversation.

Hart noted that while the nurse worked, Joan's expression remained serious but not fearful. And her eyes were no longer filled with the blistering fury he had seen when she'd realized some jackass in a van had nearly killed her daughter, then fled the scene. A lioness protecting her cub, he thought. That inner strength only enhanced her femininity. And made her even more desirable.

Clenching his hand against his thigh, he turned away from the door and drained his coffee. He wished like hell the cup held ice-cold beer instead. He damn well didn't need this, he thought as he lobbed his cup into a nearby trash can. Didn't need to get tangled up again with Joan Cooper. She hadn't wanted him before, not for anything other than a one-night roll in the hay. Considering the way she'd responded to him recently, he had a pretty good idea she wouldn't mind letting history repeat itself. Maybe repeat itself a few times.

Lord help him, he was crazy to have her.

Mentally he felt himself take a step backward. Then another. Having sex was one thing, but he would rather face a crazed maniac with a ticking bomb than allow a certain part of his and Joan's history to repeat itself. He had once lost his heart to her, and he'd suffered for it. Plenty. He had spent the past ten years in and out of relationships that barely skimmed the surface. That he was already back up to his neck with her emotionally and in danger of sinking deeper sounded a blaring alarm in his head. An alarm that had him locking the last latch on his heart.

He turned back toward the exam room in time to see the nurse hustle out the door and down the hallway. His shoulders stiffened when Joan met his gaze, her eyes filled with alarm.

He stepped quickly into the small room, his gaze going to Helena. Her knees were now clean and bandaged. Although she still cradled her left arm against her chest, the shot the nurse had given her when they'd first arrived had erased the traces of searing pain from her face. No, it wasn't Helena's physical condition that had drained the color from Joan's cheeks.

"How's it going, kid?" he asked quietly as he kept his eyes locked on Joan.

"Okay." Helena shifted around on the exam table to look at him. "The nurse is really nice. I get to ride in a wheelchair so she can take me to..." Helena wrinkled her nose. "Mom, where'm I going?"

"To radiology."

"That's where they X-ray my wrist," Helena explained. "I get to look at the pictures so I can see what my arm bone looks like. The nurse doesn't think my wrist is broken. Just sprained."

Hart ruffled her hair. "That fall sure didn't slow down your ability to speak, did it?"

"Uh-uh."

Joan slid a hand up and down Helena's good arm. "Honey, tell Hart what you asked the nurse right before she left to go get the wheelchair."

"If they had a girl here named Molly."

Hart raised a brow. "What makes you think a girl named Molly is here?"

"'Cause yesterday I was sitting on a bench by the diving pool, waiting for Ceci. We were going to take our homework to the stables where her parents work and practice our spelling words so the horses could hear us. There's a brick wall on the other side of the bench, and I heard a man talking. He said a girl named Molly's going to have an accident. I don't know Molly, but I thought maybe she got hurt like me and came here, too."

Hart's thoughts whipped to the only Molly he knew—Detective French. Thanks to her fellow officers, she'd already had several near "accidents."

"An accident, huh?" Leaning a hip against the exam table, he gazed down at Helena, keeping his expression neutral. "Did you see the man you heard talking about Molly?"

"No, he was on the other side of the wall. Then Ceci came and we went to the stables." Helena shrugged. "Well, we got almost there when I remembered I'd left my backpack on the bench. So we had to go back and get it."

"Was your backpack still there?"

She nodded. "Somebody just moved it under the bench because I'd left it on top so it wouldn't get dirty. All my stuff was still inside."

"Here we are, young lady," the smiling nurse said, rolling a wheelchair through the open door. "Let's head to radiology so we can get that wrist taken care of." The nurse gave Hart a wink before looking back at Helena. "Then, so you don't break any laws, you can go get that ice cream you told me about."

"Do you need me to go with you?" Joan asked.

"This is one where the moms and dads don't go," the nurse explained while helping Helena into the wheelchair with an efficiency that came with years of practice. "We'll do fine. You folks are welcome to wait here until we get back. Radiology isn't busy this evening, so we shouldn't be long."

"I love you, baby," Joan said, then dropped a kiss on the top of her daughter's head.

"I love you, too, Mom." Helena shifted her gaze to Hart. "Thanks for helping me in the parking lot."

He gave her a wink. "You're welcome."

His mind churning, Hart waited for the nurse to wheel Helena away, then he shoved the door closed and turned. "Helena's backpack," he began. "Is her name on it?"

"Yes. The school requires it." Joan took a step toward him. "Hart, I don't know anyone named Molly. Neither does Helena. But the other night you mentioned a detective named Molly—" she furrowed her forehead "—I can't remember her last name."

"French. Molly French."

"When Helena asked the nurse if a girl named Molly had an accident, I thought the conversation she overheard might have been about Detective French." Joan wrapped her arms around her waist. "So much has happened with the police lately."

"Too much." Hart set his jaw, his cop's mind churning with possibilities. "I damn well don't like the sound of anyone named Molly having an accident. Any more than I like knowing Helena left her backpack lying around after she heard that conversation. And that it had been moved when she went back to get it."

Joan went still. "What are you saying?"

"That maybe whoever was talking about Molly knows Helena heard." As he spoke, Hart closed the space between them and settled his hands on Joan's shoulders. "I'm not looking to scare you, Texas, but you need to hear this."

The concern in her eyes turned to fear. "What?"

"Maybe it's not a coincidence that the day after Helena overheard that conversation someone tried to run her down."

Joan's face paled. "Are you saying..." Her voice hitched as she pressed her palms against his chest. "My God, Hart, do you think the driver purposely hit her? *Tried to kill her?*"

"No, I'm not saying I think that. It's a *possibility,* is all." He tightened his fingers on her shoulders. "What Helena overheard could have been innocent. Maybe it was some concerned father predicting his daughter, Molly, will have an accident if she keeps sliding into base during T-ball games. And some other kid could have come along, picked Helena's backpack off that bench, then dropped it underneath.'' Hart dipped his head. ''I'm a cop, Texas. I look at all possible angles. What I brought up is one of those angles. As farfetched as it might be.''

''What if you're right?'' Fear sounded in her every word, glistened in her eyes. ''What if Helena was purposely hurt because she heard that conversation?''

''Okay, let's talk about that possibility.'' Releasing Joan's shoulders, he prowled toward the door of the small room, then turned. ''What she heard doesn't implicate anyone in anything. It doesn't *prove* anything.'' He paused, his thoughts racing at warp speed. ''But it might be a way to get proof of something that's bothering the hell out of me.''

''What?''

''Did you know Willie Pogue? The Lone Star's maintenance man who died in a bomb blast in his garage?''

Joan waved a dismissive hand. ''What does he have to do with Helena's accident?''

''Bear with me,'' Hart said quietly. ''Did you know him?''

''Slightly.'' As she spoke, Joan jerked the black sweatband away from her hair. ''He did repair work at the spa. A story in this morning's paper said the police believe he built the bomb that went off in the Men's Grill. And that Pogue filled a nearby closet with paint and thinner because he wanted as much damage done as possible.''

''Pogue admitted putting the paint and thinner in the closet,'' Hart conceded. ''When the evidence techs went through his place they found boxes of canvas bags and cash. A lot of cash. Most of the cops on the task force are pushing the theory that Pogue worked for the Mercado mob. And that the men who Jake saw with identical canvas bags were Mercado goons. Willie Pogue being one of them.''

''If that's true, doesn't it also mean the mob is behind

Esmeralda and the money laundering operation you unearthed?''

''One would think.''

Joan angled her chin. ''You don't sound convinced.''

''I'm not. I interviewed Pogue. I believed him when he said he stored the paint and thinner in the closet because the crew he worked on was scheduled to start painting the kitchen the following day. In my mind I wrote Pogue off as the bomber. And he sure as hell didn't strike me as a guy involved with the mob.''

''Ben Stone came by the spa this morning.'' As she spoke, Joan kept her gaze on the black sweatband, which she wrapped, then unwrapped around one wrist. ''He said Pogue had been a disgruntled employee who was upset because he'd gotten a couple of bad performance evaluations and been denied raises. Ben said the task force is sending a report to the DA's office that concludes Pogue built and planted the bomb. The report recommends the D.A. clear the case.''

''I know about the report,'' Hart said through his teeth. Whenever Stone's name came up, he didn't first think about the cop, but of the man who wanted Joan and Helena for his own. Hart knew that mind-set was dangerous, in more ways than one. At the very least, personal feelings didn't belong anywhere near a homicide investigation. ''In my opinion, loose ends still need to be tied up before this case can be closed.''

''Such as?''

''Remember I asked if you'd heard of a group called the Lion's Den?''

''Yes. I told you I hadn't.''

''There's a teenager lying in a bed upstairs who took a bad beating. Before he slipped into a coma, he told Molly French he worked for the Lion's Den, which is a group of corrupt cops. He also claimed cops were the ones who beat him.''

"My God." Joan closed her eyes. "Do you believe that?"

"I don't know of any reason for the kid to have lied." A sense of frustration had Hart clenching his fists. "For weeks I've read reports on this case, pored over photographs, conducted interviews. I don't know what might or might not be useful, so I have to keep going over everything. Thinking about every detail. All the evidence. That means I've got about a million facts floating around free-form in my head. This morning I went back to the bomb site at the Lone Star and took a metal detector with me. I knew the lab guys had already swept the rubble, but I hoped I'd find some bomb frag they'd missed. Something to help unravel a knot or two."

"Did you find anything?"

He dug into his shirt pocket. "This," he said, holding out his palm. "A gold pin in the shape of a lion."

Joan peered at the small pin which had been scarred and slightly bent by the bomb's blast. "Those pins are as common around Mission Creek as cattle on a ranch."

"Tell me about it. I see people all over the place wearing them. Yance Ingram, C. J. Stuckey, cops, the police chief, even the D.A. The other night I noticed Bonnie Brannigan has a gold lion on her charm bracelet. Spence told me the pins are community service awards."

"That's right. They've been given out for years. I'm not sure, but I think my dad had one." Taking the pin from Hart's palm, Joan held it up toward the room's glaring fluorescent light. "Why does this pin seem different?"

"Different, how?"

"I don't know. Maybe because it's bent?" She handed the small gold lion back to Hart. "Do you think your finding the lion pin at the bomb site has something to do with the Lion's Den?"

"It's a thought." He returned the pin to his pocket. "I'll just add your question to the growing list about this investigation that I have no answers to. Yet."

"One of those questions being, did Helena overhear something that put her in danger?" Joan said. "You still haven't said how that might help you prove something that's been bothering you."

"It concerns Molly French." He narrowed his eyes. "I'm trying to figure out how to make something work. If I do, I'll explain the details later."

"Fine. All I'm concerned about right now is Helena. I need to protect my child."

"I'm thinking about that, too. After we take her for ice cream, I have to go talk to Molly." And hopefully her ex-con husband, Hart added silently. "That means I'm not going to be around the Lone Star for a while. Until we know for sure who was driving that van, it'd be best if you and Helena stay somewhere else. With your parents, maybe."

Joan blinked. "My parents?"

"I've got a good memory, Texas. You used to mention how big that mansion was you lived in. I figure your parents have some spare bedrooms."

"Not anymore. My mother died last year. My father has Alzheimer's. He's in a nursing home. He doesn't know who *he* is, much less Helena or me."

Although the flash of pain in Joan's eyes had Hart wanting badly to lift a comforting hand to her cheek, he held back. He hadn't locked that last latch on his heart just to open it again. Doing so carried too many consequences. "Sorry, I didn't know."

"How could you? We didn't exactly keep up with each other after you left town. Helena and I can spend tonight with my friend, Maddie Delarue. She's the Lone Star's events manager."

"Delarue," Hart said, pulling the name from his memory. "The redhead who ran up with you in the parking lot?"

"Yes, that's Maddie."

"She walked up and introduced herself one day when

I was out on the patio. Said I should have hung around Mission Creek ten years ago. I still have no clue why the hell she said that.''

"Maddie's not shy about voicing her opinions." As Joan spoke, a look crossed her face, a quick shadow of emotion that had Hart narrowing his eyes.

"Is there something I should know about Ms. Delarue's opinions?''

"Not specifically. Hart, a lot of things happened—''

The door to the room swung inward with a clatter. "We're all done,'' the nurse chirped as she rolled Helena's wheelchair to a stop. "I was right on the money—Helena's wrist is sprained, not broken.''

Helena grinned. "I chose green,'' she announced needlessly while holding up her left arm to show off the eye-popping lime-green elastic bandage circling her wrist. "Can we go get ice cream now?''

A few hours later Hart steered his car into the dimly lit parking lot of the Saddlebag, a bar two miles from Mission Creek's town center. Years ago he and Spence had made a habit of heading there after spending their day sweating as groundskeepers at the Lone Star. Long-neck bottles of icy cold beer had helped ease the aches and pains that went along with backbreaking manual labor. He and Spence had also managed to perfect their pool games at the one table located at the bar's rear.

Hart didn't have to wonder if the Saddlebag still boasted a pool table when he opened the front door and heard the crack of pool balls. Pausing just inside the door, he let his gaze sweep the bar's interior. Nothing much had changed, he decided, taking in the dim lighting, old dark wood and faded Texas memorabilia that hung on the walls. Across the room, a sofa and armchairs sat around a huge, dark, stone fireplace, no doubt unlit due to the unseasonably warm spring weather. What might have been the same patrons who had sat at the thick wooden bar a decade ago loitered on stools while huddling over their drinks and conversing. The occasional racket from the pool table, murmured conversations and the ping of a pinball machine floated familiarly through the air.

Hart checked out the dozen or so tables that dotted the room. He noted the man with short wavy brown hair seated at a table at the rear of the bar, a long-neck beer bottle in front of him. Hart pegged Danny Gates from the description Molly French had given of her husband. That the ex-con looked as taut as a coiled spring told Hart that Molly had filled him in on the conversation Helena had overheard.

Hart nodded to Gates before stopping off at the bar to order a bottle of beer.

When he reached the table, he offered his hand. "Hart O'Brien. Thanks for agreeing to meet me."

"Yeah." Gates returned the handshake with one as hard as the look in his dark eyes. "I hope we're here because you plan to tell me who the bastard is who threatened my wife with an accident."

Hart settled into a chair and took a long swallow of beer. The anger in Gates's face looked like the leading edge of a storm that could spark into rage at any moment. Hart knew in order to divert that storm he would have to proceed with caution.

"I'm not positive your wife has been threatened. Even if I was sure and I knew who'd made that threat, I wouldn't tell you. Molly wouldn't thank me for helping you get sent to prison on a murder charge."

Gates leaned in. "You know my history, O'Brien, so let's get to the point. The only cop I have any use for is Molly. If something happens to her, I'll do what I have to and won't give a rat's ass what happens to me. During the past couple of months she's been threatened and nearly killed. *By other cops.* You call tonight, tell my wife about that little girl who overheard a threat against 'Molly.' Doesn't take much of a mental leap for me to conclude who that Molly is, and to figure whoever made that threat wears a badge.''

"You might be right," Hart said evenly. "And you're not the only one making mental leaps. It's possible the person whom that little girl overheard tried to run her down with a van this evening."

Danny's brows slid together. "Molly mentioned that. How is the kid?"

"She has a sprained wrist and skinned knees." And had been terrified, Hart thought, his fingers tightening on the bottle. "I'm fond of that little girl. *Very fond.* I want the bastard who tried to run her down just as bad as you want the ones who've been screwing with your wife since the bombing investigation started. I figure you can help me nail them."

"How?"

"Hook me up with your pal, Ricky Mercado."

Gates kept his eyes level on Hart's. "Are you saying Ricky, or one of his people, had something to do with this threat against Molly? Maybe tried to run down that little girl?"

"No." Hart slid his bottle aside. "Look, I need to back-track here so you'll understand where I'm coming from. Has Molly told you about Willie Pogue, the maintenance guy from the Lone Star who died when a bomb exploded in his garage?"

"Yeah. She said Stone's putting the finishing touches on a report that concludes the guy set the bomb at the Lone Star."

"That report also says Pogue worked for the Mercados. Stone's conclusion is that Pogue built and set the bomb on instructions from the mob."

"What reason would the Mercados have for blasting the country club?"

"A little boy saw two men lugging bulging bags out of the back of the clubhouse. Law enforcement's theory is that those bags were filled with weapons or drugs or

money. Take your pick what was actually in the bags—
that's one of those unprovable assumptions that comes up
in every case. Since mobs are known to deal in all of the
above, it's not asking a lot to accept one of those assumptions at face value. Since Pogue had identical bags
and lots of cash in his possession, it's logical to conclude
he worked for the mob. The Mercados, specifically. That
mind-set earns Pogue the label of 'murderer.' There's no
firm evidence to link the bombing to anyone but him, so
there's no charges pending against anyone in the mob.
With the prime suspect dead, the bombing case essentially
gets closed. That means *solved.* Mission Creek's citizens
will no longer have to live with the possibility that they
could be the bomber's next victim. The bomb task force
gets disbanded. The Lone Star's board receives the go-
ahead to renovate the bomb site. It's business as usual for
everyone involved.''

"You, too. You get to pack your bags and head for
wherever home is.''

"Chicago.''

"So, if everything's tied up nice and neat from your
standpoint, why the hell do you want me to hook you up
with Ricky Mercado?''

"Because I think Stone's theory is bull. I interviewed
Willie Pogue. My gut's telling me the same thing now it
did when I talked to him. He didn't set that bomb. And
he wasn't working for the Mercados.''

"If you're right, that means those bags and the cash
were planted at his house.''

"Correct. If I'm right.''

"What about the bomb he was building?''

Hart shifted his attention to the pinball machine. A man
dressed in a Western shirt, jeans and cowboy boots deftly
worked the machine's flippers, racking up points amid
pings and chimes.

"Everybody's a creature of habit, including a guy who
builds bombs,'' Hart said, looking back at Gates. "He'll

always use the same type of cords, the same type of everything, just because his way works. That means every device he builds carries his unique signature, which is as distinctive as his own handwriting. Depending upon the post-blast evidence the lab recovers, we can even tie fragments from exploded bombs to other bombs, and tell if they were built by the same person. That's the case with the bomb that exploded at the Lone Star and the one that killed Pogue. No question—the same person built both bombs. I can't prove it, but I *know* that person wasn't Pogue.''

Gates nodded slowly. ''Okay, suppose I agree to try to hook you up with Ricky Mercado. He has about as much use for cops as I do. Maybe less. What makes you think he'll talk to you?''

''If he doesn't, it's a sure thing his family will get the blame for the Lone Star bombing. That includes the death of two people. There's no statute of limitation on murder, so the bombing is something that'll hang over his family for eternity. I can't imagine Ricky would want that. If the Mercados' hands are clean on the bombing, and I'm in the position to find the guilty party, there's no reason for Ricky not to talk to me.''

''Makes sense.'' Gates sipped his beer. ''You still haven't told me how all this connects with the latest threat against my wife.''

''The bombing occurred at the Lone Star.''

''And a couple of weeks after that Molly got drugged, hauled to the bomb site and almost killed by two cops.''

''Right.'' Hart paused, thinking of the ''Esmeralda'' pages from the money laundering operation he found at the scene. And Yance Ingram and Frank Hasselman's concern over the computer run Joan made on Esmeralda. Just in case he was totally wrong about the Mercados, Hart didn't want to share with Gates the fact those pages existed. ''Other things have happened at the club that I can't get into, but they've raised my suspicions. Now someone at the Lone Star has possibly made a threat against your wife. The little girl who overheard that threat almost gets killed in the club's parking lot.''

''Hardly events one would think were the norm at a highbrow country club.''

''That's my point. Everything evolves around the Lone Star. It's my guess there's a group on the inside calling the shots. If I know for sure the Mercados aren't involved in whatever's going on, I can focus on the only group at the Lone Star in a position to pull off what's gone on there.''

''Security,'' Gates said quietly. ''Moonlighting MCPD cops.''

''Cops,'' Hart agreed.

Gates's mouth curved into a feral grin. ''Loan me that cell phone clipped to your belt. I can probably get you in to see Ricky within the hour.''

''What the hell do you mean, McCauley decided to have that little girl run down?'' Ben Stone demanded as white-hot anger stormed through his system. ''I damn well never approved that!''

''You told me to have McCauley set up an accident for Molly French,'' Yance Ingram pointed out, leaning back at his desk in the Lone Star's security office. He glanced at the wall across from his desk, flickering with a dozen monitors that displayed assorted locations across the Lone Star's premises. Other screens were tuned in to various offices and work areas so that employees could be observed by members of the security force.

Ingram nodded toward a vacant chair. ''Sit down, Ben. We need to talk.''

''I don't want to sit! And I don't see what French having an accident has to do with Helena Cooper.''

''If you'll calm down long enough to listen, I'll tell you.''

Cursing violently, Ben slapped his palms on Ingram's

desk and leaned in. "I don't want to calm down. What I want to do is put a bullet in McCauley's head. I care about that little girl, Yance. She's going to be *mine*."

"McCauley is almost certain Helena Cooper overheard him on his cell phone ordering Beau Maguire to set up French's accident."

Ben spat another curse. "So McCauley decides to kill that little girl *in case* she overheard him?"

"That's right," Ingram said levelly. "He knows she was nearby when he had that conversation because he found her backpack. I approved McCauley's plan."

"*I* run the Lion's Den," Ben snapped back. "*I* make the decisions. Not you. And damn sure not McCauley."

Beneath his neatly cropped mustache, Ingram's mouth tightened. "Ben, I took you under my wing when you were a fuzzy-pants rookie. I watched your back, protected your butt. I don't have to remind you that you're where you are today partly because of me."

"I've paid you back in spades," Ben said with snarling fury. "You were flat broke when *I* got you this job. Now, you've got more money than God because *I* cut you in on the proceeds from laundering El Jefe's drug money."

"All true. And because I owe you, I'm making sure your back continues to get watched. A lot is at stake and the last thing you need right now is to get blindsided. There are things you need to know. Trust me on this."

Because he did trust the man who had served as his mentor, Ben bit down on his anger and pulled back control. "What things?"

Ingram slid open a desk drawer, retrieved a remote control and punched buttons. "Remember I told you we installed a couple of hidden cameras around that new terrace the club built?"

"I remember."

"I'm not showing this to cause you pain. But the way things look, I wouldn't count on that little girl or her mother ever belonging to you."

Ben felt his chest tighten. "What the hell do you mean?"

Ingram punched buttons on the remote. "That night I called to tell you that Joan and O'Brien had dinner at the Yellow Rose, they also had a chat out on the new terrace. They did a lot more than talk," Ingram added as he fast forwarded the tape.

Ben dropped into a chair, staring at the TV monitor. The tape had been shot at night; the hedges and benches surrounding the dimly lit terrace had an ethereal green hue, as if being viewed through a weapon's high-powered night-vision scope. On the screen Joan's image smeared slightly when she stepped into Hart O'Brien's arms.

Ben's throat closed as a burning blast of jealousy shot through his blood.

How many nights had *he* lain awake, envisioning her in *his* arms? Of *his* mouth settling against hers, the way O'Brien's did. Of *his* fingers tangling in that silky dark hair.

Ingram aimed the remote, and the monitor went black. "Bonnie and C.J.'s untimely arrival stopped that touching scene."

"Yeah." Ben could barely breathe.

"Let's evaluate the situation," Ingram said, running a hand over his balding head. "From the tap we have on O'Brien's phone we know he found pages from our operation we overlooked at the bomb site. When the FBI agent in Denver called O'Brien back, he confirmed the pages document money laundering, so we've got a Fed who at least has a cursory knowledge of our operation. I don't have to tell you that's something we damn well could do without."

"You don't have to tell me."

"Those pages had Esmeralda printed across the top. Joan Cooper either ran the name on her computer, or she let O'Brien. Either way, you have to figure he told her why he needed that run made." Ingram inclined his head toward the monitor. "There's no denying they've got a personal relationship. Bonnie Brannigan mentioned Cooper and O'Brien met years ago when he worked here as a groundskeeper. By the way they were kissing, it's my guess there's a hell of a lot of history between the two of them."

Ben dug his fingers into the arms of his chair. He realized he'd made a mistake with Joan. He should have taken what he wanted. He would do that, as soon as he got her away from O'Brien.

Ben took a deep breath. "After I turn in my report on the bombing, the D.A.'ll close the case. Soon as that happens, O'Brien goes back to Chicago."

"I guess that depends on how interested he is in your Ms. Cooper."

Feeling his anger bubble back to life, Ben surged out of his chair. "I'll deal with O'Brien. You tell McCauley to stay the hell away from that little girl. And to make sure her accident continues to look like an *accident*." Ben shoved a hand through his hair. "Maguire could get identified as the driver of the hit-and-run van, so he's got to go."

"I don't know, Ben. Beau's been loyal to us."

"So far. If he gets picked up and booked into jail by someone other than a Lions Den member, I guarantee he'll sing like a choir. Probably get on his knees, begging to cut a deal to save his own skin." Ben sent Ingram a searing look. "I don't have to remind you what will happen to both of us if Maguire connects us to El Jefe."

"Hell, no. We'd wind up in Mezcaya, skinned and begging El Jefe to put us out of our misery long before anybody'd grant us that wish."

"Kill Beau Maguire," Ben said. "Leave O'Brien to me."

Chapter 12

Hart stood in the crisscrossing sprays of the shower, letting the too-hot water pound down on him while he went over the events of the previous night. It had taken Danny Gates time to track down Ricky Mercado. Then Gates had to do some serious negotiating to get his lifelong friend to agree to talk to a cop. The late-night meeting between Hart and Ricky Mercado had lasted several hours.

His efforts had paid off, Hart thought while the steamy water hammered his muscles. After hearing his family was about to get pegged as the prime suspect in the Lone Star bombing and the resulting deaths of Daniel and Meg Anderson, Ricky Mercado's eyes had narrowed to slits. He had assured Hart no one connected with the Mercados—or any arm of the Texas mob—had, or was, using the Lone Star as a headquarters for running drugs, weapons and/or laundering cash. They'd had nothing to do with the bombing. Nor had the deceased maintenance man, Willie Pogue, ever worked for the Mercados.

Hart knew instinctively that Ricky Mercado had told

him the truth. It wasn't a matter of guessing. Hart *knew*. Proving it was something else. As was nailing the guilty party.

After leaving Mercado, Hart drove to Spence Harrison's house and rousted the D.A. out of bed. Grim-faced, Spence had listened to Hart's summary of his meeting. Although Spence had received Ben Stone's report that concluded Willie Pogue had built and planted the Lone Star bomb on instructions from the Mercados, the D.A. had agreed with Hart's request to hold off issuing a decision on the police chief's findings.

When Hart returned to his suite at the Lone Star just before dawn, fatigue had pressed down on him like an anvil. He'd stripped off his clothes in a pile, dropped into bed like a rock and slept until noon.

The reviving rest had removed the cobwebs from his brain. Good thing, he thought, since his investigation seemed to have found its direction. Finally.

With the Mercados cleared of guilt in his own mind, he turned his thoughts to the Lone Star security personnel.

Over the past days he had learned their security office was near the burned-out billiards room. Entry to the office was controlled by a state-of-the-art system that unlatched the door only after the correct code was logged into a digital panel. During a casual chat with a janitor, Hart found out that only members of the security force had access to the office. Not even general manager, Bonnie Brannigan, or Flynt Carson, the club's current president, could enter without first arranging an escort. To Hart, that cleared Brannigan and Carson as accessories to any illegal activities the cops might be involved in. That the office seemed almost fortress-like implied it was off-limits because something inside needed hiding. Like maybe a money laundering operation using the name Esmeralda.

One essential necessity for a successful laundering operation was to have and maintain a secure collection and storage point for cash not yet laundered. Hart couldn't think of an area at the Lone Star more suitable for that type of activity than the office manned 24/7 by cops.

So, if the cops *did* use the security office for laundering purposes, where the hell did the dirty money come from? Hart wondered as he lathered shampoo into his hair. If not the Mercados, then who?

He thought back to his initial conversation with Spence about the bombing. The D.A. had voiced the theory that his former marine commander, Lieutenant Colonel Phillip Westin, had been the bomber's target. Westin had stopped off in Mission Creek on his way to Mezcaya to join a secret mission aimed at taking down El Jefe. Hart knew the Central American group distributed illegal drugs, raking in vast amounts of money. Money that required laundering in order for El Jefe to operate in certain legitimate venues. As with other infamous cartels, El Jefe wouldn't hesitate to eliminate anyone intent on its destruction.

In this case, Phillip Westin.

Was it possible the entire security force at the Lone Star supplemented their incomes by laundering money for El Jefe? And someone on that force made and planted the bomb to kill Westin in an attempt to protect that operation?

Hell, yes, Hart thought. Greed was an eternal motive. If the cops earned a percentage of El Jefe's vast profits, they wouldn't want Westin interfering with their money-making sideline.

Rinsing his hair, Hart reminded himself that his theories about the MCPD cops, their security office and Westin didn't mean squat. Investigations often took turns that seemed to be sure things only to have them fall apart. What he needed was proof that backed up his theories.

His first step in getting that proof was to take a look inside the Lone Star's security office. He had yet to figure out how to do that.

Hart turned off the shower, pulled a towel from a warming bar and dried off. Slinging the towel around his waist, he stepped out into the enormous, tiled bathroom the same instant the phone rang. He ignored the extension in the bathroom and headed for the one beside the nightstand where he kept a pad of paper and pencil.

Slicking his wet hair back from his face, he snagged the receiver and settled onto the bed's tangled sheets.

"O'Brien."

"Kip here. Glad I caught you."

"Glad you did, too," Hart said. Because of the conclusion he'd reached about Helena's parentage the previous evening at the hospital, Hart had planned to call Kip Vincent, his pal on the Dallas PD's bomb squad, first thing this morning. Sleep had gotten in the way. "Listen, Kip, if you haven't already run that check on Thomas Dean for me, don't waste your time."

"Too late, pal, it's done." Vincent chuckled. "And, yeah, you're right—trying to get a picture of a guy who never existed is a big time waster."

Pinpricks of unease crawled up Hart's spine. *"Never existed?"*

"From the sound of your voice, maybe I didn't waste my time. Hart, I ran Thomas Garrick Dean six ways from here to Sunday. Since you asked me to get his photo, the first thing I did was call a source at the bar association. I figured they'd have a picture on file of every attorney in the state. They don't have one of Dean."

"Maybe that's because he died nearly ten years ago?"

"I mentioned that to my source, so she dug through the archives. Not only could she not find a photo of the guy, she couldn't find any record that a Thomas Dean was ever licensed to practice law in Texas."

Narrowing his eyes, Hart searched his memory. Spence had described Joan's late husband as a hotshot Dallas attorney.

"I figured the next logical place to get the guy's photo was off his driver's license," Kip continued. "So I called the Department of Public Safety. Dead end—Thomas

Dean never drove in Texas. Or never had a license that said he could, anyway.''

"Go on," Hart said while the muscles in his belly tied themselves into a dozen hard and tangled knots.

"By the time I found out all of this my curiosity was going full steam, so I decided to get a copy of the report on the traffic accident in which this yahoo died. Surprise, surprise, there isn't one.''

"It's possible the accident didn't happen in Dallas," Hart said carefully. "I took for granted it did because that's where he lived. At least that was where I was told he lived.''

"Yeah, I thought you could have been wrong about the accident location. Dallas has a hell of a lot of suburbs so it's logical to figure some other department might have worked the accident. I had communications put out a state-wide request to all departments to check for information on the guy. *Any* information. We got back nada—nobody's ever heard of him.''

His fingers clenched on the phone, Hart sat motionless on the edge of the bed, feeling as if he'd just been sucker punched.

"Last resort, I called the health department," Kip said. "Brick wall there, too. The State of Texas hasn't issued a birth or death certificate for anyone named Thomas Garrick Dean in the last fifty years. Sorry, Hart, either you gave me the wrong name, or someone's leading you down a phony trail.''

"I'm right about the name," Hart managed, his voice sounding hoarse in his ears. His stomach was roiling and he couldn't seem to grab a breath of air. "And I think you're right that I just took a long stroll down a phony path.'' A ten-year-long stroll. "Sorry to cause you so much trouble, Kip.''

"No problem, pal. I owed you a favor. If you get up to Dallas, come see me. We can toss back a few beers and talk about bombs.''

''Kip, thanks for the help.''

Hand unsteady, Hart hung up the phone. He closed his eyes in an effort to get his bearings while his mind issued denials. It wasn't possible Helena was his. It couldn't be possible. Joan wouldn't—*couldn't*—have deprived him of his child.

Piece by piece, Hart put things together. He heard again Zane Cooper bellowing over the phone that he would have Hart arrested for stealing money from the Lone Star if he tried to contact his daughter again. Months later Hart had called Spence, who'd heard that Joan had moved to Dallas and married a hotshot attorney. After Spence set up his law practice, Zane Cooper hired him to draw up documents to fund a trauma wing at the hospital in Thomas Dean's name. Cooper advised Spence his son-in-law's death happened so soon after he and Joan eloped that she hadn't had a chance to change her name on all her ID. So, she'd kept her maiden name.

She'd done that because she'd never married Thomas Dean, Hart realized, the truth beating at him in every direction. How could she, when the man never existed? And therefore never fathered her child.

Helena was *his*. That gorgeous, precious little girl was his daughter. Joan and her parents had gone to a hell of a lot of trouble—and expense—to make sure no one knew. Including *him*.

The muscles in his jaw worked as he thought of Joan, of the panic he'd seen in her eyes the day he'd returned to the Lone Star. He knew now the reason for that panic. She'd borne his child. *Denied him that child.* The sense of betrayal he felt was so huge it overwhelmed everything.

Hart rose, jerked off the towel and grabbed his jeans off the floor.

He wanted answers. And, by God, he was going to get them.

Joan buttoned the short, fitted jacket of her bright-red gabardine pantsuit then checked her reflection in the full-length mirror on her closet door. Satisfied, she clipped on a sculpted silver pin and earrings. The instant she stepped into her red flats, the doorbell chimed.

A vicious case of frustration had her scowling at the clock on her nightstand. Because of Helena's accident and their spending the night with Maddie, Joan had taken the day off work. That morning she'd driven Helena to school—something she intended to do every day until she had answers about the hit-and-run accident that could have easily claimed her child's life. With the rest of the day off, she had a list of errands to run and just enough time to do them before Ceci's mom brought the girls home from their after-school Brownie meeting. Joan knew that whoever was at the door would slow her down.

The doorbell chimed again.

"Coming!" she shouted, heading into the living room. When she glanced out the peephole and saw the grimness in Hart's face, her first thought was he had information about Helena's accident.

"Did you find out something about the driver of the van?" she asked, swinging open the door.

He wore jeans and a wrinkled white dress shirt he hadn't bothered to tuck in. His hair was wet, slicked back from his face, still shadowed with the previous day's stubble. His expression looked close to murder.

"Where's Helena?" he asked evenly.

Measuring the anger in his eyes, Joan's heart stopped. Simply stopped. With the instincts of an animal that had circled a trap in which she'd at last been snared, she knew the reason for his anger.

"She insisted on going to school. Couldn't wait to show off her lime-green wrist bandage." How she managed to keep her voice even, Joan didn't have a clue.

He stalked in, shoved the door closed behind him. "She's mine, isn't she? Helena's mine."

Swallowing hard, Joan took a step in retreat. She was

certain she heard her bones creak like rusty hinges with the dreamlike movement. "Hart, I—"

He took a swift step forward. "Answer the question. Helena is my daughter, isn't she?"

Joan nodded. Cold, she was suddenly so cold.

"Dammit, say it!"

"Yes." The word came out perilously close to a sob. "Helena is your daughter."

"Why?" His gaze cut like a blade. She'd never seen anger so cool, so controlled. "Why didn't you tell me?"

She crossed her arms protectively across her middle. She might be the one who'd stepped into a trap, but they both knew damn well he'd left town without a word to her. That there'd been no way she could have told him. "You know why."

His hands whipped out snake quick and gripped her elbows. She felt his fingers press down to the bone. "Yeah, I do. I figured out a long time ago all you wanted from me was one night of hot sex. The spoiled country club girl whispered a few lies, lost her virginity to a dirt-poor groundskeeper, then hightailed it back to Daddy's mansion. Maybe you even put a notch on your bedpost."

"How dare you?" She shoved at his arms in a futile attempt to frcc herself.

"*How dare I?* We have a child, and you kept her from me. For nearly ten years." There was more than fury in his eyes now. There was torment. "Damn you, how could you not tell me I had a daughter?"

"You left!" Joan shouted. "How could I tell you anything when you disappeared and never came back? When I had no idea where you'd gone?"

"Like hell." Whirling her around, he backed her up against the door, pressed her against the hard wood. "I fell for your lies that one night, sweetheart, but don't expect me to do it again. I called and left messages for you with about every servant your daddy had. I wrote you a couple of times to let you know where I was. All you had to do was pick up the phone. Write a damn letter."

She felt the blood drain from her face. "There were no—"

"But letting me know you were pregnant with my child wouldn't have been good for your image, would it?" he ground out. "Telling *me* the truth would have meant you'd have to admit to all your country club pals that a piece of trailer trash with a lush for a mother had fathered your child. No, it was much better, more *presentable* to invent Thomas Dean, the successful attorney."

"Stop it!" Shoving Hart back, she sidestepped away from the door as ten years worth of regrets, resentment and frustration bubbled to the surface. "I didn't lie to you that night. *You* lied to *me*. You told me you loved me, wanted me, then you left." Her hands balled against her thighs. "*You left*. You didn't come back. Didn't call. Or write. I presumed you didn't want to be bothered with anything that had to do with me. That included our child."

"I didn't lie to you that night. When I said I loved you, I meant it." His voice was low, deadly, terrifying. "I'm not lying to you now. I did call you. I wrote."

"I never…" Her voice faded as uncertainty pressed in around her. "I swear I didn't get…" Appalled, she pressed her fingers to her lips as an agonizing realization set in. "Oh, my God."

"Your parents," Hart grated, voicing the conclusion she had reached. "All they cared about was where I stood on the social ladder. Which wasn't even on the bottom rung."

"That morning, after they found us together in the parking lot at the club, my mother gave me a huge lecture on how appalled she was over my forgetting my upbringing. When my dad got home they closed ranks and forbade me to see you again. Ever." Joan shoved a trembling hand through her hair. "I didn't care what they said."

"Didn't care?" Hart countered. "You can stand there and say it didn't matter when you heard your father accuse me of stealing money from the club's golf shop? Or that my mother was a drunk who'd written a hot check and had a warrant out for her arrest? You didn't care?''

''I knew you hadn't stolen that money!''

''How? How did you know?''

''I knew *you*. That whole summer I chased after you, flirting with you, tempting you. You did your best to hold me at arm's length, insisting I stick to my own class. A man who so adamantly refuses to take what he believes isn't his doesn't go around stealing. As for your mother, I didn't care that she drank or that she'd written a hot check. I was in love with her son—that's all that mattered to me.'' Unconsciously Joan rubbed the heel of her hand between her breasts as if to force the air in and out. ''The first chance I got, I packed a suitcase and sneaked out of the house. A friend picked me up and drove me to the trailer park where you lived. I wasn't going to leave until I talked you into eloping. The trailer you and your mother had rented was empty. The manager said you'd left no forwarding address.''

Hart pressed the heels of his hands to his eyes and uttered a vicious oath. ''Leaving a forwarding address isn't a smart thing to do when you're running from the law.''

''I kept asking, but you never sent for your final paycheck from the club. Spence didn't know where you'd gone. It was as if you had vanished off the face of the earth. By the time I found out I was pregnant, I knew you weren't coming back. I believed you'd lied about loving me. If you'd loved me, you would have come back for me.''

''That's what I planned to do. It took me a couple of months to find a place in Chicago near my mother's stepbrother and get her straightened out. I had to force her into rehab. There was no way I could leave to come back here until I knew I could trust her to stay off the booze. When that time finally came I called Spence. He told me he'd heard you'd moved to Dallas and gotten married. What the hell was I supposed think? That you wanted your one-night fling to show up to meet your new husband?''

Hart's hands clenched. "Your new husband," he repeated softly. "You told everyone you married Thomas Dean. That Helena was his. Admit it, Joan, it wasn't your pregnancy you were ashamed of, but the fact that your child was an O'Brien.''

"*I* wasn't ashamed." Feeling as if her legs might give out, she walked to the nearest wing chair, gripped its back for support. "My parents were. When I told them I was pregnant, my father was livid. He insisted I have an abortion. I refused, so he sent me to Dallas to live with his sister. I loved my aunt. She was understanding and didn't judge me. She owned a spa, I worked there while I was pregnant and after I had Helena. Two years later my aunt sold the spa and moved to Los Angeles. I considered going with her, but decided I wanted to raise Helena in Mission Creek, not L.A. My parents had made a couple of trips to Dallas, and I could tell they had grown to love her. The night before they moved us home, they told me about Thomas Dean. About how they'd announced to everyone in town that I'd married this lawyer, conceived a child with him and become a widow when he died in a car wreck. They'd already funded a trauma wing at the hospital in his name. Donated stained-glass windows to the church in his memory. Built a playground in his honor. I was stunned.''

"Stunned, maybe. But you went along with their story.''

"That's right, I did," she shot back. "I didn't care what people thought of me, but I did and do care what they think about Helena. My parents' story about Thomas Dean prevented my child from being labeled illegitimate.''

"*Our child.*"

"Our child." Joan closed her eyes. "You weren't here, Hart. For all I knew you were dead. I did what I thought was best for Helena. Dammit, you weren't here.''

"I'm here now. Have been for weeks. Remember what you said to me that day in the elevator? 'Let's agree that we simply prefer to avoid each other,'" he ground out. 'Perhaps your stay at the Lone Star will be more pleasant for both of us if we have as little contact as possible.' You were trying to set ground rules so I wouldn't see Helena. You weren't going to tell me about her."

"You're right, I wasn't. Not then." She lifted her chin. "I wasn't going to let you hurt her like you hurt me. No way would I let you matter so much to her that you ripped out her heart when you left and never came back."

"Dammit, I wouldn't do that to her. I wouldn't have done that to you if— Hell!"

The swirl of emotion in his eyes battered her heart. "I know now you'd never do that to Helena, but I didn't know then. I ached for her when she started looking for you every day the minute she got home from school. She bonded with you, talked about you incessantly. I truly thought it was all one-sided on her part. That night the three of us ate dinner at the Yellow Rose, I realized it wasn't only Helena whose feelings were involved. You weren't just acting like you cared about her, the way I thought you'd done with me." Joan felt a tear sneak past her defenses. "I knew then that I had to tell you the truth. Last night at the hospital when we were waiting for Helena to get back from radiology, I started to tell you, then the nurse wheeled her in."

As if going back to that point in time, Hart shifted his gaze. While a muscle worked in his jaw, he stared toward the sheer-curtained, sliding-glass doors that fronted the balcony overlooking the club's extensive grounds.

The silence overwhelming, Joan caught herself rubbing her hands together.

"All right," he said after a moment. "Let's say you were going to tell me at the hospital."

"I *was* going to tell you." She felt a quick twist of relief, knowing he believed her.

"I'm not the only one who's been kept in the dark," he continued. "What are you going to do about the fact you've lied to Helena every day of her life? Told her that her father is some invented guy who conveniently died? That even after I showed up you kept the truth from her that *I'm* her father?"

Guilt, with a terrifying edge, descended around Joan like clammy heat. "I've always planned to tell her the truth. When she's older. When she can understand."

"You think she'll ever be able to fully understand?"

"I don't know." She took a choked breath, struggling not to cry. "Right now I'm not sure *I* understand anything. All these years I thought you'd lied when you said you loved me. After you left I lay awake nights praying you'd call or write. Come back. I cried myself sick for weeks. My parents knew how miserable I was. *How hurt.* They could see how much I loved you, needed you. I was carrying your child, for God's sake, yet it's obvious now that didn't matter to them. I always knew they cared about maintaining appearances. I just didn't realize it was to the extent that they would sacrifice my happiness."

As Joan spoke, a rush of useless emotions—anger, outrage, hurt swept over her. She needed time. To think. To deal with the burning around her heart. "I know we have to talk about Helena—"

"Damn right. She's mine." Hart walked to where she stood. "I want her to know that. I want to spend time with her here. For her to come spend time with me."

In Chicago. Joan's throat seemed to fill with sand at the thought of Helena living chunks of her life so far away.

"We...can talk about everything. Work things out. Right now...I need time to think. Hart, please just go."

"I don't think so."

"Please." She swiped at the tears streaming down her cheeks. "I need to...need to...get used to..."

"The fact your parents deceived you? Deceived *us?* That they purposely kept us apart because they were ashamed we'd created that beautiful, lovable little girl? You think that's something either of us will ever get used to? Either of us deserved? Including Helena?''

''No. All of this… It's too much.'' Feeling as though a vise was around her heart, squeezing, squeezing, she lifted her head, met his gaze. ''I don't know how I feel. I don't know what to do about any of this.''

''I don't know how I feel, either. But I damn well know what I want to do.'' His eyes were dark and fierce as he closed a hand around her throat. Beneath his fingers her pulse jumped and scrambled. ''I want to claim what your parents denied me. My daughter. You.''

''Hart, wait—''

''I've waited ten years. I'm damn well done with that.'' Quick as a snake his hands moved. Clenching her shoulders, he yanked her up on tiptoe and closed his mouth over hers.

The kiss was hot, greedy and full of edgy need. Blood roared in her head. The realization that she, too, wanted—*needed*—to reclaim the man whom she had loved, who had so cruelly been denied her had her clinging to him, her mouth wild and willing.

Passion erupted inside her like lava spewing through ice, frenzied, unexpected. Dangerous.

Without a thought to reason, without a thought to consequences, she groped at his shirt, fought the buttons, pulled it open. Her fingers cruised over the dark circling hair of his chest, feeling the sinewed muscles beneath. She smelled the soap from his shower, the clean, masculine scent of his skin.

Desperate to sate her hunger, she dragged her mouth from his and sank her teeth into his shoulder.

Groaning, he shoved his hand through her hair, fisted his fingers. He arched her head back and savaged her throat.

A moan of pleasure slid past her lips; time and place were nothing against the hard, driving need inside her.

He shoved the jacket off her shoulders, her slacks pooled at her feet. Beneath she wore wisps of black lace and dark thigh-high hose. He deftly unclipped her bra, tossed it aside, then slid his hands beneath her bottom and lifted her. His head dipped, his mouth fastened on one of her nipples.

"Hart..." Pleasure lanced like a spear through her system.

His mouth reclaimed hers as he moved into the hallway then into her bedroom where the sun poured gold through the curtains. She kicked off her shoes as he fell with her onto the peach-colored comforter.

Feeding greedily on her mouth, he fought off his clothes. Between one heartbeat and the next, he was between her knees, using his thighs to part her legs and open her to him. A scrap of midnight-colored lace was the only barrier between them. Seconds later he peeled it and her hose off in one dark tangle.

With their mouths fused in a rough, desperate kiss, his hands streaked over her, hotly possessive, invasive.

Trapping her wrists in one hand, he stretched her arms over her head, arching her breasts upward. Lifting his head, he gazed down at her. The feral emotion in his eyes had her nipples drawing into tight buds.

"I've thought about you," he said, his voice a raw whisper as his free hand slid over her belly, down between her spread legs, cupping her. "Thought about having you like this for ten long years."

She felt herself go damp against his palm. "I've thought...about you, too." She could barely breathe against the ache of need pounding in her veins. "Wanted you inside me. Only you."

She saw the change in his eyes, the deepening, the darkening of them before he leaned and suckled one nipple, then the other.

Heat flared beneath her flesh as he took his fill of her. She moaned, fruitlessly wrenching her arms against his grip in an effort to free them—not to push him away, but to hold him. To hold on to the man she had loved and lost so long ago.

His fingers slid inside her while he continued to suckle, his tongue laving her nipple. Her breath snagged, then caught as she felt herself climbing through waves of heated sensation.

The climax hit her like a blow, searing her breath out of her lungs in burning gasps. He released his hold on her wrists; for dazed minutes she lay trembling, panting, her bones molten and her mind reeling.

''Again,'' he said his voice ragged. He slid his hands beneath her, yanked her hips high and used his mouth on her. He drove her up to a blinding, shattering release.

With her body still shuddering from the onslaught, he plunged inside her, deep and hard. His mouth crushed down on hers, feeding there as she arched in welcome.

Inside her, fire raged out of control as his hips pumped against hers, mating. Taking. Claiming.

His chest heaving, he groaned her name while her sweat-slicked body matched the fast, furious rhythm of his hips. When her muscles clenched around him, she watched his eyes turn to green smoke.

Her moan of dark pleasure echoed through the still air seconds before his own.

Hart stood on the balcony off Joan's living room, staring out at the Lone Star's pristine grounds, now bathed in the glow of late-afternoon sunlight. Although his physical need had been sated, his jaw was locked tight and his hands clenched on the balcony's wrought iron rail.

Sweet heaven, he was a father. Having finally allowed himself to feel the emotion accompanying that knowledge, he was almost brought to his knees.

How was it Helena had been born and he hadn't felt something? Shouldn't he have experienced some upheaval inside himself? Shouldn't he have *known?*

He scrubbed a hand over his jaw, felt the thick, coarse stubble. He had probably made a mistake by not leaving when Joan had asked him to. He acknowledged that he needed time where she was concerned. Time to step back, gain some distance for a more objective look. And while he was at it, he had to figure out why the need to reclaim the woman he had once loved had felt like claws tearing at his throat, his heart, his loins. Determine why he had taken her so ruthlessly, as if that one act could somehow inflict revenge on those who had cheated him of so much.

Including *her*.

His fingers tightened on the railing. Logically, he knew Joan wasn't to blame for his losing years of his daughter's life. She had been lied to. Deceived. Still, he felt a tiny splinter of resentment in his gut over the fact that *she* hadn't been deprived of their child. *She* hadn't been conned out of all those irreplaceable years with Helena.

When he heard movement behind him, he turned. Joan nudged aside the sheer curtain that fluttered in the breeze over the sliding-glass door. Stepping out onto the balcony, she left the door open behind her. She was dressed in a yellow T-shirt and trim black slacks. A clip pulled her dark hair back from her pale face. Her eyes were intent, watchful as though she didn't know what to expect from him.

Hell, he didn't blame her. He didn't know, either.

She paused halfway between him and the door. "I thought maybe you'd gone," she said quietly.

"Not until we get some things settled."

"I agree, we need to do that. Hart, I need to know what you're thinking. What you want to do."

"What I want is to go back ten years and tell your father what he can do with his threats against me and my mother." He leaned a hip against the wrought-iron rail. "Then I want to be there to watch my daughter come into this world. Hear her say her first word. See her take her first step. Drop her off for her first day of school. That's what I want."

Joan pressed her lips together. "I wish we could both go back and change things."

"Yeah." He glanced behind her toward the door, his thoughts going to what had happened between them in the rooms beyond. "Look, you were right when you asked me to leave. Give you time. I should have gone. Shouldn't have... I was rough. Too rough and I apologize." He shoved a hand through his hair. What had happened between them hadn't just been sex, deep down he knew that. Still, the pain twisting inside him had him adding, "I made a big mistake."

Her color faded at that. "It seems we've both made mistakes. So, let's not complicate this more than it already is. Since we can't go back and change things, let's talk about where we go from here."

"All right. First thing, I want you to tell Helena I'm her father."

"I will."

"When?"

She closed her eyes, opened them. "You have to give me some time. I just can't spring this on her. I need time."

Her words touched an already raw nerve that sent a red mist across his vision. "I've lost nearly ten years with her, and you need *time?*"

"Look, you and I are both angry and upset, but we have to put that in the background. We have to think about Helena. About what's best for her. She's the one who matters."

Hart bit down on his roiling emotions. He was a father. He needed to start thinking like one. Joan was right— Helena's feelings had to be considered first. Their daughter was the one who could be hurt most by this. The truth would forever change her life and it was a sure bet she would resent having been lied to. He had no guarantees she would want him as a father. No assurances she wouldn't hate him for showing up and turning her secure, happy world upside down.

"I agree," he said evenly. "Helena is the one who matters. If it's better for her to find out she's my daughter when she's older, then I'll wait." Pushing away from the rail, he moved to where Joan stood. The warm, haunting scent of Chanel clung to her skin, to the air, to his senses. He felt everything at once—need, annoyance, anger, resentment. "But I won't let you keep her from me. Whether as a father or a friend, I *will* be a part of Helena's life."

"I don't want to keep you from her. I just don't want her hurt."

"Then we both want the same thing." He stared down at Joan, saw the small lines of stress at the corners of her eyes and mouth. She was the woman he had wanted, craved, dreamed about for a decade. She was the mother of his child. Right now his feelings for her were so tangled up he couldn't name them, much less sort them out. He pressed his lips together and tasted her again. He wondered if he would ever rid himself of her taste. If he wanted to.

"I'd better go," he said.

"Yes."

He followed her to the glass door, waiting while she edged back the sheer drapes. The instant she stepped into the living room, she froze. "Oh, my God. Sweetheart."

Hart moved in behind her, a knot forming in his throat as he caught sight of Helena. She stood just inside the balcony door, her expression distressed, her eyes teary.

Joan started toward her, arms outstretched, but Helena backed away.

"Is it true?" she asked, her voice thin and quavering. "Is it true that Daddy—that he isn't my real father? That you lied to me?"

"Sweetheart, listen to me—"

Helena shrank back and looked at Hart with tear-filled eyes. "Are you really my daddy?"

He swallowed hard. Having no real clue what to say, he went with gut instinct. "Yes, I just found out today. I feel lucky that you're my daughter, Helena. I hope you'll let me spend time with you so I can get to know you even better. And find out what it's like to be a father.''

"How can a dad not know about their kid?" Helena choked out in confusion. "My real dad had to have known I was his and he would've come seen me."

The betrayal in her dark eyes clawed at Hart's gut. He had no answer for that. He met Joan's distressed gaze, a sick dread snaking through him that he might lose the precious little girl he'd only now found.

Chapter 13

Watching the tears stream down Helena's face, Joan felt as if she were dying on the inside. She had no idea how much of her conversation with Hart her daughter had overheard, but it was enough to know she'd been deceived her entire life. By her mother.

Joan took a step forward. "Honey, listen—"

"Why did you lie to me?" Helena's tear-stained cheeks were as red as the T-shirt layered beneath her denim jumper.

"Sweetheart, listen." Joan reached out for the hand that extended past the lime-green elastic bandage circling her child's injured wrist. "There's a good reason. It's the only way—"

When Helena backed away, Joan's heart began bleeding. She could feel it. She crouched, trembling so badly she could barely keep her balance. She was aware of Hart standing behind her, wished she could find comfort in his presence, but she knew that wasn't possible. He was as hurt and angry as Helena.

Sensing her child was about to break down, Joan decided to try a firmer approach in an attempt to avoid it. "Helena, I'm sorry you had to find out like this. I was going to tell you. When you were older and could grasp—"

"You say it's wrong to lie! You even punish me for it." Helena's eyes glinted with emotion. "You taught me that it's wrong. You know I *hate* liars. And you have always been lying to me."

Because the grandparents you love were ashamed of your father. Because when I brought you back here to live I didn't want the whole town to know what liars my parents were. Because they made me believe your father hadn't loved me.

"Helena, please—"

Her heart breaking, Joan watched her daughter race away and disappear into the hallway. Seconds later the door to her bedroom slammed. Panic that she'd forever lost her child's love pounded like an anvil at the base of Joan's skull. If Hart hadn't gripped her arms and eased her to her feet, she'd have sunk into a small huddle on the floor.

"What do we do now?" he asked quietly. As if realizing her shaky condition, he kept his hands on her arms. "Do we give her time to get used to this?"

We, Joan thought. For the first time a decision about Helena wasn't totally hers to make. Helena's father was involved now. Would forever be involved.

"She does need time, we all do," Joan said, despair pressing against her heart. "But she's so upset, so hurt. I…we can't let her stay in her room without trying to talk to her."

"All right." Hart looked down at her, his green eyes somber. "You're the expert here. I'll follow your lead."

His words tightened the knots of guilt and regret in her stomach. If he'd been given a chance to be a part of their daughter's life, he wouldn't now have to depend on her to know what to do next. God, if only she had believed in him enough years ago to know he'd meant it when he said he loved her. If only she'd known he had tried to contact her. If only she'd put aside her own hurt pride and tried to find Hart. If only her parents had loved her enough to put her feelings ahead of their unbending need to maintain appearances. *If only.*

Her pulse pounding painfully, she fought an instinctive urge to lean into Hart's arms for support. He had made it clear he considered the intimacy they'd shared that afternoon a blatant mistake. For him, taking her had apparently been a man's symbolic reclaiming of the woman who had so deviously been denied him. Now that the act was done, he might be forever through with her on a physical level. Their coming together had meant far more to her, but she didn't have time to think about that right now. She had another, more immediate concern. And that concern was no doubt crying her eyes out in a bedroom down the hallway.

She pulled back from Hart's hold. "We need to see if Helena will talk to us. Somehow we need to get her to listen."

Minutes later, with Hart beside her, Joan tapped softly on the door to Helena's bedroom. The sound of her child's muffled sobbing tightened Joan's chest. "Helena?"

"Go away!"

"Sweetie, please, we need to talk."

"I don't want to talk to you! Ever again!"

Joan leaned against the wall. She understood the sense of hurt and betrayal that had Helena lashing out. Though Joan's mother was dead and her father's mind gone, she too, felt the need to strike out at them for what they'd done.

Biting her lip, she turned back to the door. "Baby, I made a mistake. I understand why you don't want to talk to me right now. We'll do that later. But you shouldn't be mad at Hart. He didn't know any of this until today. None of this is his fault. Will you talk to him?''

After a long silence came a quavering, "Yes. Just him."

Joan met Hart's gaze. She could read nothing in the unfathomable darkness of his eyes. "She's very angry, that's obvious."

"She has every right to be," he said levelly.

"Yes." Joan pulled in a deep breath, forcing herself to think. "Hart, she may sometimes sound more like an adult than a child, but Helena's just a little girl. She won't understand the circumstances of all that happened between you and me, so don't try to explain. Just let her know you're here if she needs you. That you're not going to make a lot of demands on her."

"I have a whole list of demands where my daughter's concerned."

Like wanting her to live at least a part of the time with you, Joan thought weakly. Maybe all of the time. She lifted a hand to reach for Hart, then dropped it to her side. He stood a foot away from her and she could feel the distance between them grow by leaps and bounds.

"I'm the one you need to talk to about those demands." Her voice trembled as she spoke. "You have to give Helena time. Be patient. She needs a chance to get used to the idea that you're her father. Don't pressure her. *Please.*"

His hand gripped around the knob on the door of Helena's bedroom, Hart watched Joan turn and walk down the hallway, her spine stiff. When she disappeared into the living room, he rested his forehead against the door. She was hurting. Terribly. Horribly. Over a series of lies perpetrated by the very people who should have done anything—*everything*—to ensure her happiness.

He was trying not to resent the fact she'd chosen to believe those lies. Why couldn't she have believed *him*, instead? Dammit, they'd only shared one night of intimacy, but those few hours had rocked both their worlds. She should have *known* he would come back for her, no matter what. If she had believed him, he could have been with her during her pregnancy. Seen his child take her first breath. Watched her grow up.

Somewhere inside him, a spark of logic told him his blaming Joan was unreasonable. He, too, had believed lies he'd been told about her. With guilt balling in his throat, he reminded himself he needed to let his emotions settle before he could even begin to figure out how he felt about her. That wouldn't happen until—*if*—his anger cooled over the fact that even after she'd discovered her parents' lie about Thomas Dean, she'd still gone along with it. Maybe she had made what had seemed to be her best choice at the time, but it had been the wrong one. And her action had robbed him of knowing his child.

His child. Hart looked down at his fingers clenched on the doorknob and was hit by the monumental realization that he was about to have a life-altering talk with his daughter.

He could disarm a case of dynamite wired to a motion sensor, but he knew damn well what now faced him held a different potential for destruction. If he could manage this, he thought as he eased open the door, he could pull off anything.

Helena huddled on her bed against a bank of pillows, her face tear-stained, her thin arms hugging a large white stuffed dog. Her long, dark hair hung in a tangled mess to her waist.

"Hi," he said, shutting the door behind him. "Thanks for agreeing to talk to me. How are you doing?"

Rebellion settled in her tear-blotched face. "She lied to me," she said flatly. "She's always saying I should tell the truth, and punishes me when I don't." Her eyes narrowed. "She lied to you, too, didn't she?"

As he moved across the room, Hart noted a dresser and small desk in the same whitewashed pine as the twin sleigh bed on which Helena had sought refuge. Gossamer curtains covered the windows; wallpaper stenciled with pale-pink flowers rose from the waist-high white wainscoting. A padded keepsake box wrapped with fabric matching the wallpaper sat on the nightstand. The room might be straight out of a fairytale castle, but the little girl who lived there currently looked nothing like a happy princess.

Meeting Helena's stormy gaze, Hart settled a hip on the edge of the mattress. He wanted to reach out and take her small hand, but resisted the urge. Right now he didn't know how she would react to him. To anything.

"People make mistakes," he began carefully. "No one's perfect, not even your mom. Some of her mistakes were made even before you were born. I left Mission Creek and your mother didn't know where I'd gone. I thought she did, but I was wrong. And because…"

He curled his hand on his jeaned thigh. Joan was right—he'd be up to his eyeballs in alligators if he even tried to explain the circumstances that had led to this mess. "For certain reasons, I didn't contact your mother. That was a mistake on my part, because she didn't know how to find me to tell me about you. I hope you know that if I had known about you, I never would have allowed you or your mother out of my life."

Helena picked at the hem of her jumper. "Grandma Kathryn and Grandpa Zane kept telling me what a nice man my daddy was. That his name was Thomas Dean and he loved me, though he went to heaven before he ever got to see me. I heard Mom say Grandma Kathryn and Grandpa Zane made him up." Her bottom lip trembled. "They lied to me, too."

Big-time, Hart thought. Seeing his child suffering tightened the ache in his chest.

Testing the waters, he reached out, put a finger beneath her quivering chin and lifted. Her expression was angry, verging on forbidding, but there was a fresh gleam of tears in her eyes. Although he would have liked to place the blame for her pain squarely where it belonged, he knew that would hurt and confuse her even more.

"Your mother told me how much your grandma and grandpa loved you," he said quietly. "I think deep down you know that. And you also know your mother loves you. A lot."

"They all lied!"

"Yes, they did. Helena, sometimes adults tell a lie to someone they love because they truly believe it's the best thing to do."

"But, because they all lied to me, I didn't know you were my daddy. And you didn't know about me. How was that the best thing?"

"Turns out it wasn't." He ran his knuckle along the baby-soft line of her jaw while he groped to find some way to explain.

"When I look for a bad guy, I have to follow clues and leads and make fast decisions. After I close a case I look back over what I've done. Sometimes I can see I would have found the bad guy sooner if I hadn't been wrong about certain things. It's easy to spot stuff like that when you've got all the answers. That's the situation your mother's in right now. She was wrong years ago not to tell you I'm your real father. Looking back, it's easy for her to see she made a mistake."

Still clutching the white dog, Helena leaned forward abruptly. "A couple of kids in my class have divorced parents. They have to live with both of them at different times. Will I live with Mom or you or both places?"

Hart paused. He had forgotten Helena's penchant for asking questions. "That's something the three of us need to decide. But not now. We're all surprised and upset by what's happened. That isn't a good time to decide things. All I can tell you right now is that I'm not going to ask you to do anything you don't want to."

"Everything's going to change." With fresh tears

streaming down her cheeks, Helena moved in close, snuggling beneath his arm. "I like you, Hart. I really do. It just hurts to find out you're my real daddy and not who I thought was."

"I'm sorry, Helena. I'm so sorry you're hurt."

Helpless to do anything else, he held her close, stroking her hair while she cried against his shoulder. After a while her tears slowly dried but she didn't move away. "Did you mean it?" she asked, her voice muffled against his chest.

"Mean what?"

"When you said you feel lucky I'm your daughter. Did you mean it?"

Inching his head back, he looked down at her. Her nose was red, her eyes bloodshot, her dark lashes spiked with tears. He hugged her. "You bet I did."

"Good." She slid an arm around his back. "I guess I'm going to find out what it's like to have a real daddy."

In the space a heartbeat, Hart O'Brien truly fell in love with his daughter.

While Hart lingered in Helena's bedroom, Ben Stone stabbed the doorbell to Joan's suite. He had just come from the Lone Star's security office where Yance Ingram had summoned him on important business. For Ben, hearing the tape of that morning's phone call between O'Brien and a Dallas PD bomb tech had the same effect as waving a red flag before a bull.

It was a *fact* Joan and O'Brien had known each other ten years ago. A *fact* they were now more than just friends—the video tape of their recent tête-à-tête on the terrace proved that. Finding out that Joan had claimed Helena's father was a man who'd never existed was all the proof Ben needed to know that Hart O'Brien had sired Helena.

That gave O'Brien an overwhelming reason to extend

his stay in Mission Creek. Hell, the cop might even decide to move there.

Which was something Ben neither wanted nor would abide.

While he waited in the corridor, he shifted his gray uniform Stetson from one hand to the other. He thought grimly about his own daughters, how their mother had divorced him, taken them to live in California with another man whom they now called Daddy. Many times he had imagined dark-haired, dimple-cheeked Helena Cooper calling him that. Imagined Joan lying under him, her body slick with sweat as he took her. With O'Brien in the picture, Ben didn't have a hell of a lot of hope either of those things would happen.

Personal concerns weren't the only reason Ben wanted O'Brien gone. The D.A. had yet to make a determination on Ben's report in which he'd concluded Willie Pogue, acting on instructions from the Mercado mob, had set the bomb in the Men's Grill. Ben knew that Spence Harrison wanted the bombing case closed as badly as he, so Ben had checked around when the D.A. hedged. According to a source, O'Brien had told Harrison the cops jumped the gun when they pegged the dead maintenance worker as the bombing suspect.

Ben didn't know how O'Brien had reached that conclusion. It didn't matter. He'd stuck his nose in too deep. Ben had worked long and hard to get where he was. He had no intention of allowing the bastard to threaten his association with El Jefe. O'Brien was going to have an accident. Soon.

At that instant Joan pulled the door open. Her simple yellow T-shirt and trim black slacks didn't prevent her body from looking like a fantasy of curves. A clip pulled her dark hair back from her chalk-pale face. Ben didn't have to guess the reason for her ashen skin and red-rimmed eyes. O'Brien had no doubt confronted her after talking to the Dallas cop.

"Ben, I—"

"My God, Joan." He stepped in quickly, giving her no chance to ask him to come back later. "What's happened? What's wrong?"

"I…have some things on my mind." Although he now stood inside the suite, she made no move to close the door.

"Pretty heavy things, it appears." Turning, he walked into the living room, setting his Stetson on the coffee table in front of the deep-cushioned couch. She was upset. Vulnerable. What better time for a woman to reach for a man for comfort?

He looked back at her. She gripped the door, her body as stiff as a marble statue. "I apologize for not phoning ahead, but I've got some news about Helena's accident. I went by the spa to tell you. Sonji said you'd taken the day off. On a hunch I stopped by here." Since there was no way she would ask him to leave without hearing what he knew about the accident, he added, "If you'd prefer, I'll come back later when you don't have so much on your mind."

"No." She closed the door, then walked to where he stood. Her warm scent smelled erotically of woman. "Have you found out who purposely ran down Helena?"

"I'm not sure I'd say 'purposely.'" His gaze traced the long, slender length of her throat while he imagined his mouth doing the same. She would taste sweet, he thought. Like spun sugar.

"Looks more like it was what we thought in the first place—a hit-and-run *accident,*" he continued. "The sheriff's office found the van wrecked and in a ditch west of town. We know it's the one that hit Helena because her friend, Ceci, had spotted damage to one of its rear doors."

"What about the driver?"

"We don't have a lead on him. Yet." Beau Maguire was dead. No one would ever find the body of the cop who went on the lam weeks ago after screwing up Ben's orders to kill Detective Molly French. Maguire was one less problem on Ben's plate.

"Do you know who the driver was? Who owned the van?"

"No to the first question, yes to the second. A used-car lot reported the van stolen the morning of the accident. The lab techs say it had been wiped clean of prints, so that's a dead end."

"In other words, you won't ever find him," Joan said fiercely, her voice quaking with anger. "You won't ever find the bastard who hurt my child."

"I'll find the scum. You have my word." With her emotions so unsettled, Ben decided this was a good time to make his move. Stepping forward, he placed a hand on her shoulder. "Joan, I care about that little girl like she was my own. You know that. And I care about you, too."

"Ben—"

"We could be good together. The three of us. If you'd just give us a try."

"I can't." She shook her head. "I... Ben, go. Just go."

His eyes narrowed when she shifted away. She'd moved just enough to tell him he had no right to touch. The pain of that boiled through him like acid. Dammit, she was *his,* and she needed to understand that.

"I can see you're upset," he said, forcing his voice to remain level. "Maybe my timing is off here, but I want you to know I'm willing to give you and Helena anything. *Everything.* All you have to do is give me a chance. I don't think that's too much to ask."

"Stone, the lady asked you to leave."

Ben's gaze whipped toward the hallway. Shoulder leaned against the wall, arms crossed over his chest, O'Brien gave him a flat, cold stare. Ben had an uncomfortable image of being sized up by a dangerous hunter.

"I heard her, O'Brien."

"Then why are you still here?"

"We have business to discuss."

Joan turned, looked at O'Brien, her gaze searching his face. "Ben came to tell me they found the van that hit Helena."

"So I heard." Moving into the living room, O'Brien kept his gaze locked with Ben's. "I was just leaving, too. Why don't you and I go talk about what your men are going to do about finding the driver?"

Ben knew the cop had just sent him a message. Since O'Brien had heard that part of Ben's conversation with Joan, he'd heard the rest. Ben could understand O'Brien's resentment over another man trying to move in on his daughter—he'd had to endure the same thing himself. The difference was, O'Brien didn't need to worry about working out visitation rights to see his kid: he wouldn't be alive to visit anybody.

Knowing that cooled Ben's anger. The bottom line was that he would win. Winning was all that mattered.

"Fine, O'Brien. Let's you and I go have that talk." Ben snagged his Stetson off the coffee table, turned to Joan. "I'll talk to you later."

"All right."

"So will I," O'Brien said, shifting his gaze her way. "Helena's asleep now," he added quietly.

A look crossed Joan's face, a quick shadow of despair. "That's probably best."

It wasn't lost on Ben that, instead of him, it was O'Brien whom Joan's gaze tracked toward the door.

Chapter 14

Three days later Hart was still angry. Angry that he and Joan had been set up by her parents. Angry that Joan had gone along with her parents' lie about Thomas Dean that had caused *him* to miss out on nine years of his daughter's life. Mad and filled with guilt that he had taken Joan ruthlessly and with so little care when the overwhelming force of those lies had hit him.

Every time he'd seen her over the past few days she'd looked fragile, her eyes bruised and waif-like. And each time, his body instantly responded to the sight of her, even as his mind took a step in retreat. He could no longer deny that she still moved something in him, no matter how hard he tried to stand against it while he attempted to figured out how he felt.

That, too, stirred his temper. He had finally come to the conclusion that he was angry for reasons he no longer knew, and was fed up with trying to get a handle on those reasons.

So he turned his attention to the other, pressing issues

on his plate: the most important, learning how to be a father.

At Joan's suggestion he had taken Helena to breakfast each morning, then driven her to school. He picked her up in the afternoons and brought her back to the Lone Star. Last night he and Helena had appeared at their first official function when he'd escorted her to the annual father-daughter banquet. Hart didn't know much about fatherhood, but he had no doubt that raising a child alone couldn't be easy. Joan, he thought, had done a hell of a job on her own…which she wouldn't have had to do if it hadn't been for all the damn lies.

When Hart felt his anger again stir, he thought perversely that he was glad he was about to execute a plan Spence termed "dangerous." Doing so required total concentration on the task at hand, not on his personal problems.

Dressed in a black pullover, black jeans and black, rubber-soled boots, Hart strolled past the Lone Star's security office without giving the access-controlled door a glance. He didn't need to check his watch to know it was just after two o'clock in the morning. He had surveilled the pair of off-duty cops who worked the graveyard shift long enough to know that they left the security office exactly at two o'clock each morning and returned one hour later. They spent that hour in the kitchen, eating meals prepared by the twenty-four-hour room-service staff.

The security cops had walked out of the office and headed in the direction of the kitchen minutes ago.

Hart paused at the plywood door that led to the bomb site and slid the key into the padlock. Bypassing the portable lights sitting just inside the door, he pulled a small flashlight out of the black pack slung across one shoulder. As he made his way toward the front of the Men's Grill, the flashlight's beam fanned out, touching dark heaps of rubble. Sidestepping the bomb's crater, he ducked through the charred opening into the burned-out shell of the billiards room. He retrieved the ladder he'd placed there earlier and positioned it against the far wall.

The Lone Star's security office was on the other side of that wall.

After pulling on latex gloves, Hart scaled the ladder, then shoved back several charred panels on the drop-down ceiling. He repeated the process on a few panels over the empty security office. That done, he shimmied over the wall, his rubber soles landing soundlessly on top of the room's single desk.

The fluorescent lights had been left on; still crouching on the desk, he clicked off his flashlight and took in his surroundings. The wall directly across from him flickered with a dozen monitors displaying assorted locations across the Lone Star's premises. Other screens were tuned in to various offices and work areas. Hart narrowed his eyes. He doubted the employees who worked in those offices knew they were under constant observation by members of the security force.

The only sound in the office was the far-off hum of a distant piece of machinery.

At the rear of the office were two doors—one, Hart knew, provided outside access to the back of the clubhouse. If his suspicions were right, the second door guarded a space large enough to store cash waiting for laundering. He hoped to find some of that cash tonight.

Easing off the desk, he crossed the carpeted floor while pulling his pick set from his pack. After studying the door's lock, he selected a pick and tension wrench. Minutes later the lock clicked and he swung open the door on what was indeed a large storage closet. He felt an instant flare of disappointment as he gazed at the closet's bare shelves.

At least they *looked* bare, Hart thought, pulling the remaining item out of his pack. The black, EGIS explosive detector was a sensor that resembled a handheld vacuum. The detector operated on the same principle as a vacuum, however, instead of pulling in dirt, it sucked fumes into a collection cartridge. By inserting the cartridge into a high-speed gas chromatograph, it could be determined if an explosive had ever been stored inside the closet. If so, the chemical composition of that explosive could also be determined.

After running the detector over each shelf, Hart replaced it in his pack. He relocked the closet door, moved to the desk and went soundlessly back over the wall.

Five hours later Joan answered the door to her suite. She knew it was Hart who'd rung the doorbell—he had arrived each morning at seven on the dot to take Helena to breakfast before driving her to school.

Just as it had each day, the instant he stepped through the doorway the sorrow of his distrust enveloped her. As did anger. She also had been lied to. Deceived. She had believed Hart hadn't loved her. *He* had left Mission Creek without a word to *her.* She'd gone along with her parents' story about Thomas Dean because she had no reason to believe she would ever see Hart again. She had done what she thought best for Helena.

All of Joan's senses told her that Hart resented her for having had nine years with their child when he hadn't known she existed. The fact that Joan had loved him, cried herself sick for him, would have given *anything* to have him a part of her life during those years didn't seem to matter to Hart.

Her hurt and bitterness felt even more keen and brittle because she now realized that, sometime over the past weeks, she had fallen in love with Hart O'Brien all over again. She knew there was no point in questioning it, debating it or denying it. She loved him. But she damn well didn't have to admit it to anyone but herself. Certainly not to the man who now stood in her living room, gazing down at her with unreadable green eyes. The man who had reached out for her when they'd both discovered the agonizing truth. The man with whom she had shared the most intimate of acts, who had touched her in ways no other man ever had, then with humiliating detachment informed her those acts had been a *mistake*.

"Morning, Joan." He no longer used his nickname for her.

"Good morning." She slid her tensed hands into the pockets of her gray silk slacks. "I just checked on Helena. She'll be ready in a minute."

"Okay. I have to leave for the state lab in Austin after I drop her off at school. It's a long drive and I probably won't get back until tonight. Can you pick her up this afternoon?"

"I planned on talking to you about that, anyway. The candles she's sold to help her Brownie troop earn money for a trip to Six Flags came in yesterday. She asked me to take her and deliver the orders this afternoon."

Hart angled his chin. "Are things going better between you two?"

Joan glanced down the hallway, then remet his gaze. "She doesn't seem as angry at me as she first was." Because Joan knew that was largely due to Hart, she added, "Last night Helena told me you asked her if it made her feel better to stay mad at me. She admitted it didn't. That it made her heart hurt. Then she hugged me." Joan pressed her lips together to keep them from trembling. "Thank you for that."

"You don't need to thank me." He lifted a hand as if to touch her cheek, then let it drop back to his side. "She loves you, Joan. She's hurt. We're all hurt."

"Yes, we are."

Just then Helena zipped out of the hallway, dressed in a long red T-shirt, black leggings and her high-top red tennis shoes. "Hi, Hart, ready for breakfast?"

The pleasure that glowed in her face at seeing her father had emotions warring inside Joan. She was truly thankful for the closeness developing between father and daughter.

Glad for their easy camaraderie. She was also desperately afraid that when the time came for Hart to return to Chicago he would insist on taking Helena with him. And that she would want to go.

"I'm ready, kid." As though he'd been doing it for years, Hart snagged her blue backpack off the coffee table and anchored it over one of her shoulders. "I told your mom that after I drop you off at school I have to take off for Austin."

Helena's fingers gripped the strap of her backpack while she looked up at him with enormous dark eyes. "Are you coming back this time?"

When Hart's gaze slid across Joan's, she saw anger, frustration and hurt flash in his eyes. It would take time, she knew, for Helena to trust that he would forever stay in her life.

He leaned, looked Helena in the eye. "I'll always come back," he said quietly. "You and I will always be together. Count on it."

Hours later, Hart sat at a U-shaped counter in the state crime lab. Around him, white-coat-clad chemists worked while instruments hummed and lights blinked. On a counter across the pristine lab sat boxes containing brown paper bags and envelopes sealed with bright-red evidence tape.

Spread out in front of Hart were the reports and photographs he'd brought on the Lone Star bombing. He planned to review the paperwork again while he waited for the gas chromatograph to analyze the contents of the cartridge from the EGIS explosive detector. It wasn't, however, the reports or photos spread before him that currently claimed his attention, but the small gold lion pin he'd retrieved from the rubble.

His thoughts went to Joan, standing in the hospital treatment room while she examined the lion. "Why does this pin seem different from the others?" she had asked.

Was the pin he'd found somehow different? Hart wondered. If so, what was the difference?

He recalled the photos of Daniel Anderson taken at the bomb scene. A few had been close-ups of the dead man's battered upper torso. Hart shuffled through the photos in his file until he found one of those close-ups. Pinned to the bloodstained collar of Anderson's shirt was a gold lion pin. Hart snagged the attention of a female chemist wearing thick, black-rimmed glasses.

"I need to see if there's a difference between this pin and the one in the photo. Can you set these up on the comparison microscope?"

"Sure thing, Sergeant O'Brien. Follow me."

Minutes later, the chemist looked up from the scope's lens. "There's a difference, all right," she pronounced. "A slight one."

"What?"

"On the actual pin you brought in the lion is standing at an angle where only three legs are visible." As she spoke, the chemist rose off her stool so Hart could look through the lens. "The pin on the man's shirt shows all four of the lion's legs."

"I'll be damned." Hart leaned back from the scope, pulled out his cell phone and dialed Spence.

It took the D.A. only a half hour to check the information Hart had asked for. When he called back, Spence said, "The only lion pins the city has ever awarded have four legs visible."

Hart thought of the lion pins he'd seen worn by various cops, including Ben Stone. "Spence, call Molly French. Have her take a covert look at the pins some of her fellow cops wear. I've got a hunch if she sees a lion with only three legs, she's found a member of the infamous Lion's Den."

"Sounds logical," Spence said. "Speaking of Molly, she called from the hospital an hour ago. Bobby J. is improving. The doctor thinks he'll come out of the coma soon."

"Good. Maybe he'll give us an ID on the two cops he claims beat him. Since he's the one who first talked about the Lion's Den, let's hope he can help us there, too." Hart paused. "Who's keeping an eye on Bobby?"

"Molly's husband, Danny Gates. As a former enforcer for the Mercados, he knows how to make sure Bobby stays safe."

After hanging up, Hart ascertained that he had another half hour to wait for the gas chromatograph's results. He returned to his stool and began shuffling the bombing reports and photographs back into the file folder. When he slipped the gold lion pin into his shirt pocket, it hit him that Joan had given them the biggest break so far in the case.

Joan. When he felt something shift inside him, he tried to put himself into the same mind-set he used when he disarmed a bomb. Separate himself from emotion. Enter a dimension devoid of sensation. He tried to get to there, but failed. Now that some time had passed, he found he could no longer distance himself from his feelings for her.

So, he stopped trying.

With his mind off the tight leash he'd kept it on for days, he allowed himself to think about Joan. About the coolness he now saw in her dark eyes whenever she looked at him. About the pain he glimpsed in her face when she thought he wasn't watching. About how she'd stood before him this morning, looking beautiful and vulnerable and immensely relieved over the fact Helena's anger toward her seemed to have cooled. About how *his* relief over that had almost equaled Joan's.

He had desperately wanted to touch her, Hart conceded. Cup his hand against her cheek and pull her against him. He had known instinctively how right it would feel to wrap his arms around her and just hold her. Comfort her.

Instead he had held back. Now he acknowledged how

much that gesture had cost him. Through no fault of their own, he and Joan had spent ten years apart. The events that had led to that estrangement continued to keep them at arm's length. What price would both pay if they never righted the wrongs others had done to them?

To *both* of them, he added ruthlessly. Over the past days he hadn't thought much about Joan's feelings, but of his own anger and pain and sense of betrayal. He could resent all he wanted the years he'd lost with his daughter but in his heart he knew that loss wasn't Joan's fault.

Their past hung between them, dense with complicated facts and feelings. He could do nothing to change that. Yet he could take certain steps so that past events didn't have a devastating impact on their future.

Joan Cooper was—and always had been—the one woman who could tangle up his mind, rip open his heart and leave him helpless. Whatever was between them had a long reach and a hard grip. He knew now she was the one person from his past from whom there was no moving on. A woman he was destined to carry around in his heart for the rest of his days. He had loved her when they were young, and he had lost her. He loved her again. Hell, he had probably never stopped. Why else had he never been able to get close emotionally to another woman? Never allowed any relationship to dip below the surface. Never wanted any woman the way he'd always—forever— wanted Joan.

Are you coming back this time? Hart closed his eyes while Helena's question echoed in his ears.

"Oh, yeah, baby, I'm coming back," he said quietly. "For you and for your mother."

"Mom, where do you think Chief Ben is?" Helena asked while they stood on Ben Stone's front porch.

"I'm not sure." Shifting the box of candles from one arm to the other, Joan glanced back toward the driveway, squinting against the low rays of the setting sun. "His car's here."

Helena scrunched her nose. "Maybe he's in the backyard, playing with Warrant. Chief Ben says he and Warrant play Frisbee every day when he gets home from work."

"I bet you're right."

"Can we go around and look? We can use the gate we went through the night Chief Ben cooked us steaks. He'll probably let me play with him and Warrant."

For the first time since Helena had found out the truth about her parentage, Joan's heart felt light. She and her child had spent several pleasant hours this afternoon delivering candles. Helena had asked to eat dinner at the Mission Creek Café, which featured brownie ice cream sundaes on the dessert menu. Joan knew rough spots over what had happened were inevitable, but as long as she had her child's love—and it seemed she did—she could endure anything.

She glanced down at the open box holding the numerous colorful, scented candles Ben had ordered. She suspected a divorced man had little use for designer candles and he had made this purchase solely for Helena's sake. His was the last order they had yet to deliver, and Joan knew Helena was anxious to keep her promise to her customers that they would receive their candles today. Plus, Joan needed to talk to Ben. She hadn't seen him since the day he'd stopped by her suite to tell her the police had recovered the van that had hit Helena.

Because Joan had been beside herself with worry over Helena's finding out about Hart, Ben's attempt to get close had prompted her to reject him with zero finesse. For that she owed him an apology. She and Ben were friends and he had shown her child immeasurable patience and kindness. Joan wanted to make sure he knew how much she appreciated that and valued his friendship.

"Okay, sweetie," she said. "Let's check to see if Chief Ben's in the backyard."

Helena bounded off the front porch in her high-topped tennis shoes, then zipped around the side of the house. Joan followed at a more sedate pace on the clean-swept sidewalk edged with flowers that wrapped around the side of the house.

By the time Joan caught up with Helena, she had the gate open. Warrant pounced around her with canine glee, a sloppy, doggy grin on his face.

Giggling, Helena tossed the Frisbee, which the golden retriever sailed after. "Look, Mom, the door to Chief Ben's workshop's open, and there's a light on. I bet he's in there."

Joan glanced at the workshop on the far side of the newly mown lawn. The white-painted wooden structure gleamed in the rays of the setting sun. The workshop had one small window beside the door through which light shone. "Let's go see."

Helena's dash across the yard halted when Warrant bounded up, tooth-pocked Frisbee in his mouth. She tugged on the plastic disk, sent it sailing across the yard, then headed for the workshop, Joan on her heels.

"Chief Ben! We rang your doorbell, but you weren't there," Helena said, running toward the rear of the structure where Ben Stone busied himself at a bench against the wall. "We brought your candles."

Dressed in full uniform, Ben swung away from the bench. His eyes glowed in the glare from the long-armed light attached to the bench.

Joan froze in the doorway, panic threatening to swamp her as she took in everything at once. The mountainous stacks of paper money on the benches lining the workshop's other walls. The vicious-looking automatic weapons hanging above those benches. The sticks of dynamite spread on the bench in front of which Ben stood. *Money laundering,* she thought numbly. *Bombs.*

"Helena, come here," she said, her voice trembling.

"Too late." Ben clamped one massive hand around the child's thin upper arm and jerked her back against him.

Fright searing her eyes, Helena twisted and turned in an ineffective attempt to free herself. "You're hurting me," she whimpered.

Ben locked his other hand around Helena's throat. Immediately she stopped struggling.

"Baby, stay still." Joan's hoarse voice shook. Although yards separated them, she reached an unsteady hand out to her daughter whose eyes glistened with terrified tears. "Just stay still."

Ben nodded at Joan. "Set the box on that bench nearest you."

She hadn't even realized she was still holding the box of candles. Hands trembling, legs weak, she complied.

"Now shut the door behind you and bolt it." His steel-edged gaze flicked to Helena, then lifted. "I don't have to tell you what'll happen if you make a run for it."

He would kill Helena. "I won't run." Sick with her own impotent terror, Joan bit her lip so hard she tasted blood. Turning, she did as ordered. With the door closed and locked, the building effectively became a prison.

Ben's face looked gray in the artificial light. "You should have called to let me know you were coming." His voice agonized, he moved his hand from Helena's arm to his holstered weapon. "Dammit, why the hell didn't you call first?"

Chapter 15

"**D**ynamite," Hart said into his cell phone as he steered his car south toward Mission Creek. With the slate-blue sky fast transforming into evening's gloom, he reached and switched on the car's headlights.

"No question?" Spence asked. "You're sure dynamite was in the closet at the Lone Star's security office?"

"Gas chroms don't lie. You now have a link between the security cops and the bomb that exploded at the Lone Star."

"The cops guard that office like a fortress. They can't claim someone planted the explosive so they'd take the rap for the bombing." Spence's voice carried an edge of grim satisfaction. "That's enough to get a warrant to search the house of every man who works security there. We suspect they're into money laundering, so we'll dig into their financial history. Seize computer hard drives. I'll have a couple of my assistants meet me at my office. We'll get those warrants drawn up and served tonight."

Hart glanced at his watch. It was just past seven. "I

should be back in Mission Creek in less than an hour."
He thought of Joan. He wanted to go to the Lone Star and
find her. Tell her he loved her, had always loved her. "I
have an important stop to make. After that I'll be at your
office," Hart added before hanging up.

He was about to punch in the number to Joan's suite
when his cell phone chimed.

"O'Brien."

"I got your kid and her mother. Want to see them
again?"

The stark words hit Hart with the force of a fist to the
gut. His lungs stopped working. And his heart.

"Who is this?"

"I ask the questions. You want to see them alive or
not?"

He kept his eyes focused on the road. Although his insides were churning, he couldn't think like a lover or a
father. He had to think like a cop. The caller was a man;
his voice was muffled, as though he were talking through
a thick cloth. Hart couldn't ID the voice, but it almost had
to be one he would recognize. Else, why the disguise?

"Yes, I want to see them alive."

"Go to the Lone Star Country Club. There's a maintenance road that winds past the west side of the golf
course. At the end of the road is a groundskeeper's shed.
That's where they are. You know where it is?"

"I'll find it." Hart knew the shed well. The summer
he'd worked there they'd stowed riding lawnmowers, tools
and other supplies inside. He'd had to stop by the shed
almost daily.

"Come alone. I see anyone but you, the little girl gets
to watch her mother die. Then it's her turn."

Hart's hands clenched on the steering wheel while his
mind worked on logistics. If the caller used a night scope,
he could surveil the maintenance road in both directions.
"How do I know they're not already dead?"

"Ask another question, they will be."

"Let me talk to them."

"You don't want to come, don't. They'll die knowing you had better things to do."

Hart clenched his jaw when the line went dead. On the off chance the call had been a hoax, he stabbed in the number for Joan's suite. No answer. He phoned the Lone Star operator and had him dial her pager. The operator got no response.

The bastard had Joan and their child. The sick realization had Hart flooring the car's accelerator, sending the speedometer needle quivering.

He knew he wasn't dealing with kidnappers. Their goal was not to harm, but to keep their captive safe to collect a ransom. Hart had received no assurances that Joan and Helena would remain unharmed if he cooperated. Whoever had them in that shed wanted only one thing: Hart to join them.

Definitely an ambush.

He couldn't have backup go in with him, but he had to have support. If something happened to him, Joan and Helena would be totally vulnerable. Defenseless.

He punched in Molly French's phone number. When the detective answered, Hart ran down what he faced. "You can't get spotted, so don't try to move in too close to the shed," he added. "I need you and any other cops you trust in position to help Joan and Helena in case something happens to me."

"I'll bring Joe Gannon," Molly said, referring to the senior detective on the bombing task force. "Hart, be careful."

"Yeah." Clicking off the phone, he tossed it into the passenger seat while the car blew by a black Porsche. The thought that some faceless bastard had his daughter and the woman he loved sent cold terror racing through his veins. The idea of their getting hurt made him homicidal. He would kill for them. Kill to keep them safe. He *had* to keep them safe.

* * *

Since he expected an ambush, Hart avoided the maintenance road.

The moon was beginning to rise, covering the landscape with a silver light as he nosed his car into the trees bordering the eighteenth green. He had no idea if what he faced was about bombs or spur-of-the-moment retribution or something else. So he had to be prepared for anything. At least his going in on foot would give him the element of surprise.

When he slid out of the car, a gentle, enveloping silence closed around him.

Quietly he opened the car's trunk, thankful he'd stowed his field kit there for the trip to the lab. He opened the kit, grabbed his black equipment vest. It had dozens of pockets and loops that held metal and wire cutters, an electronic stethoscope to listen to the inner workings of a bomb, night vision binoculars and other essential hand tools.

Reaching back into the kit, he retrieved his holstered 9mm Glock. In a smooth, practiced move, he clipped it onto the waistband of his jeans.

With the snug weight of the Glock against his waist, he used the darting silver images of moon and stars to guide him through the trees. With each silent step he took, the sick dread in his stomach increased. His senses screamed that Joan and Helena were in perilous danger. His family. His life. He had to keep them safe.

He crouched when he reached the edge of the treeline. The maintenance shed sat in the distance, moonlight glinting off its pale metal walls. Once he moved out of the treeline there would be no cover between him and the shed. He'd be an easy target in the silvery moonlight.

The shed's front had a double door and one window. The pane looked like a dark eye with no light behind it. There was no sign of life inside.

Hart knew it was possible Joan and Helena were in there, already dead. The thought had him struggling to maintain control over the emotions seething inside him. He couldn't think about that right now. Couldn't even consider it.

Sensing that the bastard orchestrating this scenario was also watching from somewhere inside the treeline, Hart shifted his attention. While his gaze ran slowly over the edge of the clearing, he rolled up the sleeves of his denim shirt. He needed his arms bare in order to feel any thin wires hooked to booby traps stretched around the shed's perimeter.

Reaching inside his vest, he pulled out the night vision binoculars. Again he scanned the clearing, now transformed into an eerie green by the specialized lenses. A minute or two passed before he caught sight of the green-hued figure, crouched a few hundred feet away. The figure leaned against a tree, his body pressed into the shadows. Hart couldn't ID who it was, but the build spoke male.

Stiff-jawed, Hart traded the binoculars for his Glock. Dragging air into his tight lungs, he hunkered down and moved. Advancing slowly, his feet silent on the soft dirt beneath the trees, he adjusted his course to approach the man from behind. When the crouched figure again came into view, Hart noted the MCPD uniform, the holstered automatic. With the man's back to him, Hart couldn't ID the cop.

Hart eased his finger onto the Glock's trigger. He felt nothing now, his concentration so focused on his prey that nothing else registered. He took several soundless steps forward. As if sensing another presence, the crouched figure half swiveled, his hand going for his weapon.

"Freeze!" As Hart advanced, the silver shadows highlighted Ben Stone's profile. "Raise your hands, Stone."

Stone glared up at him, his face full of malice. "You didn't get as far as I hoped, O'Brien."

"Yeah, you want me inside the shed. Or close to it. I said raise your hands. Slowly."

"Sure." When he did, Hart saw the radio transmitter

gripped in the cop's left hand. Hart's nerves pulsed. The only logical reason for Stone to have the transmitter was to arm a bomb. All of Hart's senses screamed the bomb was in or near the shed. As were Joan and Helena.

"Lay it down," Hart ordered between his teeth. "Put down the damn transmitter or I shoot."

"Wouldn't want to get shot." Stone's left hand lowered. Just as he set the device on the ground, Hart heard a distinct click that seemed to echo on the still night air.

"Better run, O'Brien," Stone advised.

Cursing, Hart smashed the Glock into the side of the cop's head. Stone's body slammed against a tree trunk before he slumped unconscious at its base. Hart grabbed the weapon out of Stone's holster and tossed it away. Jerking the handcuffs off the loop on the cop's belt, Hart cuffed Stone's thick wrists around the tree trunk.

No longer worried about wires or booby traps, Hart dashed toward the shed. Logic told him Stone had the transmitter because he'd intended to wait to activate the bomb's timing device until he spotted Hart enter the shed. Clearly, the chief's goal had been to kill Hart, Joan and Helena in one blast. With gasoline stored inside the shed to fuel the club's lawnmowers, Hart felt sure Stone planned on explaining their deaths had been due to some freak, accidental explosion.

Lungs heaving, heart pounding, Hart reached the shed. Although he wanted to rip open the door, he had to make sure it hadn't been triggered to blow when opened. Switching on his flashlight, he examined the door's exterior. It looked clean. He then stepped to the window and aimed the beam inside.

His mouth went dry when he saw Joan and Helena sitting in chairs backed up to each other. They were both gagged, their arms and legs bound to their chairs. Slowly Hart lowered the flashlight's beam to the cement floor. Beneath Joan's chair a green LED timer strapped to sticks of dynamite counted down the minutes. *Ten,* he thought weakly. He had ten minutes to get them out.

The flashlight's beam had Joan jerking her head toward the window. Above her gag, her eyes glinted with fear.

"The door," Hart shouted, hoping to hell she could hear him through the glass. "Did you see Stone do anything to the door? Put any wires on it?"

She gave her head a frantic shake.

Hart rechecked the timer. *Nine minutes, thirty seconds.* He didn't have time to check to see if Stone had left any hidden triggers Joan didn't know about. He had to go in now. Turning to the door, he gripped the handle, sucked in a breath and pulled it open.

Nothing blew. Sweat broke across his forehead.

Hart dashed inside the shed, the flashlight's beam bobbing. He didn't dare flip on the overhead light—Stone could have rigged the switch to trigger the bomb.

When he reached the chairs, Hart saw the thin wires coiling around both Joan and Helena's legs. His chest felt like a boulder had slammed into it. Touching those wires could detonate an explosion. He couldn't just untie Joan and Helena and get them to safety. His only option was to defuse the bomb.

He swept the light over Joan's gag, checking for wires. When he saw none, he pulled it down gently.

"Save Helena," she choked. "Hart, get her out of here."

"I'm getting you both out." He checked Helena's gag, then eased it down. Her face was white, her dark eyes filled with pure terror. Tears streamed down her cheeks; when she whimpered, his heart broke.

"Helena, baby, listen to me." He touched her cheek, felt her uncontrollable trembling. "I need you to sit really still." If she so much as shifted in her chair, she could trigger the bomb. "Real still. Can you do that for me?"

"Okay…Daddy," she sobbed.

Daddy. This was the first time she'd called him that.

Hart knew it might be the last. He fought back a raging, tearing sense of helplessness. He wanted to wrap his arms around her, tell her he would make everything all right. If only he knew he could.

Scrubbing a hand across his sweat-filmed face, he crouched and peered at the bomb beneath Joan's chair. The timer clicked on eight minutes, twenty seconds. Blocking out the sound of Helena's soft sobs, he forced himself to concentrate on the device attached to the LED display. Three sticks of dynamite were taped to a timer bristling with wires. Too many wires. He needed a day to sort them out, not the seven minutes, fifty-nine seconds he had left.

"Hart, please." Joan's voice was a whispered sob. "Take Helena and run. I beg you…"

He lifted his gaze. Her eyes were huge and dark, her skin so pale it was nearly translucent. She was a mother begging for the life of her child. What she couldn't know—*wouldn't know*—was that he felt as helpless as she. The only way to save their child was to disarm the bomb counting down the seconds. He wasn't sure he had enough time to do that.

"Steady." He put a palm against her thigh. She was trembling, her body drenched in sweat. "Just hold on."

When he looked back down at the bomb, his own sweat dripped into his eyes. Using his forearm, he swiped it away and concentrated.

He identified what looked like the bomb's arming switch. But Stone had soldered a metal cover to the device, and Hart knew beneath it could be a completely different switch. One that would fire if he tried to pry off the cover.

The one hope—the only *sure* hope—they had for survival was to sever the wire that sent power from the 9-volt battery to the timer. He couldn't just pull out the battery in case Stone had built in a surge monitor. The monitor would sense if the battery had been disconnected and would automatically fire the detonator. To disarm the bomb, Hart had to cut the wire that supplied all power. Problem was, he didn't know what the hell wire that was, and he had less than five minutes to figure it out.

His hands were rock-solid steady as he slowly separated the wires, isolating the single red one that jutted from the timer. *Never cut the red wire.* The age-old litany hammered in his head, along with the ache brought on by his nearness to the dynamite.

As he worked with the wires, he glanced at the timer. Less than a minute. He looked up at Joan while he pulled a pair of wire cutters from his vest. "Stone did a good job on this. Almost too good. I'm taking a guess here."

She stared down at him, her eyes going even darker when the meaning of his words settled around her. "Save yourself," she whispered. "Hart, you can leave—"

"No, I can't." He closed his eyes, opened them. "I love you. Both of you. No way am I leaving you."

"I love…you…too…Daddy," Helena sobbed. "I love you…Mommy."

"Baby…" Tears rolled down Joan's cheeks. "I love you."

His chest so tight he could barely breathe, Hart slid the teeth of the cutter around a black wire. He hesitated. This felt wrong. All wrong.

"Joan, did you see Stone do any work on this? Anything at all."

"Right before…he put the bomb under my chair…he soldered different colors of wires together." Her lungs were heaving, her voice shaking, barely audible. "A yellow wire…to a…blue. Black to white. Then he wrapped… tape around all the ends of the wires…to hide the difference in color. Does it…matter?"

"A lot." So much so that Hart knew he couldn't chance cutting any wire.

His gaze shot to the timer. *Fifteen seconds.*

The only option left was to break the connection between the 9-volt battery and the timer by removing the battery. That was *all* he could do. Praying that Stone hadn't built in a surge monitor that would backcharge and fire the detonator, Hart gently lifted the battery. Holding his breath, he detached the little silver snaps at its top.

The timer stopped with one second to go.

Chapter 16

For Joan, the remainder of the night was a blur. After Hart released her and Helena from their bonds, he'd spirited them out of the shed. By that time Molly French and several other cops had arrived. Detective French looked extremely satisfied when she transported Ben Stone to jail.

Spence Harrison had shown up at the shed, several of his assistant D.A.s in tow. Flynt Carson—the Lone Star's current president—put in a grim appearance. As did general manager Bonnie Brannigan, her fiancé, C.J. Stuckey and several members of the media.

After briefing Spence, Hart had swept Joan and a sobbing Helena back to their suite at the Lone Star. He'd insisted the Lone Star's on-staff physician examine them both. Even though the doctor gave Helena a mild sedative, it had taken several hours and two cups of hot cocoa until she stopped trembling. Finally she'd fallen into an exhausted sleep sometime after dawn.

Now, rays of noonday sunlight beamed through the

sheer curtains that hung over the balcony's sliding glass door. Joan sat on the couch in her living room, dressed in a T-shirt and slacks, clasping a mug of coffee between her palms. Gauze circled both of her wrists, made raw from struggling against her bonds. A remembered swirl of the panic and nausea she'd felt while imprisoned in the shed had her setting her coffee aside.

"Last night I called the governor's office," Spence Harrison said from one of the chairs facing the couch. Fatigue shadowed the D.A.'s eyes. His white dress shirt and black suit looked as if he'd slept in them. His tie was missing. "I outlined the suspected widespread corruption inside the MCPD," Spence continued. "I asked the governor to authorize the Texas Rangers to serve the search warrants at the homes of everyone who worked off-duty security at the Lone Star. The gov did."

"Good move," Hart said from the opposite end of the couch from where Joan sat. His face was haggard, the stubble on his jaw dark and heavy. Although he'd pulled her into his arms and held her after they'd escaped death, they'd had no time to talk after that. *I love you,* he had said while the bomb slowly ticked off the time. Had he meant it, or had the words been a result of the terrorizing emotion she'd seen in his eyes as he worked to disarm the deadly device?

Spence sipped his coffee before continuing. "At Stone's house, the Rangers confiscated dynamite, bomb parts, hundreds of thousands of dollars in cash and money laundering records from the backyard workshop. They also unearthed a map marking a tunnel into Mexico from a Laredo car wash."

"So, the money came from Mexico," Hart said. "Any idea who on that side of the border sent it through the tunnel?"

"Yes," Spence answered. "Stone's not talking, but

Yance Ingram is. He's desperate to work a deal with my office for a light sentence. According to Ingram, Stone's previous financial straits left him a prime target for El Jefe. Stone's job was to pick up the money at the tunnel's Laredo end, then get it laundered. Stone needed a secure place to store the money before it got washed. Basically a spot under constant guard. He also needed someone he could trust to keep his eye on the money.''

"Yance Ingram," Hart stated.

"Right. Ingram was Stone's mentor at the PD. Ben knew that Ingram's savings had been wiped out by his wife's terminal illness and that he owed thousands of dollars in medical bills. So Ben got Ingram the job running the club's security detail. Ingram got a cut of the profits from the laundering operation and made sure the only cops hired were rogue ones who belonged to the group Stone formed.''

"Don't tell me," Hart said. "The Lion's Den. The group Bobby J. mentioned before he fell into the coma.''

"Bingo." Spence's eyes widened. "Speaking of Bobby J., Molly called while I was driving over here. He's out of the coma. He's still disoriented, but he managed to ID Kevin Neely and Bryce Evans as the cops who beat him.''

"Do you know yet why?''

"It's still conjecture at this point. All we know for sure is that Bobby worked for the Lion's Den. Running errands, things like that. The beating came after he told them he wanted out.''

"What about the lion pins?" Joan asked. "Are they connected with the Lion's Den?''

Spence nodded. "Ingram said Stone designed his own version of lion pins which he gave to the group's members. Something along the line of fraternity pins, I imagine." Spence raised a shoulder. "The entire security force helped launder El Jefe's cash, mostly by converting it to money orders and cashier's checks.''

Hart's eyes narrowed. ''You can buy a money order and not fill out who it's payable to. Not a cashier's check. Who did the Lion's Den members have the cashier's checks made out to?''

''Esmeralda.''

Joan leaned forward. ''*Who* is Esmeralda?''

''Not who, what,'' Spence explained. ''It's a shell corporation, within about twenty other shell corporations owned by El Jefe.''

''Speaking of El Jefe, I take it we were right about the motive for the bombing?'' Hart asked. ''To kill Phillip Westin before he joined the mission in Mezcaya to take down the cartel?''

''You've got it,'' Spence confirmed. ''Ingram says everything went smooth until word of Westin's mission leaked. Stone handled explosives in the military, has dabbled in them ever since. He built and planted the bomb, intending to kill Westin.''

''And you,'' Hart reminded him. ''Don't forget, you were also a part of Westin's party.''

''I haven't forgotten,'' Spence said grimly. ''Four things went against Stone that day. One, little Jake Anderson spotted some of the Lion's Den members moving money in canvas bags. Two, our golf game ran long, so Westin wasn't in the Men's Grill when the bomb exploded. Three, Daniel and Meg Anderson died in the blast. Four, unbeknownst to Stone, Willie Pogue had stored paint and thinner in the closet. It ignited, burned the billiards room and nearly incinerated the security office, too. If that had happened, about a hundred thousand dollars of El Jefe's money would have gone up in smoke, and Stone would have been accountable. With fire investigators conducting inspections for days after the blast, Stone had to move the money laundering operation to his workshop.''

Hart nodded. ''Since the minute that bomb blew, Stone's done his best to blame the Mercados. Willie Pogue paid for that with his life.''

''Ingram named every member of the Lion's Den. They're all sitting in jail right now. I intend to make sure they pay for what they've done.'' Spence's mouth curved into a feral grin. ''There's a statute in the Texas Penal Code titled Engaging in Organized Criminal Activity. When three or more subjects are arrested during the same incident, we can enact that statute. It raises each offense one degree higher than what could be charged otherwise. That means a third-degree felony can be filed as second-degree felony, and so on. Doing that ups the jail time and fine each subject's looking at.''

''That's one for the good guys,'' Hart said. ''What about Stone? You think he'll try to plea out?''

''No. He'll keep his mouth shut and go to trial.'' Spence shifted his gaze to Joan. ''You'll have to testify about the kidnapping. How Stone set the bomb. I'll try to make sure Helena doesn't have to testify, too.''

''Thank you.'' Joan attempted a smile that didn't gel. ''Did Ingram know anything about the van that hit her? The driver?''

''If he does, he's not saying. Not right now, anyway. My people will keep talking to him. I'll let you know if we find out anything.''

Spence glanced at his watch and rose. ''Hart, I owe you big-time for all you've done on this investigation.''

''So, buy me a drink sometime,'' Hart said, joining his friend on his way to the door.

''I'll do better than that. How about a job? After last night, the MCPD has a few vacancies that need filling.''

''You think the department's going to recover from this?''

''I wondered that same thing last night while the Rangers served the warrants on all those cops. Believe it or not, I got a call this morning from Flynt Carson. To put it mildly, neither he nor the club's board of directors is happy knowing that every cop on the Lone Star's security staff is corrupt. Flynt told me he's making a large donation to the MCPD. He wants honest officers hired. Pronto.'' Spence angled his chin. ''That, Sergeant O'Brien, would be you.''

Hart glanced at Joan, his eyes unreadable. ''I'll keep that in mind.''

When Spence left, Joan realized she and Hart were alone for the first time since the day he had found out he was Helena's father. She rose off the couch, thinking that day seemed a lifetime ago.

Gathering her and Spence's coffee mugs, she walked into the kitchen. She clung to a simple and steady hope that Hart would take Spence up on his job offer. But wishful thinking was all it was. The possibility existed that Hart might return to Chicago. If so, it was only natural for him to want to take Helena with him. Give himself a chance to get to know his child. And her him. Joan's hands trembled when she set the mugs in the sink and turned on the water. She would want to do the same thing if her and Hart's positions were reversed.

She didn't realize he'd followed her into the kitchen until his hands settled on her shoulders. ''We need to talk.''

''I know.'' She closed her eyes. She loved him and he might leave soon. Might insist on taking their daughter with him. *She'd* had nearly ten years with Helena. Hart needed time, too. He deserved that time. She understood that. Still, the thought of her child being so far away clawed at Joan's throat.

"Texas." With the lightest of pressure on her shoulders, he turned her to face him. "I need you to listen to me."

"Are you going to try to take her away?"

He reached behind her, shut off the water. "What?"

"Helena. Her whole life, you didn't know you had a daughter. What my parents did, what I did wasn't fair to you. I know that." She was speaking so fast that the words tumbled over each other. "Any judge will agree. Are you going to go to court and ask for full custody? If you do, I'll understand why. But I'll also fight you. I can't just let you take her away. I *won't.*"

He cupped her face in his hands. "Do you really think I would do that?"

Joan curled her hands against her thighs. "I don't know what you'll do. I don't know how you feel."

"That's right, you don't. In fact, I didn't know myself until yesterday afternoon at the lab. That's when I finally let go of being mad and allowed myself to think. I was on my way here last night to tell you how I feel when Stone's phone call sidetracked me."

"I begged him to let Helena go. To just take me and let her live." Joan fought back the memory of the icy cruelty she'd seen in Ben Stone's eyes. Of her child's terrified sobs. "You saved Helena. When I think about what would have happened to her if you hadn't come. I haven't thanked you—"

"Stop it. We both love Helena. We would both die for her. She's a part of this, a big part of what we are, but she's not all." His hands slid into her hair, tilted her head back. "Do you know what it would have done to me last night to lose you? You matter to me more than life itself."

Joan's lips parted. She couldn't get a word out past the knot in her throat.

''For ten years I tried to live my life as if you'd never existed,'' he said quietly. ''I couldn't quite pull that off because I never forgot you. Believe me, I tried. I know now that ridding my system of you didn't work, because I never stopped loving you. Never.''

''Never?''

''That day I saw you in the lobby, I thought you were a ghost.'' He dipped his head, slicked his mouth against hers. Instantly heat swarmed into her blood. ''The one who'd faded away every time I tried to reach out and touch her over the past ten years. Turns out you were real. If you think I'm going to let you get away this time, think again.''

She *had* to think, Joan told herself. Despite the fact her knees were weak, her blood pumping and her head spinning, she pulled from his arms. Took a step away. Then another. ''That day, when you found out Helena is yours. Our...having sex, you said was a mistake. A big mistake.'' She searched for calm, knowing it was the best way. ''It's one we won't make again.''

She saw the barest glint of panic in his eyes. ''I was mad. Hurt. Even though deep down I knew you did what you thought was best for Helena, I felt betrayed. To top that off, I'd been rough with you. Careless. I hurt you that day and I'm sorry.'' He scrubbed a hand over his stubbled jaw. ''What happened between us was more than just sex. We both know that. We made love.'' He stepped toward her. ''No other woman has ever made me feel the way you do. No one ever will. I love you, Texas. I need you in my life. I want to live here with you and Helena. Be a father to her. Help raise her.''

''You have a life in Chicago. A job. Why would you sacrifice all that?''

''It isn't a sacrifice. I have an *apartment* in Chicago. Mission Creek is your and Helena's home. I've never had a real home, Texas. As for my job, I'm a cop. I can be a cop anywhere. You heard Spence. Doesn't sound like I'll have a problem hiring on to the MCPD.''

She stared at him, not quite believing all she wanted was suddenly within her reach.

When she made no response, he scowled and gripped her arms. ''Dammit, you and I were both cheated ten years ago. No matter what, we can't change that. I'm done with regrets. Now I'm fighting for what I want. *You.* I said I love you. That I want forever with you. You've said nothing about how you feel about me.''

She had been holding back as a means of self-preservation. Afraid of the pain she would suffer when he walked away again. He wasn't leaving, she realized with a jolt. The emotion she saw in his eyes was real. It had been real ten years ago. He loved her. She loved him.

''Hart, since the moment you walked into that lobby I've been in an impossible situation.'' She pressed her palms against his chest, felt the steady, reassuring beat of his heart. ''I never let go of you, either. Never could. I love you. I've always loved you.''

His fingers tightened on her arms. ''You're sure?''

''Yes.''

He tugged her against him. ''Marry me, Texas.'' He buried his face in her hair. ''You have to marry me.''

Her heart stuttered, then picked up its beat. She inched her head back. ''You want to get married?''

''I want the whole ball of wax. You. Helena. A home. More kids.'' He was kissing her face now, her cheeks, her temples, her jaw. ''Will you marry me?''

''Looks like I'd better. Especially since we have a child.'' She slid her arms around his neck, twined her fingers in his dark hair. ''And it seems both of us want more.''

''When?''

"It takes nine months."

"*When* are we getting married?"

"I have to check to see when my maid of honor can make it."

"Who?"

"Our daughter."

Hart grinned. "I was thinking about asking her to stand up with me."

"With both of us," Joan said. "She'll stand with both of us."

* * * * *

You are cordially invited to attend
this year's most exclusive party at the
Lone Star Country Club, where three very
different young women discover that
wishes can come true!

LONE STAR COUNTRY CLUB:
THE DEBUTANTES

Coming to Silhouette in May 2002!

Silhouette®

INTIMATE MOMENTS™
presents:

Romancing the Crown

With the help of their powerful allies,
the royal family of Montebello is
determined to find their missing heir.
But the search for the beloved prince
is not without danger—or passion!

Available in May 2002:
VIRGIN SEDUCTION
by Kathleen Creighton (IM #1148)
Cade Gallagher went to the royal palace of
Tamir for a wedding—and came home with
a bride of his own. The rugged oilman thought he'd married to
gain a business merger, but his innocent bride made him long
to claim his wife in every way....

This exciting series continues throughout
the year with these fabulous titles:

Available only from Silhouette Intimate Moments
at your favorite retail outlet.

Silhouette®
Where love comes alive™

Visit Silhouette at www.eHarlequin.com

SIMRC5

April 2002 brings four dark and captivating paranormal romances in which the promise of passion, mystery and suspense await…

Experience the dark side of love with

DREAMSCAPES

WATCHING
FOR WILLA
by *USA Today*
bestselling author
Helen R. Myers

DARK MOON
by Lindsay Longford

THIS TIME FOREVER
by Meg Chittenden

WAITING FOR THE
WOLF MOON
by Evelyn Vaughn

*Coming to a store near you
in April 2002.*

Visit Silhouette at www.eHarlequin.com   RCDREAM6

INTIMATE MOMENTS™

and *USA TODAY* BESTSELLING AUTHOR

RUTH LANGAN

present her new miniseries

Lives—and hearts—are on the line when the Lassiters pledge to uphold the law at any cost.

Available March 2002
BANNING'S WOMAN (IM #1135)

When a stalker threatens Congresswoman Mary Brendan Lassiter, the only one who can help is a police captain who's falling for the feisty Lassiter lady!

Available May 2002
HIS FATHER'S SON (IM #1147)

Lawyer Cameron Lassiter discovers there's more to life than fun and games when he loses his heart to a beautiful social worker.

And if you missed them,
look for books one and two in the series

BY HONOR BOUND (IM #1111)
and
RETURN OF THE PRODIGAL SON (IM #1123)

Available at your favorite retail outlet.

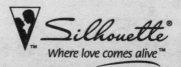

Where love comes alive™

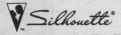

ANN MAJOR
CHRISTINE RIMMER
BEVERLY BARTON

cordially invite you to attend the year's most exclusive party at the **LONE STAR COUNTRY CLUB!**

Meet three very different young women who'll discover that wishes *can* come true!

LONE STAR COUNTRY CLUB:
The Debutantes

**Lone Star Country Club:
Where Texas society reigns
supreme—and appearances
are *everything*.**

Available in May
at your favorite retail outlet,
only from Silhouette.

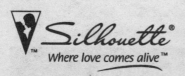